Jeremiah

A Walker Brothers Novel

Seven Sons Ranch in Three Rivers Romance™
Book 4

Liz Isaacson

ISBN-13: 978-1-63876-365-9

1

Jeremiah Walker ignored Stony's snuffle of displeasure as he strode past. "I have to get to town, Stony," he said over his shoulder, wondering when his life had been reduced to talking to horses.

Oh, that was right. When Whitney had gone completely cold and silent on him. When Liam had moved in with his wife next-door. When Micah had gone back to Temple and was still tying up loose ends.

"Skyler's coming home in a couple of days," Jeremiah yelled to the horse, happier about his brother returning to Seven Sons than he dared to admit. Wyatt had gone back to normal, and he still hadn't told anyone who he'd been sneaking off to see in the evenings. Jeremiah, of course, didn't ask. He was just glad he didn't have to spend his evenings alone anymore. Those couple of weeks in January had been dark, dark days for him.

But with Skyler home, and Wyatt, Jeremiah had something to look forward to again. Rhett and Evelyn had taken a springtime trip to the Texas Hill Country to see the wildflowers bloom, and they'd be home by the time Skyler was too.

Jeremiah had been planning a feast for the past week, and he needed to get to town to get the groceries. Orion and Dicky, Simon and Wallace, would handle all the chores on Wednesday, and Jeremiah would spend the day in the kitchen.

Excitement ran through him—another indicator that his life had reached a low point. Who was actually excited to spend the day laboring in the kitchen?

It wasn't his lowest point ever, and for that, he was grateful.

He showered quickly and swiped his truck keys from the peg by the door leading to the garage. He was the only one who parked in the garage, as he seemed to be the only permanent resident at the homestead. Wyatt had been there for a year and a half now, though. Jeremiah wondered if he'd spend the rest of his life alone. When Laura Ann had left, he'd thought he would.

But now, with some time and distance between where he was now and that terrible moment when he realized his fiancée wasn't going to come out and become his wife, he'd changed. Healed. Well, at least a little bit.

His thoughts automatically betrayed him and went to Whitney Wilde. He may have put the truck into gear a little bit too hard with that woman on his mind, and he pressed his teeth together to get her to leave.

Four months. That was how long it had been since he'd heard from her. And her sudden disappearance from his life made no sense. She'd called him for a solid six months before he'd allowed her onto the ranch to shoot.

"She was using you," he told himself for probably the hundredth time. But she hadn't ever brought one of her brides. Or a family. Or anyone. She'd merely wandered the ranch with him, taking a picture for Liam, and *poof.* Disappeared.

Jeremiah was still trying to figure out what he'd done wrong. He'd held her hand that night. Bought her dinner. Been a perfect gentleman, with great conversation, and laughter, and he'd even thought about kissing her.

A scoff came out of his mouth, and he really wished he could get Whitney out of his mind. Funnily enough, when she'd been harassing him about shooting at the ranch, he never gave her a second thought. Even after he'd hung up on her.

But now?

Now she tormented him in his quiet moments and haunted him at other times. Even after four months, Jeremiah was still hung up on her.

"That's because you fall too hard, too fast," he told himself as he caught sight of the outskirts of Three Rivers. He'd just get to Wilde & Organic before they closed, get everything he needed for the feast, and get back to the ranch.

He went to town quite a bit, actually. Out of everyone, he was probably considered the most social. He was the public face of the ranch, and he went to ranch ownership meetings every other week. He attended church, though he still felt somewhat removed from the Lord. He did the shopping. He went to all the town celebrations. In fact, attending them had become somewhat of a family tradition.

No, he didn't go to the summer dances, which would be starting up again in about a month.

"Maybe you should," he told himself. But he couldn't imagine finding someone his age at a dance in the park. That felt more like something people in their twenties did, and Jeremiah would be forty-three in August.

Nope, he wasn't going to go to the summer dances.

He pulled into the parking lot at Wilde & Organic, thinking it would be darker than it was. He reminded himself that May had dawned last week, and maybe he hadn't had to rush into town so quickly.

Wilde & Organic was only open until eight o'clock, though, and he'd taken to shopping in the late afternoon or evenings to make sure he wouldn't run into Whitney. She'd told him once that she worked in the morning, stocking the produce before the store opened, so he wouldn't see her if he shopped later in the day.

Plus, he knew this was the perfect light she liked for

shoots. "Golden hour," he muttered to himself, sick of talking to horses or thin air.

Determined not to say another word unless it was to a human, he headed for the store. He had a long list that included premium cuts of meat and at least twenty produce items. He loved everything about Wilde & Organic, and he wasn't surprised to see Molly, Whitney's mother, working the only register open. She didn't look toward Jeremiah, but she'd chat him up as she rang him out.

He liked Molly a lot, and she hadn't acted differently toward Jeremiah in the last four months. Of course, no one had known about his relationship with Whitney, if it could even be classified as such.

He selected his honey whole wheat bread, a round of sourdough, plenty of cheese and lunch meat, a huge rack of lamb, pounds and pounds of organic chicken and ground beef, and then moved over to the produce section.

"Shoppers, Wilde & Organic will be closing in fifteen minutes. Please make your final selections and make your way to check out four."

Jeremiah glanced up at the sound of the female voice, and he wondered how many people were still in the store. He hadn't seen many people, and he was the only one left in the produce section.

Working quickly now, he finished up his list, adding a bottle of mayonnaise last, and heading for the check out.

"Jeremiah," Molly said, that warm smile on her face. "How are you, darlin'?"

"Just fine, ma'am." To his surprise, he found himself smiling. He supposed Patsy couldn't control her daughter any more than Jeremiah could.

"Looks like you're planning a big meal."

"Yeah," Jeremiah said. "Skyler's coming home from college on Wednesday. Everyone's coming for dinner."

"I hear you're a good cook," she said.

"I'm decent," he said, though he knew he was a good cook. Movement caught his eye near the automatic doors. A dark-haired woman entered, and it took Jeremiah less than a blink to realize it was Whitney.

He sucked in a breath. Molly said something, but he had no idea what. White noise sounded in his ears, and all he could do was stare.

As if in slow motion, Whitney glanced in his direction. She didn't look long enough to truly see him, and she turned away a moment later, clearly not recognizing him. She set a basket on the ground and reached for a poster on the bulletin board near the exit.

Somehow, without even knowing it, Jeremiah had walked away from Molly and toward Whitney. He breathed, and he got a nose full of Whitney's perfume. "Hey," he said.

Whitney turned, barely looking at him. She jerked back to him, her eyes widening. "Jeremiah."

Even with the shock in her tone, he wanted to hear her say his name over and over again. "What are you doing?"

She just stared at him, almost like he was the one who'd gone silent four months ago.

"Jeremiah?" Molly said, and he turned back to her mother. She'd finished with his groceries, and he wanted to pull out his wallet and toss it at her. Instead, he looked back at Whitney.

"Don't disappear, okay?" He backed up a couple of steps, just making sure she didn't bolt for the door the moment he'd finished talking. She didn't, and he returned to the check out counter to pay for his cart full of groceries. "Thank you, Molly," he said as she flipped off the light on her check out station.

Jeremiah pushed his cart toward Whitney and watched as she stapled a new poster to the board. This one was the usual newborn picture. A darling, sleeping baby, probably only five or six days old, this one nestled among bright flowers—tulips, crocus, and bluebonnets—and tons of greenery. Vegetable greenery—kale, cabbage, and butter lettuce.

"Do you know Lake Winters?" he asked, indicating the poster.

"Not well," she said evasively.

"Why would anyone want a picture like that?"

Whitney stood back and looked at the poster. She stepped down the bulletin board a few feet and took down a flyer for a cooking class that had happened last weekend.

If Jeremiah had known she'd be there, cleaning up the bulletin board, he wouldn't have come. Or maybe he would've made sure to come tonight.

He honestly didn't know.

"I think they're sweet," she said. "The baby photos."

"I guess," Jeremiah said. "I think they're weird." He wished he could bite back the words. He didn't want to argue with her. Or even disagree. He had so many questions for her, but he couldn't ask any of them, with her mother only a few feet away, and the store about to close.

He pushed his cart behind her and leaned closer to her. "If I called, would you answer?"

Before she could answer, the main lights in the store went out, leaving only the glowing light of emergency lights. "You should go," she said, which wasn't the answer he wanted.

He had so much more to say, but he simply did what she wanted. He left the store, holding his head high as he marched away from her.

Every step tore at him a little more, but he clenched the pain tightly inside him. Cinched it close to his heart as a reminder that he couldn't trust women and that he would be just fine with only ranching and cooking in his life.

He would.

2

Whitney Wilde's heart pounded in her chest for several long minutes after Jeremiah had walked out the door. Not only did she not like being in the store by herself, but that man was her biggest regret.

Would you answer if I called?

Whitney had wanted to blurt *yes. Yes, I'd answer.*

But then she'd have to tell him why she'd *stopped* answering. Humiliation burned through her. She just wanted to forget about Blake Thurston, the man that was like a recurring nightmare in her life.

He'd come into her life almost two years ago and swept her right off her feet. That relationship had only lasted eight months. Then he'd broken up with her to go to farrier training. But he'd dropped out of that and worked as a loper for a horse farm in Oklahoma instead of returning to Three Rivers—and Whitney.

When he'd come back to Three Rivers, Whitney had fallen for his charms again. This time for only five months. Then Blake was off again, this time to Florida for some other job. And he'd come back just after the New Year, after a nine-month absence.

And Whitney had been sucked into his charms again. She had a horrible weakness for the man, who made her feel beautiful and sexy and like she was the only woman for him. Maybe she was—but only until he got bored of his job, bored of this town, bored with her.

Her heart wailed as it continued to pump, and she looked up at the new poster she'd just tacked up of her latest spring newborn shoot. Jeremiah's words spiraled through her mind, and she seemed to be able to remember every single thing the man had said to her.

So he didn't like the baby photography. He wasn't the only one. But somehow, his opinion carried more weight than anyone else's, and she could never tell him she was Lake Winters now.

Carrying the pseudonym was getting tiresome, and Whitney just wanted to put her own name on the cards and stop maintaining two websites, two phone numbers, two of everything. She wasn't sure why she'd wanted to keep the baby photography separate from her regular stuff in the first place.

Oh, wait, yes, she was. Blake had suggested it, and Whitney seemed to think everything the man said was made of pure magic. Whitney had done what he said. She wore what he liked. She laughed at everything he said. When he called, she answered.

She hated the person she was when she was with Blake, and she was glad his time in Three Rivers had only lasted eleven weeks.

Embarrassment and humiliation had kept her from texting Jeremiah, though she had a wedding that would be *perfect* if it were out at Seven Sons. But she didn't want him to think she was using him, because well, if a man did to her what she'd done to Jeremiah and then called about using the ranch...she'd think they were using her.

And Jeremiah was a smart man. A very smart, very handsome, very sexy cowboy.

Whitney's breath whooshed out of her lungs, and she started piling everything into her basket. Her mother had left when she'd turned off the lights, and Whitney didn't normally like being in the huge supermarket alone. She went up the stairs with her supplies and into the office on the second floor.

With another sigh, she collapsed into the office chair there and looked out the one-way window that showed her the store below. Eerie shadows draped across the ends of aisles and mounds of oranges and other produce.

She simply sat, trying to figure out what she wanted her life to be. In Jeremiah's absence, she'd turned thirty-six, and her mother had spent the entirety of Whitney's birthday dinner talking about boyfriends and marriage and babies.

Things Whitney wanted, sure. Of course. She simply didn't have anyone knocking down her door.

"But you do," she muttered to herself. "Kind of."

If Jeremiah called, Whitney would answer. The problem was, he wasn't going to call. Whitney could feel it way down deep in her soul. *You have his number*, she thought, her gaze sweeping across the meat department.

Her stomach grumbled, but she made no move to get up and feed it. She didn't want to order another meal to be eaten alone. And she certainly wasn't going to cook tonight. She'd most likely drive through somewhere in town and eat it in her car, tossing the bag into the outside trashcan on her way into the house.

She'd sit in front of her computer and edit the senior pictures she'd done yesterday. Exhaustion moved through her body, because she'd booked six more seniors for that week alone. Tonight was the only night she didn't have anyone to shoot, and she had one in the morning on Saturday and one in the evening too.

She loved March, April, and most of May because she was so busy, but she hated them at the same time. Senior pictures and weddings paid her bills, though, and she didn't want to be ungrateful for the business the Good Lord sent her.

After all, if her photography couldn't pay the bills, she'd have to work at Wilde & Organic full-time. While she loved her family, she sure didn't want to be here with her parents, her older sister, and one of her older brothers.

No, thank you, Whitney thought. She liked getting together for Sunday lunches and holidays. She went and saw her sister a couple times a week, but that was more for Dalton than Patsy.

Whitney opened the desk drawer in front of her, because Michael kept his favorite chocolate candy bars there for when he had a full day of paperwork ahead of him. He'd never miss one among the dozens he kept there, and Whitney wondered how he managed to eat them and stay trim and fit.

All she had to do was look at a bowl of macaroni and cheese or a plate of ribs and she'd gain ten pounds. Since Blake had left, Whitney had been eating chips or chocolate and counting them as meals, so she did carry a few extra pounds.

Her mind didn't seem to be able to settle onto any one thought, and she finally got to her feet. She moved her basket to the top of a filing cabinet, so Michael wouldn't get irritated when he arrived in the morning.

Whitney herself needed to be here in less than twelve hours, so she checked her pockets for her keys and headed downstairs. She hadn't parked out front, and she had to walk through the shadows to the back exit.

Her skin caught a chill as she hurried through the frozen section, and by the time she made it to the black, plastic door that led into the warehouse behind the storefront, she was almost running.

The exit lay directly in front of her, and Whitney

exploded through it, though the darkness beyond wasn't much more comforting.

She'd parked right beneath the bright outside light on the building, and relief spread through her as the heavy, metal door slammed behind her. Whatever phantoms that had been chasing her through the store had been sealed inside. She turned back to make sure that door was locked, because if she didn't, and a robbery happened, she'd never be trusted in the store again. Her siblings already gave her sideways looks for how little she was involved in the family business, but Whitney had never minded.

With the door locked, Whitney turned back to her truck.

A man stood there.

Whitney sucked in a breath and screamed as loud as she could, spilling backward toward the door she'd just checked.

Her eyes didn't leave the man standing next to her driver's door, his cowboy hat bathing his face in darkness. He lifted both hands and said, "Whoa, it's fine. It's just me."

Even through her distress and the echoes of the screams, Whitney's brain connected the dots and "Jeremiah?" came out of her mouth.

"Sorry," he said. "Sorry." A nervous chuckle came out of his mouth. "You have no idea how long I sat in my truck, trying to decide if I should go on home or wait to talk to you."

She pressed her palm against her chest and sagged against the door behind her. "Jeremiah," she said again as if she needed to convince herself that it was him and not someone else.

He hadn't taken a single step away from her truck, and a healthy distance remained between them. "I'm so sorry," he said. "I...." He closed his mouth and ducked his head in that adorable way he had, and Whitney straightened as a smile touched her mouth. Maybe her first smile in a long time, actually.

"I'll let you get on home," he said. "I know you're busy right now."

"How do you know I'm busy right now?" She took a step closer to him, then another one. It wasn't particularly cold outside, but she fought against a shiver.

"Uh, maybe I spend too much time on social media." He raised his head and looked right at her.

A thrill shot through her bloodstream with the sight of those beautiful, intense, dark eyes holding onto hers. "You're right. I'm shooting a lot right now."

"So if I maybe called during the day, it would be better?"

"Did you circle the store and pull behind my truck to wait for me to ask me when you could call?" Whitney teased, glad when the ghost of a smile touched his lips. She'd never had the privilege of kissing that mouth, but oh, she wanted to.

Thank goodness it was dark and the light there threw

shadows around, because her face heated to a dangerous level.

"You still stockin' shelves here in the morning?"

"I do the produce section," she said, stopping just out of reach from Jeremiah. Their whole relationship had been like that. He was always just out of her reach.

But closer than he's been in a while, she thought.

"I've told you that so many times," she said, shaking her head.

"That's what I meant," he said. "What time do you finish filling up the produce section?"

"Before we open," she said. "Daddy wants everything pristine for the very first customer. Michael has adopted that stance." With only a couple of other grocery stores in town, Wilde & Organic didn't have a lot of competition, but her family wanted to provide the best experience. "I usually have to work in the back a little bit before I'm really done."

"So ten-thirty?"

"Closer to eleven before I leave here."

Jeremiah leaned against her truck like he wasn't going anywhere. "Do you always come tearing out the back door like the devil himself is chasing you?"

Whitney heard all the flirtation in his voice, and if she could see those eyes more clearly, they'd be sparkling like pure diamonds. "Yes," she said simply.

"Mm hm," Jeremiah said. "Well, maybe I'll call tomorrow then." He straightened and held her gaze for one more moment before circling toward the hood of her truck.

"Maybe?" she asked when he'd reached the far corner. She could barely see the light glinting off the chrome on his big, black truck. It seemed to melt right into the night, and Whitney promised herself in that moment that she'd never come to the store after dark and stay alone again.

Jeremiah looked over his shoulder at her. "You have my number, too, you know."

"Yeah, well, maybe I'll use it tomorrow then."

He grinned, tipped his hat, and continued to his truck. It purred as he started it, and he backed away from her vehicle. He didn't leave though, and Whitney hurried to get behind her own steering wheel and get the engine turned over.

She preceded him out of the parking lot, warmth moving through her like her momma had just pulled her favorite blanket out of the dryer and draped it over her shoulders.

"Please let him call tomorrow," she whispered to the sleepy town before her. She tilted her head back and added, "Please, Dear God. Give him the courage to me call tomorrow."

And if the Good Lord could do that, then Whitney would somehow find the strength to answer the phone when Jeremiah called.

3

Jeremiah muttered to himself the entire way back to Seven Sons Ranch. There were plenty of names in there, like, "idiot," and "stalker," to name a few. He'd never tell anyone what he'd just done, as he could still hear the terror in Whitney's scream when she'd turned around and found him standing between her and her truck.

Frustration built inside him, the same way it had while he'd loaded his recyclable bags into the backseat. Truth be told, he was irritated too. At himself. At her. At the world. At God.

And he hadn't been able to drive away. He'd tried to talk himself out of waiting at least a dozen times before she'd come racing out the backdoor. She'd stopped as suddenly as she'd appeared, and by the time she'd checked the lock on the door, Jeremiah had slid from his truck and rounded hers.

"I didn't even know she had a truck," he said to himself as he turned off the main highway. Of course, he hadn't spoken to the woman in almost four months, so there was probably a lot he didn't know.

"Like why she cut you out of her life," he said. "And then sort of talked to you in the store, and then flirted with you in the parking lot."

At least Jeremiah had thought Whitney had been flirting with him. He hadn't been in the dating pool for a while. In fact, he didn't even own a pair of swimming trunks to get near the pool.

Whitney had been the only woman he'd even remotely felt anything for in years, and her disappearance from his life had set him all the way back to the day he'd been left at the altar. His thoughts had been circling so many damaging thoughts, and the stories he told himself about who he was and what he could be for someone else had turned dangerous.

He'd started driving to town to meet with Tug Wagstaff, a counselor who'd helped Jeremiah start to change some of his damaging thought patterns.

Broken ran through his mind as he eased his truck past Wyatt's. At least his brother was home tonight. He had never said where he'd disappeared to earlier this year, and as far as Jeremiah knew, Wyatt wasn't dating anyone.

And Jeremiah didn't feel as broken as he had previously. He still wasn't sure God cared all that much about him, but he and Tug didn't base his mental health on his faith, something Jeremiah was actually grateful for.

He still went to church with his brothers and their wives—those that had them—but Jeremiah simply wasn't sure if he'd ever be able to feel the calming influence of the Lord in his life again.

Wyatt opened the garage door leading into the house before Jeremiah had even gotten out of his truck. "There you are. I was just about to call the police."

"You haven't even called me," Jeremiah said, grabbing his phone and glancing at it. Nope. No missed calls.

He wondered what his pulse would do if the screen lit up and Whitney's name and picture sat there. He put the thoughts away, because Dr. Wagstaff had encouraged him not to live inside of if's.

It was good advice for Jeremiah, because then he wouldn't have to think about what might happen if he allowed another woman into his life, into his heart. Onto his ranch, which had become Jeremiah's sanctuary from the rest of the world.

"I was about to," Wyatt said. "Liam called and said he's making toasted marshmallow ice cream, and we should head next door whenever we want."

"Help me with the groceries," Jeremiah said. "And we'll go." He opened the back door and started handing his brother a couple of bags. Together, they took everything inside, and Jeremiah automatically looked for Penny to come greet him.

The cattle dog didn't. Rhett brought her out to the ranch most days, but she didn't live here anymore, and Jeremiah missed her. He'd known he missed the dog for months now, but he'd been so busy doing other things with his time and mental energy that he hadn't done anything about it.

"I'm going to head into town and get a dog tomorrow," Jeremiah said. "You want to come?"

"You want a dog tomorrow?"

"I think it's time." Jeremiah pulled out the milk he'd bought.

"Well, go to the animal shelter if you want. Boone'll have something for you. But if you want, there's a cowboy out at Three Rivers who has blue heeler puppies. He might have one or two left."

"A blue heeler?" Jeremiah asked. "Don't know anything about them."

"They're cattle dogs," Wyatt said. "Love to run. Need to be working."

"We do plenty of that here."

"Yep. I'll talk to Bennett if you want. I don't know how much he's charging."

"Yeah, I might not be able to afford it," Jeremiah joked, shaking his head. "Yeah, talk to him."

"I'll call him right now." Wyatt probably just didn't want to help put away the groceries. He got annoyed when Jeremiah moved where he put the pudding mix or when he put the cucumbers in the bottom drawer after

Wyatt had put them in the top one. So, fair enough. Jeremiah liked things in a certain place, and he did do ninety-nine percent of the cooking in the homestead.

Wyatt stepped away while Jeremiah continued unpacking produce and meat.

"Heya, Bennett," Wyatt said. "My brother wants one of your pups. Do you have any left?"

Jeremiah kept one ear on the conversation as Wyatt said, "A boy and a girl. I'll ask him."

"Both," Jeremiah said without thinking.

"You want them both?" The surprise on Wyatt's face wasn't hard to find.

"Yes," Jeremiah said. "If he'll let me have both of them, I'll take them."

Wyatt went back to Bennett, and only two minutes later, he said, "Great, I'll bring you the money tomorrow. When can he pick them up?" He gave Jeremiah a thumbs up. "End of the month. Right. Thanks, Ben."

He hung up and said. "You got 'em both." He grinned at his brother. "Look at you, getting two dogs." Wyatt chuckled and cocked his head. "What happened in town?"

"Nothing," Jeremiah said quickly. "I went grocery shopping."

Wyatt picked up a container of organic chicken stock Jeremiah bought from the butcher. It really was so much better than anything put in a can. "Wilde & Organic. Interesting."

"I shop there every week," Jeremiah said, practically ripping the box of chicken stock from Wyatt's hands.

"Did you see anyone there tonight?"

"It was late," he said. "I was practically the only one in the store."

"I see."

Jeremiah sucked in everything he wanted to say. He didn't want to argue with Wyatt, and he didn't want to extend the conversation. "Skyler's leaving Amarillo about ten on Wednesday," he said, clearly changing the topic.

"Which means it'll be closer to noon," Wyatt said with a chuckle.

"Yeah, probably." Even Jeremiah could laugh about his younger brother's tardiness. "But I'm pretty sure he said he had to be out of his apartment by ten."

"Oh, he'll charm the check-out student and maybe give her fifty bucks and then start throwing everything he owns in boxes."

The two of them laughed heartily after that, and Jeremiah finished putting everything away. He hadn't eaten dinner yet, but it was already late, and he went with Wyatt over to the Shining Star Ranch, where Liam lived with Callie now.

The scent of fiery, toasty marshmallows filled the house, and Jeremiah took a deep breath as he walked through the front door. "We're here," Wyatt called, and Jeremiah needed to remember to do that.

He loved Callie and Liam, but he didn't need to walk in on them making out again. The first time had been enough, and he'd done it a few more times since.

"In the kitchen," Liam called, and Wyatt and Jeremiah walked past the office and formal living room at the front of the house.

Happiness spread through Jeremiah when he arrived in the kitchen. The whole house had been remodeled only a few months ago, and Jeremiah had done a lot of the work. Rather, he'd *overseen* the work, which was just as hard as lifting a hammer.

The island in the kitchen was covered with treats, from shredded coconut to hot fudge to graham cracker crumbles. Liam really was a genius with desserts. He didn't cook much, but he made a killer last course.

"I love you," Jeremiah said.

"Rough day?" Callie stepped next to him, and he put his arm around her easily.

"A little," he said, because he was really trying to be truthful about how he felt. Another tactic from his therapist. He was also supposed to record how many hours he slept each night, and it was depressing to see the low numbers. "Just tired."

She leaned into him for a moment and then stepped away. Jeremiah didn't blame her—she was married to his brother, after all. He harbored absolutely zero romantic feelings toward the woman, and he never had. But she had been his first friend in Three Rivers, and they'd had a special friendship.

But he would never do anything to hurt one of his brothers, or Callie. So if she had to be a little more distant than she'd been in the past, he could shoulder it.

He was tired, and he didn't feel like talking, so gratitude streamed through him as Wyatt started up a story about something one of the Ackerman kids had done out at Three Rivers Ranch that day. Jeremiah could laugh as he ate a delicious bowl of ice cream that tasted just like the s'mores he'd enjoyed as a kid.

By the time he got home, he was ready for the solace of the master suite in the homestead. It was a huge room—way more room than one man needed. But Jeremiah never felt like the room was too big for him.

He had a desk in the corner where he kept his crossword puzzles and other books he might read when he woke early in the morning. He didn't allow a scrap of ranch business in his bedroom, as he had an office out in the stables.

Recently, he'd brought in a yoga mat so instead of lying in bed, wishing he could go back to sleep, or solving another puzzle, he could meditate. At first, he'd had no idea what to do. He didn't know what to think about, and even a minute had felt like an hour.

He was getting better and better at it, and he'd reported to Dr. Wagstaff last week that he'd made it to thirty minutes per day for his meditation. He wasn't as tired as he used to be, he knew that. He wasn't as broken, no matter what Wyatt said.

Dr. Wagstaff said he wasn't broken at all, but Jeremiah still had his doubts. As he laid down and immediately started to doze off, he supposed he'd find out tomorrow...if he could work up the gumption to call Whitney Wilde.

4

Whitney flew through her morning produce replenishment, mostly to prove to Michael and Patsy that she could come in a few minutes late and it wasn't a national event. She didn't clock in and out like a normal employee, and she didn't need to be glared at by her brother, who was twelve years older than her, because she was fifteen minutes late.

Patsy had given her a look and said, "If you were Dalton...."

"Well, I'm not," Whitney said as she pulled on her gloves. She didn't need her sister to treat her like she was a fifteen-year-old. Besides, Dalton was a good kid. He got good grades and he was kind. So what if he didn't want to work from dawn until dusk? Who did?

Maybe Michael.

Whitney smiled at her own internal joke. She also

finished laying out the organic eggplants with lightning fast precision, quickly moving onto the apples that had just come in from Mountainland Fruit Farms.

She finished right on time, despite being a few minutes late, and she hurried through her paperwork in the back room that had held demons last night. She left Wilde & Organic by ten-forty-five, and eleven came and went while she drove through a coffee shack to get her energy for the day.

With a shoot at six, Whitney had the day to edit the senior from earlier that week and maybe catch a nap.

And hopefully, talk to Jeremiah for a few minutes.

She kept a close eye on her phone, seemingly checking every few minutes. Then every minute. She swore she even checked once before the numbers had rolled over.

Jeremiah hadn't called.

"He's busy," she reminded herself. He hadn't said he could call right at eleven, and her stomach growled a few minutes past noon, reminding her that she hadn't eaten yet that day. She'd finish the picture on the screen in front of her, and then she'd decide what to do.

Sunlight spilled through the windows in front of her, and Whitney got up to close the plantation shutters. She loved editing in the natural light, just like she only shot the photos in an outdoor environment. She'd been taking classes in the art of lighting, and she'd done a few shoots in the hills south of Three Rivers.

But her favorite light came right from the sun as it rose

or as it sank, and she focused on the pretty girl on the screen. Jean Jenkins probably wouldn't be categorized as the most beautiful girl in her class, but Whitney had posed her just right. Jean had even said, "Thank you for making me feel pretty," as the shoot had concluded.

Whitney loved taking ordinary people and bringing out the extraordinary in them. Photography had provided her with a way to do that, and she couldn't imagine working more than the few hours she did at the family grocer or farm.

The sore shoulders and cramped back, all the aches and pains of getting the just-right shot, were worth it when she got the appreciation for delivering flawless photographs.

Her love of producing something artistic and beautiful had transferred to her pseudonym, and she hoped her new poster at the store would yield another handful of newborns she could place on her garden table.

After all, the bluebonnets would be in bloom for another month, and there was nothing better than blue-bonnets layered with carrots that still had their greenery and sugar snap peas—the whole plant if she could sneak one away from Johnny, her brother who ran and worked the family farm for fifty hours a week.

The last time he'd caught her taking the beets, Whitney had bought him the fanciest steak from Musca-dine's. The dish's price wasn't listed on the menu. Instead, it said "Market price," and Whitney's price for the beets had been a sixty-dollar steak dinner for John.

But out of her three siblings, Whitney got along with John the best. He didn't constantly ask her to help out with her nephew, not that she minded spending time with Dalton. But John didn't simply want her to get the job done. He didn't care if she was married or not. And he didn't have any expectations for her whatsoever.

Her father's expectations had lessened the closer to full retirement he got, but her mother would probably never stop lecturing Whitney about getting married.

And her blasted phone still hadn't rung.

Reaching for it, she felt a bit outside of her head. She didn't normally call men. Even with Blake, while she'd been desperate to be with him, he'd always called and texted her. He set up dinners and hikes and dates. Maybe according to his own pleasures and whims and schedule, but at least he called and invited her.

She pulled up Jeremiah's number and hit the green phone icon, her nerves shaking with the force that would register on the Richter scale. The line rang and rang, and Jeremiah didn't pick up.

She ended the call, a pinch starting behind her lungs and expanding outward quickly. Wow, what an unending pain. Whitney swallowed, trying to get the feeling to go down into her stomach, but it didn't settle any better there.

If this was how he'd felt when he'd called her and she hadn't answered, she had some serious repenting to do.

She wouldn't want to inflict this kind of agony on anyone, least of all the man she hadn't been able to get out of her head for ten months now.

Ten, long months.

They'd gone on one date, and held hands a few times, and still, he'd been a better boyfriend for her than Blake.

And Jeremiah could hardly be considered her boyfriend. He probably didn't even want to be.

To distract herself, she pulled up another picture of Jean, but her focus had fled. She'd only have to redo any work she did, so she abandoned her spot in front of the computer, picked up her keys, and headed out to her grandfather's truck.

She loved the old rust bucket, though it wouldn't get her out to Seven Sons Ranch very fast. Didn't matter. Then she'd have plenty of time to talk herself out of going. Of talking to Jeremiah while he kept his focus on his work instead of her. In the past, she'd liked that, because it meant he had feelings for her he didn't want her to see.

But now, she was sure those feelings would be borne of anger, not attraction. And she didn't want to be beside an angry Jeremiah. She pulled over to the side of the road and sighed. Maybe the sound was more of a huff. She wasn't sure.

"What should I do?" she asked, reaching up and rubbing the back of her neck. She rolled her shoulders out and checked her lipstick before she got back on the road. She wasn't sure if God was giving her an extra push, or if her granddad's voice was the one that told her to *keep going.*

The whisper that ran through her mind often sounded like his aged, raspy voice, and a keen sense of missing him hit her in the back of her throat. She tried to swallow it away too, but it didn't even go down. So Whitney let herself remember the man who'd always loved her, who'd learned how to text so he could ask to see pictures of any newborn pictures she'd done lately.

Granddad had been alone for a decade after Gran's death, and Whitney had gone to see him at least four times a week. They shared lunch together, sweet tea on the back porch, a walk around the block with Granddad's new dogs. The old ones too.

He always asked her what she was doing to make a good life for herself, and Whitney gripped the steering wheel with both hands, hard. "I'm trying, Granddad," she said. "I'm taking lighting classes for my photography, and I'm going to see this man I really like. Maybe, if you're close by, you could put in a good word with the Good Lord about us? I sure could use it about now to help Jeremiah forgive me."

Whitney knew that was what she needed. Forgiveness. And Jeremiah wouldn't give it easily.

She turned onto the packed dirt road that led to the Seven Sons and the Shining Star Ranches. The first ranch that came into view was her goal, and she drove through the open gate with all the stars on it. Her eyes lingered on

Jeremiah's name, enjoying how very Texan the Walker brothers were.

After parking in front of the house, she couldn't get herself to get out of the truck. If Jeremiah had come into the homestead for lunch, he hadn't come out to greet her. Maybe she'd never get the forgiveness she sought.

On wooden legs, she climbed the front steps to the door, and knocked. No one came to the door, even when Whitney rang the doorbell once, twice, three times.

Another huff, this one mixed with a scoff, and she turned back to the ranch. Jeremiah probably wouldn't like her trespassing, even if it was to beg him to talk to her. Thankfully, she caught sight of a cowboy walking on the pristine path between the backyard and the first ranch buildings, and she raised her hand and called, "Ho, there!"

Orion Roundy turned toward her, surprise etched on his face she could see from ten yards away. "Whitney," he said, a smile blooming on his face. "What are you doin' here?"

Whitney pressed her lips together to ensure they'd be as red as possible, though she wasn't trying to impress Orion. The cowboy had asked her out once or twice in the distant past, but they'd never actually shared a meal together.

"I'm looking for Jeremiah Walker," she said, though his last name wasn't needed.

"Oh, he's in town on Tuesday mornings," Orion said easily.

"Town?" Whitney looked over her shoulder as if she could see Three Rivers from here. Of course, she couldn't. "What's he doing there?"

"He'll have to tell you that," Orion said, and Whitney's curiosity increased. "He's usually back around one, and he brings food." He pulled his phone out of his back pocket and checked it. "I haven't heard from him today, though."

"I called him, and he didn't answer." Whitney dug her own phone out of her pocket. "Should I try him again?"

Orion wore an unreadable expression. "I'm sure he'll call you back when he's...when he can."

Only twenty-five minutes needed to pass before one o'clock, and Whitney pointed to the house. "Could I wait on the porch?"

"Yeah, sure," Orion said. "Try to find out if there will be lunch or not." He touched the brim of his hat and continued down the path. Whitney returned to the front porch and sat in the shade on the top step.

She loved this ranch, and she'd only been here twice. A sense of peace and tranquility existed on the land, as if God himself had touched it with the tip of his finger. She felt like she could be exactly who she was here, and it would be good enough. She would be good enough. Unmarried. Childless. Just a produce stocker for Wilde & Organic.

When the clock struck one, and Jeremiah hadn't come, Whitney called him again.

"Hey," he said after the second ring. Relief flooded her. He'd answered, and this new feeling of acceptance was a thousand times better than his silence. The rejection she'd tried to push away.

"Where are you?" he asked.

"Sitting on your front porch," she said, smiling like a fool. "Where are you?"

He started laughing, and the sound would be so much better in person. "Well, we have a problem, don't we?"

"We do?"

"I'm standing on *your* front porch."

5

Jeremiah reveled in the sound of Whitney's laugher, even if it was through the phone line. "How did you even figure out where I live?" she asked.

"Oh, well, that was easy," he said. "I called your mother."

"Tell me you didn't." She sounded horrified.

"I just told her I had a question about photography and I was in town, and where might I be able to find you?" He chuckled, hoping she wouldn't be too upset. "She rattled off the address easily. You know, I think she likes me."

"Of course she does," Whitney said. "You're handsome and rich and you buy groceries from our store."

Jeremiah shook his head, smiling at Whitney's landscaping. "A lot of people do that. And I doubt your mother cares about how handsome I am." Still, it sure did feel nice to have Whitney say such a thing. She clearly spent time in the yard, or paid someone to, if the perfectly trimmed rose bushes and green clipped lawn were any indication. A cluster of trees stood in the corner, with a flowerbed bare and ready to be planted.

"Oh, she might not care for herself," Whitney said. "But she lectured me for a solid hour the other day about getting married. She has no idea what I'm waiting for, you know?"

Jeremiah's throat closed at the mention of getting married. His therapy session that morning had centered on his last, failed attempt at marriage, and Dr. Wagstaff had asked him what he needed to do in order to take that step again.

Jeremiah had originally said he would never take that step again. But that Dr. Wagstaff was a tricky fellow, and he'd started asking Jeremiah questions about who he wanted to spend the rest of his life with. Who would be there with him when he left this world. What he'd have to show for his time on Earth.

And Jeremiah could admit that he didn't want to live at Seven Sons alone. And the ranch would just be passed to someone else. Land was just land. Money was just money. He couldn't take any of it with him.

His thoughts had been revolving around Whitney since—and maybe even before that. Maybe way back in January when Wyatt had called him broken, Jeremiah had had the insane thought of finding someone who would marry him just to prove to his brothers that he was the opposite of broken.

And the woman on the other end of the line was the only one he'd been thinking about since.

"Are you still there?"

"Yes," he said. "And no. I'm on my way to you now."

"Orion wanted to know if there would be food."

"I'll drive through and get burgers and fries. Don't leave, okay?"

"I'll be right here," Whitney promised, and Jeremiah's pulse pounded out of control. Every moment of the next twenty-five minutes seemed to take an eternity to pass, but he finally pulled into the garage at the homestead, the sight of Whitney and those bright, kissable, red lips made him chuckle to himself as he parked.

"Pull it together," he told himself under his breath as he turned off his truck and gathered the brown bags of food. He didn't need to go broadcasting how he felt about Whitney. He wasn't going to ask her to marry him today, but he did wonder if he could get to that point with her in the future.

Instead of pure fear, something akin to joy moved through him. For the first time in almost four years, Jeremiah could see himself with a woman again. Taking risks. Learning to love all over again. Becoming vulnerable.

"Hey," Whitney said, and he handed her a bag of food. "Bless you. I'm starving."

"Sorry," he said. "Guess we should've planned better."

"I called you earlier," she said. "Before I drove out here."

Jeremiah didn't get calls while he was in counseling, but he wasn't sure he wanted to reveal where he'd been quite yet. "Hmm, I didn't get that call."

"No?"

"No."

"Where were you? Inside a cave or something?"

He liked it when she teased him, and he simply passed her a drink carrier with four colas in it. Thankfully, Orion opened the door and said, "Thank the Texas stars. Dicky was about to chew on my arm."

Jeremiah met Whitney's eyes for a moment and then focused on his ranch hand. "Well, we wouldn't want that." He went up the steps and into the mudroom, Whitney right on his heels. He introduced her around to the boys, adding, "Orion, Dicky, Wallace, Simon. How'd everything go with Oprah?"

"Oh, she's still pregnant," Orion said.

Noticing Whitney's confused look, Jeremiah handed her a cheeseburger. "Oprah's our pregnant mare. She's bein' stubborn about lettin' that foal come out."

"You named a horse Oprah?" she asked, giggling immediately afterward. Jeremiah wondered what would happen to his pulse if she giggled like that after he'd kissed her. Surprise darted through him, as did that healthy dose of fear he was used to when it came to having a real relationship with a woman. He'd only really talked to the

Foster sisters in the four years he'd lived here, and he'd never once thought about kissing any of them.

"Well, Dicky did," Jeremiah said, indicating the other cowboy. "He has a soft spot for afternoon television."

"That Dr. Phil is wise," Dicky said, lifting his hamburger to his lips.

Jeremiah just shook his head and dumped his fries onto a plate. He took two cheeseburgers and headed over to the table to eat with everyone. Thankfully, Whitney joined him without any awkwardness, and lunch commenced.

"I'll go check on her this afternoon," Jeremiah said. "I need everyone on the fields this afternoon."

No one argued, though checking on their newly planted crops wasn't an exciting job. They needed to make sure their watering systems worked, and things were growing properly, and that the planting had gone as planned.

"Just a couple more days," he said. "Then we'll be back to regular chores." He glanced at Whitney, who simply gazed at him like he was solving the world's hunger problems one corn field at a time. He wasn't, but in that moment, Jeremiah felt like he could conquer the world.

He looked away, and Wallace ate like he hadn't eaten in days, so he was finished. "I'm going now," he said. "Remember I have that thing tonight?" He met Jeremiah's eyes, who nodded.

"Thing?" Orion asked. "That's so specific."

"We all have things," Jeremiah said, switching his gaze to his foreman. He was the only one who knew where Jeremiah went on Tuesday mornings, and he wondered what Orion had told Whitney. He trusted the blond cowboy who'd been at Seven Sons for almost a decade, and he had no reason to suspect that Orion had said *Jeremiah goes into town for therapy sessions every week*. He'd asked Jeremiah about them once, and he'd simply said, "They're really helping."

And they were.

"It's a date," Dicky said, ribbing Wallace. "With Molly Schuyler."

"No," Orion said, his voice awed. "Is that true?" He looked at Wallace.

"I mean, maybe." Wallace grinned, so his secret was definitely out.

"Wow," Orion said, looking around at the other cowboys. "I'm impressed. She doesn't go out with anyone."

"No," Wallace said. "She didn't want to go out with *you*."

"Oh-ho," Dicky said, laughing loudly. All the cowboys did, even Simon, who was a little more reserved than the other boys, and Jeremiah joined in as well. Lunch broke up then, though he'd only eaten one of his cheeseburgers. He watched the boys go out the back door, leaving him and Whitney alone.

"They're fun," she said.

"Are they?" Jeremiah unwrapped his burger, wondering

what her definition of fun was. Sitting around while a few cowboys joked and teased each other didn't really seem like his version of fun, but he had enjoyed eating lunch with them on Tuesdays for the past few months. Anything where he got to have real adult interactions with other human beings was good for Jeremiah's soul, and he once again toyed with the idea of going to the summer dances when they started up at the end of the month.

One glance at Whitney, and that idea was out. Completely.

"I like them," she said.

"You like everyone and everything that's a bit special," he said.

Her expression grew serious. "What does that mean?"

"It means you have a good heart," he said, a measure of embarrassment slipping through him. "And you don't mind the oddballs."

She ducked her head, smiling. "Maybe that's true."

Several beats of silence passed, and Jeremiah finished his cheeseburger. "Look, I didn't mean to say anything about the baby photography," he said.

"What?"

"I mean, that lady who does the vegetables and babies? She must be a friend of yours."

"She...is."

"I didn't mean to say anything mean about it. It's good photography."

"Was that your photography question?" she asked, leaning forward onto her elbows, a flirtatious look dancing across her face now.

He laughed and shook his head. "No. I didn't actually have a photography question. You knew that, right?"

Whitney nodded, oh-so-slowly. "I need to apologize too."

"Yeah? For what?"

"Not answering you." She swallowed, those big, dark eyes almost swallowing his whole soul when they were mournful. "When I called you earlier, and you didn't answer. Wow." She shook her head, her dark hair swaying slightly. "That hurt, and…I'm sorry if I made you feel like that."

Jeremiah experienced the tightness in his chest, the helplessness, the anger that had come when Whitney hadn't picked up his calls or answered his texts. He nodded, the only acceptance of her apology he could muster.

He got up and picked up her plate, then his. He slid the trash into the garbage can and set the plates in the sink, his mind telling him to confide in her about where he'd been that morning, but his heart screaming out a warning to keep his secrets.

Secrets.

How he hated those.

"How about a deal?" he asked.

"A deal?" Whitney got up and joined him, the island separating them.

"You want to walk around the ranch? See what spring is like out here?" He rounded the island and extended his hand toward her.

She put her fingers through his, and all the things in Jeremiah's life that had been skewed suddenly aligned. A sigh physically passed through him, and he couldn't help smiling. "Here's the deal," he said when they got to the back door. The air outside wasn't super-heated today the way it would be in July, August, and September, and for that, Jeremiah was grateful.

"I'll tell you why I didn't answer this morning, if you'll tell me why you disappeared in January."

Whitney stayed silent as they crossed the deck and went down the steps to the lawn. She said nothing as they left the homestead behind and stepped onto the ranch. "All right," she said. "You have yourself a deal." She looked at him. "You go first."

Jeremiah suddenly needed a lot of steps to find the right words for her. He took her out to the horse pasture, where Lightfoot and Stony snacked on grass. "All right. I couldn't answer, because I actually put my phone in a locker during my counseling sessions. It's a device-free zone."

He looked at her, so many things now laid open, at least for him. "Your turn."

She blinked, clearly not expecting him to say that. "My turn? You're in counseling?"

"Yes," he said simply.

"For what?"

Oh, she didn't get to know about Laura Ann and the failed wedding yet. "That wasn't part of the deal."

"Will I get to find out?"

"Depends on how long you stick around this time," he said, not intending to be unkind. He still saw her face fall. "Sorry," he muttered.

"No," she said, her voice pitched a bit high. "No, I deserve that."

He took a butterscotch candy out of his pocket and unwrapped it, waiting for Whitney to take her turn and tell him why she'd cut him out of her life four months ago. She took a deep breath as if she'd start talking, but then she didn't.

"Whenever you're ready," he said, withdrawing another candy for Lightfoot, who'd been slower than Stony in coming over to the fence for a sweet.

6

Whitney wanted one of the treats from Jeremiah's pocket. She reached over, palm up, and he placed a wrapped peppermint in her hand without comment. He really was too good for her. And what would he think when she told him the truth?

She thought about making something up, but her brain spun, unable to land on any one story that sounded reasonable. Plus, she didn't want to lie to him. She knew from experience that good relationships weren't formed on a foundation of untruths.

"There's this guy," she started, wishing she'd chosen any other way to begin. "My former boyfriend, I guess. He seems to come in and out of my life whenever he wants, and...." She shrugged. "For some reason, I let him."

Jeremiah said nothing, and when Whitney dared to look at him, she found him studying the horizon. His gaze centered somewhere past the horses she knew he loved, and a muscle in his jaw jumped.

"It's really over with Blake this time," she said.

"Is it? Or did he just leave town?" He sucked in a breath in tandem with Whitney. "I'm sorry," he said instantly. "I didn't mean that. I apologize."

Whitney reached for his hand, somewhat surprised when he let her touch him. He might have flinched; she wasn't really sure. His fingers curled around hers, sending warmth down to the coldest part of her soul. And while she'd just said her relationship with Blake was over, she hadn't really believed herself.

She did now.

His touch was nothing like Jeremiah's, which had fireworks exploding through every cell in her body. He was mature, several years older than Whitney, and she sure did like the silver which salted his sideburns. But her attraction to him was so much more than physical.

"You know," she said, sure this stream-of-conscious talking was going to land her in serious trouble. "When I first met you, I thought you were just this grumpy cowboy. Good-looking, sure. But with a huge ego, and all this land he didn't want to share with anyone."

Jeremiah turned his head and looked at her, those dark eyes devouring her in less time than it took to breathe.

"But I wanted to shoot on this land, and so I called you." She edged closer to him, feeling wild and reckless and absolutely unstoppable. She'd always wanted a relationship where she could talk about how she really felt, and Blake had never allowed that. No one had. And here was Jeremiah, just waiting for her to say whatever she wanted.

"And called you. And texted. And you weren't all that nice." She bumped him with her hip, glad when the tension in his shoulders relaxed slightly. "And then, some-time in between all the calls, and all the times you hung up on me, I started to like you. You know, *like* you."

She could see the sweeping romance before her, and she could only imagine telling it to her children one day. Whitney reminded herself that she was standing at the fence with Jeremiah and two horses. This was reality, not fantasy.

"And then, one magical day, you called and asked me to come out to the ranch. I thought I'd maybe died and gone to heaven. Not only were you nice, but I got to come out to this beautiful ranch?" She sighed and shook her head at the beauty spread before her. "I love Texas, and Three Rivers, and you own a mighty amazing piece of it. You take good care of it, almost like you can feel the spirit of the land the way I can."

"I can," he said quietly.

"Anyway." She exhaled, taking a moment to appre-ciate that he did feel things on a deep level. Of course he did. That was why he'd held her at arm's length for so long. It was why he'd made this deal. He wanted to know what he was getting into if he offered her his forgiveness.

Please, she prayed, unable to add more to the plea.

"Anyway," she said again. "The photo shoot was amazing. Holding your hand is life-changing. I had *so much fun* at the New Year's Eve parade."

"And yet, you cut me off after that," he said, the hurt right there in between every syllable, every letter.

"I know," she said. "I don't know how to apologize enough." She leaned her head against his bicep, wishing he'd curl that arm around her and hold her against him. He remained as unyielding as she'd suspected he would. "Blake was only here for eleven weeks, and now he's off somewhere else. My mother and sister told me to get over him. Move on."

"How long have you been with Blake?"

"Actual physical time? Probably over a year, spread out across two and a half. Blake always has some wonderful thing he wants to do. Some amazing job in another part of the country." Whitney heard the bitterness in her words as it coursed through her whole body. She didn't even try to bite it back. "And I'm not that wonderful, or that amazing." She shrugged again, her mouth tightening as she fought back tears. "Maybe I should be in therapy." A half-laugh, half-sob came out of her mouth. "I'm sorry. I really am."

Jeremiah nodded a few times and looked away from her. Without being able to see his face, she had no idea what he was thinking. Not long passed before he said, "I think you're wonderful and amazing, Whitney Wilde." He looked back at her. Right at her. "Would you go to dinner with me this weekend?"

"Yes," she said without any hesitation, the utmost relief running through her the way fast-moving water did as it flowed downhill. "Yes, I'd love to."

A smile touched that mouth she'd spent far too long dreaming about, and he pressed his lips to her forehead. "I can get you in with Doctor Wagstaff. He's really good." He tugged her away from the fence. "It's way too hot to stand out here in the sun. I put a swing in the oak tree out front. Did you see it when you came in?"

"No," she said. "I was a mess when I got here."

"You were?"

"Oh, come on," she said, glad the mood between them was lighter. "Don't tell me you weren't nervous as you climbed my front steps and knocked on my door."

"Maybe a little," he admitted.

"Yeah, a little," she said, grinning at the chickens as they passed. They walked in companionable silence through the yard to the giant oak tree that stood guard in the front yard at Seven Sons Ranch. She'd seen it in all its glory at Christmastime, and she almost wished the brothers decorated it for all the holidays. Red, white, and blue streamers or stars for Independence Day, perhaps.

He held the swing still while she sat, and then he took his place beside her. He pushed them with his foot every time they moved forward, and he did lift his arm and curl it around her shoulders when she leaned into him this time.

"This isn't the whole reason I'm going to counseling," he said. "But what prompted it was when Wyatt called me broken." He cleared his throat. "So I apologize for hanging up on you last year. And laughing when you called. And anything else that may have upset you. I was a little broken, I suppose."

"The counseling helps?"

"A lot," he said.

They moved forward and back, forward and back.

"Will you cook for me sometime?" she asked, almost in a whisper.

"I tried that once," he said. "I ended up throwing all that food away."

Whitney pressed her eyes closed as a wave of pain cut through her. "I'm sorry."

"We don't need to spend our time together apologizing," he said. "And if your boyfriend comes back and you want to be with him, I'd rather you just told me. I'm not a baby. I can handle the truth."

"Deal," she said, wondering how many more she'd make with this gentle, strong, gorgeous man. She hoped a lot, and she thought, *Thank you,* as he continued to rock them back and forth, the Texas sun shining down but the oak tree protecting them from the heat of it. And inside the circle of Jeremiah Walker's arms, Whitney felt protected from everything that could possibly go wrong, ever. She felt safe. She felt cherished. And it had been a long, long time that she'd felt any of those things.

————

"Hey, Dalt," Whitney said as she walked into her sister's house. "Where you at?"

"He's in the backyard," Billie said from her spot in the giant beanbag. She held a screen in front of her face and didn't look at Whitney as she walked by.

"Heya, Bill," she said.

"Oh, wait, Aunt Whitney." She launched herself out of the beanbag, an earnest look on her face.

"Yeah?" Whitney paused before entering the kitchen, where she'd continue to the backyard. She should've gone straight there in the first place. She knew Dalton hated being in the house when his mother was home. Whitney wasn't too happy with Patsy at the moment either, so she understood how her nephew felt.

"Momma said I should ask you to come take some pictures at youth group next week."

Of course she did, Whitney thought. "What for?" she asked, keeping all the weariness out of her voice. People were forever asking her to take pictures for this or that or the other.

"Just for group," Billie said. "Head shots. It'd be an hour."

Plus editing. "What time?"

"Seven."

"Indoors?"

"Yeah."

Whitney could use some of the techniques she'd been learning about in her classes. "Tuesday?"

"Yes," Billie. "Could you?"

Whitney wanted to say yes, surprisingly. But she had a zillion seniors right now. She pulled out her phone and looked at her calendar. "Tuesday...Tuesday...." She had a shoot with a boy named Zach Olsen.

"I could, but I wouldn't be able there until seven-thirty." She looked up at her niece. "How many kids are in your youth group?"

"Seven."

Whitney could shoot seven twelve-year-old girls in twenty minutes. "Ask your group leader if seven-thirty is okay."

"I'll call her."

"Okay." Whitney started through the kitchen. "Let me know, 'kay?"

"Okay," Billie chirped after her, and Whitney slid open the door and stepped into the backyard.

"Ready, Dalton?" she called to her nephew.

Dalton laid on his back on the trampoline, perfectly still. Even the Texas air was deathly quiet. Whitney paused for a moment, looking for the earphones or some other indicator that he hadn't heard her.

There was none. She started across the lawn, recognizing the soft snores coming from him. She smiled fondly at him, wondering how her sister could see anything bad in him. Part of her wanted to leave him to his happy, evening nap. The other part of her knew he'd be upset if they didn't get to go driving. He only had an hour left to complete his driving requirements, and then Whitney would take him to get his driver's license.

"Dalton," she said again, this time reaching out to jostle the trampoline.

Her nephew yelped as his eyes opened, his hands coming up as if to ward off any unwanted attackers.

"It's just me," Whitney said. "Do you want to go driving, or should I let you go back to sleep?"

He looked at her, recognition in those dark eyes, so much like Whitney's own. "Driving," he said with a groan. "And you can take me to get my license after school tomorrow, right?"

"Yeah, that was the deal," Whitney said. "I'll be in the car, okay? Don't take forever, because I'm starving and you promised me barbecue from that stand on the east side of town."

"I can't afford that place." Dalton moved to the edge of the trampoline and jumped down.

"Promised," Whitney said as she walked away.

Dalton came with her, smiling. "Fine, but you're buying."

"I always buy," she said.

"I'll be out in two seconds," he said, veering toward the

house while she opted for the sidewalk that led beside the garage. She waited in the car for only about thirty seconds before her nephew came out. He got behind the wheel and started his pre-driving check. Mirrors. Seat position. Radio. Cell phone on silent and in the console.

"Ready?" he asked, turning the key in the ignition.

"Ready," she said. "And I think you were going to tell me about Lucy May."

"I was not," Dalton said, putting the car in reverse. Whitney grinned as his neck and ears turned red. Well, the ear she could see anyway.

"Yes," she said, teasing him now. "You said Lucy was talkin' to you at lunch, and you said—" She cut off, because that was where Dalton had halted the story too. "Then your mom called, and you never finished."

"Nothin' to finish."

"Dalton," Whitney whined. "I've been dyin' to hear what you said to her."

He shook his head, though Whitney knew her insane desire to know everything he did at school, everyone he talked to—especially girls—everything he liked, pleased him.

"Did you ask her out?"

"Maybe."

"Maybe!" Whitney started laughing. "Well, I'll have you know that you're not the only one with a date this weekend."

Dalton looked at her and then back to the road. Her

again. "Are you kidding? You can*not* go out with that loser again!"

"I'm not—"

"I'll cancel my date, and we can hang out," he said. "I'm not letting you go out with Blake again. Nope. Not happening." He shook his head, his fingers clenching tightly around the steering wheel. "Aunt Whitney, he's all *wrong* for you."

"I know," she said.

"Then why are you goin' out with him again? Didn't he just run off to, to…I don't even know where he went this time!"

"Signal," she said. "Turn right here so we can go out to the barbecue place."

"That won't take us an hour," he said. "I need another hour." He put on his blinker, but it was to turn left.

"Fine," she said. "I suppose you want to go downtown."

"Yeah," he said. "I need the practice in traffic."

Whitney's stomach threatened to claw itself out, but she didn't say anything.

"Call Lucy May," he said, and Whitney jerked her attention to him.

"Why you callin' her?"

"I ain't letting you go out with that no-good lowlife again."

"Calling Lucy May."

"Don't call Lucy May," Whitney said, stabbing at the

screen between them, where her voice-activated car had started to dial. The call ended, thankfully. "I'm not going out with Blake."

"Oh." He looked at her. "Then who are you going out with?"

Whitney rolled Jeremiah's name around inside her head, savoring all four syllables for just a few more moments.

Then she said, "Jeremiah Walker."

Dalton jerked the wheel, nearly sending them over the curb.

"Dalton," she scolded.

"Are you serious? Jeremiah Walker?"

"Yeah." She looked at him. "Why? Is that so shocking that he'd want to go out with me?"

"'Course not," Dalton said quickly. "I mean, a Walker." He sounded awed.

"What's so special about the Walkers?" she asked, though she had a few reasons of her own.

"Number one, they're super rich." He looked at her as if she didn't know this. "Number two, Wyatt Walker is like the ultimate cowboy. Did you know he's won more rodeo championships than anyone, ever? In roping, bronc riding, and bull riding? He's like, a legend."

"I said Jeremiah," she said. "Not Wyatt, though I could probably introduce you to him."

"Really?" Dalton nearly careened into oncoming traffic this time. "Could you?"

"Don't kill us," she said. "I may have bought Grand-dad's truck, but I need this car."

Dalton waited until he'd come to a stop at a red light. "Really, Aunt Whitney? Could you introduce us?"

"Let's see how my date goes first," she said. "Now, you start talkin' about Lucy May, or no one's meeting Wyatt Walker. Ever."

7

"Hey, there he is," Jeremiah said, laughing as Skyler came into the kitchen with a blue duffle bag in one hand and the other toting along a rolling suitcase. "How was the drive?"

"I got a ticket," he said, grinning as if getting a traffic citation was the best thing that ever happened to him. "I just can't seem to slow down coming out of Laverne." He dropped everything and stepped over to Jeremiah.

They embraced, and Jeremiah closed his eyes for a moment. Things were going to be so much better with Skyler home. Maybe Jeremiah would have someone to eat lunch with, though he knew all he had to do was text Orion, and all four cowboys would come to the homestead for food.

Food Jeremiah could order or cook.

"Somethin' smells good," Skyler said, looking around the kitchen and dining room.

"Braised short ribs," Jeremiah said. "Mac and cheese."

His brother chuckled. "It's so good to be home." He did look relieved, and Jeremiah wondered if college life wasn't everything Skyler wanted it to be. He'd only been gone for one semester, but he certainly had enough money to eat well. He didn't have to be the starving student most others were.

"How are things going?" he asked, watching Skyler's face. "With school and stuff?"

"Good," he said, putting a smile on his face. "Fine." He didn't look directly at Jeremiah though, which meant something was definitely off.

"You seeing anyone in Amarillo?" Jeremiah asked.

Skyler's face took on a completely new glow. "Tons of people."

Jeremiah rolled his eyes and shook his head. "Forget I asked."

Skyler let loose with a loud laugh. "Hey, it's good to be single among so many younger women."

"Do they know you're thirty-five-years-old?" In Jeremiah's opinion, that was way too old for a twenty-one-year-old. Heck, some of those "women" were only eighteen. They were girls.

"Don't ask, don't tell," he said with a wicked grin.

"You're ridiculous," Jeremiah said, honestly not understanding Skyler at all. How could he not be serious about who he went out with? Why was it a party to him?

Jeremiah turned away from his brother and said, "Want help unloading?"

"Yeah, sure."

Before they could go back out to Skyler's truck, the back door opened. Rhett and Liam walked through it, and another chorus of "You're back," and "It's so good to see you," filled the kitchen.

Jeremiah hugged Rhett too, who'd been away for a few weeks as he and Evelyn went on one last trip before their baby came. "How was the Hill Country?"

"Spectacular," Rhett said. "I'm thinkin' of buying something down there."

"Something?" Jeremiah asked. "Like a small something or a big something?"

"A big something," he said. "There are entire ranches full of miniature horses. The land is beautiful. Gorgeous. You'd love it there."

"I'm not going to the Hill Country," Jeremiah said, his voice maybe on the barky side of things.

Rhett simply grinned at him. "Oh, me either. I'm just saying."

What was he saying? Jeremiah honestly didn't know. "Let's go help Skyler get unloaded," he said, and the work was easy with four of them instead of just two. Jeremiah put his suitcases and boxes in the room he'd been in before, when he'd lived here for only a month.

"Micah's not here?" he asked, glancing at the empty room in the quad that took up the entire west wing of the homestead.

The twins' room was likewise empty now that Liam and Callie were married, and Tripp had that big estate on the east side of town. Rhett had been gone for a long time, and Wyatt and Jeremiah had bedrooms kitty-corner from one another.

"No," Jeremiah said, a pull of sadness moving through him. "He said he had some loose ends to tie up in Temple. I just don't think he knew how loose."

"What's the problem?" Liam asked.

"It's a who," Jeremiah said. "Her name is Stephanie."

"Oh, boy," Rhett said.

"Maybe I should call him," Liam said. "I mean, I had a hard time leaving Austin because of a woman."

"You do that," Jeremiah said. "He doesn't listen to me."

"Like he's going to listen to me," Liam said with a scoff. "Rhett should call. He's the oldest."

"And say what?"

"Whatever," Jeremiah said. But if he were Rhett, he wouldn't call either. Micah was a good man. A fine brother. But he'd always marched to a different beat. He did what he wanted, when he wanted to do it. Their mother had often said, "Oh, it's just Micah. He'll come around to my way of thinking soon enough."

And that was that. Everything had to be his idea, or it wasn't worth doing.

"Wyatt should do it," Rhett said. "They're the closest."

The brothers continued squabbling as they went back into the kitchen. Jeremiah began to make coffee, enjoying the new life that had entered the homestead the moment another Walker had. He grinned around at everyone so much that Liam finally asked, "What is wrong with you?"

"Nothing," he said quickly, straightening and bringing his coffee mug to his lips to hide the smile.

Liam glared and cocked his head, his eyes narrowing.

"How's your project?" Jeremiah asked.

"Something's going on." Liam ignored his question entirely. "Does he seem...happier to you?"

"Definitely," Rhett said.

"And I saw a strange truck here a couple of days ago," Liam said.

Jeremiah's pulse pounded, and he turned away. He could deny that he had anything going on—again—but he wouldn't. In a household of seven brothers, he'd learned a few survival tricks, and one of the biggest ones was silence. Nothing to interpret if nothing was said.

"What kind of breed were the mini horses?" he asked Rhett.

"You're right," he said to Liam, also ignoring Jeremiah's question.

"I've got to get back to the boys," he said, heading for the exit though Orion and the other cowboys were not expecting him on the ranch that day. No, today was about family and visiting and getting Skyler settled in. Jeremiah should've known his brother would live out of his suitcases for at least three weeks before he decided to hang up a single item of clothing.

Rhett stepped in front of him, probably the one person Jeremiah respected the most. Well, he respected a lot of people. The cowboys he met with at his ranch owner's meetings. The men who worked for him. The Foster sisters.

Whitney.

Her name entered his mind, and it was almost like Rhett could see the seven letters of it flashing on his forehead.

"Oh, this has to do with a woman," Rhett said slowly, his eyes widening.

"No," Jeremiah said.

Liam joined Rhett, creating a virtual wall of Walker muscle between Jeremiah and the exit. His insides tightened, tensed, while he tried to figure out if he should flee or fight.

"Whitney?" Liam asked. "Was that her truck here the other day?"

"It was just yesterday," Jeremiah practically growled.

Rhett hooted, the laughter coming soon afterward. Liam just stood there and watched Jeremiah. "What?" he asked.

"You're...going out? Or...what?"

"Yes," he said coolly. "We're going out this weekend."

"When?"

"I don't know."

Liam cocked both eyebrows. "Where?"

"Unclear."

"So you don't have a date with her." Rhett looked a bit perplexed too.

"I asked her out," Jeremiah said stiffly with a glance at Skyler. He watched Jeremiah too, but his expression carried more amusement. Rhett seemed worried, and Liam simply looked...resigned? Disinterested? He sure was staring a lot for someone who didn't care if Jeremiah went out with the gorgeous photographer or not.

"She said yes," he finished. "That's it."

Broken echoed through his mind, only amplified when Liam said, "Wow. Are you ready for that?"

The truth was, Jeremiah didn't know. He wanted to be ready. He wanted to spend time with Whitney. A lot of time. He wanted to know everything about her, and see if he could tell her precious things about him too. He'd dreamt of kissing her, getting that red lipstick all over his mouth too.

His face heated, and *broken* ran through his mind again. "I'm capable of dating," he said stiffly.

"I didn't say you weren't," Liam shot back.

"Whoa, okay." Rhett held up his hands and made a triangle with the three of them instead of a face-off. Skyler edged around him, and Rhett backed up to make room for him. "Jeremiah, we just want to support you. Do we need to have a family meeting? Then you can tell us what's going on."

"Nothing's going on," he said. "I'm going to text her and set something up for Friday or Saturday. I'm allowed to date."

"I'm just shocked you want to," Rhett said. "Who's Whitney?" He looked at Liam.

"Dark hair. Bright red lips. He held her hand at the New Year's Eve parade."

"Oh, of course." Rhett looked back at Jeremiah. "I thought she ghosted you."

Jeremiah winced, the words so sharp and so raw...and so true. His pulse accelerated, his flight mode fully employed. After all, that was what Jeremiah was good at. Running away. Hiding in the homestead, away from the prying eyes of everyone in town. Keeping everyone except his brothers at double-arm's length. He didn't trust anyone he wasn't related to, except Callie. He didn't feel anything for anyone except his blood relatives.

"Well?" Liam asked.

"I guess she did ghost me," Jeremiah said. "But I ran into her, and the old boyfriend isn't in the picture anymore, and—"

"Whoa, whoa, whoa." Rhett actually held up his hand. "She ghosted you for an *old boyfriend*?"

Jeremiah wasn't going to answer that. He already had.

Rhett settled onto his back leg, his expression edged

now. With what, Jeremiah couldn't quite be sure. "Wow, Jeremiah. I can see you really like her."

"You know I do," he whispered. "You both know. I've talked to you about her."

"Family meeting," Rhett declared. "Tonight."

"I'll call Tripp," Liam said.

"I'll tell Wyatt," Skyler said, and Jeremiah felt betrayed by the man who'd hardly said anything.

"We can do it right after dinner," Rhett said, like he just got to decide everything, and everyone would fall into line because he said so.

Funnily enough, Jeremiah didn't argue. Maybe he did need the help of his family. Maybe, if he told them how he was feeling, he wouldn't mess things up with Whitney for a second time.

JEREMIAH STAYED at the kitchen sink even after Rhett said, "Family meeting." He really didn't want to have this conversation, and he didn't understand why they couldn't just have a nice dinner to welcome everyone back to Three Rivers and Seven Sons.

"Jeremiah," Rhett said, absolutely no emotion in his voice at all.

He finally turned away from the already clean kitchen and glared at his brother as he entered the living room. Thankfully, none of the wives had come for the family meeting, and Jeremiah was glad Rhett had some sense.

"All right," Tripp said. "What's going on?" He looked from Rhett to Jeremiah, as if he knew the two men were in a battle of wills. Jeremiah's fists clenched, and he deferred to Rhett. After all, he'd called the meeting.

Rhett stared steadily back at Jeremiah, as if he should start. Several long moments passed in pure awkwardness, and Rhett finally sighed and looked away. He had always been so calm and steady, and Jeremiah did envy him that.

Of course, he hadn't been standing at the altar while his almost-wife was fleeing the scene as fast as her feet could take her. Still in her wedding dress. As if the thought of becoming his wife was the worst thing in the world.

Jeremiah swallowed, his throat narrow even though he'd been working through these feelings for four years.

"Jeremiah has a date this weekend," Rhett said.

All eyes swung to him, though this really couldn't be a surprise to many of them. Maybe Tripp, who'd been scarce around the ranch since Christmas.

"And he's nervous about it," Rhett said. "And he might need some extra support."

Jeremiah relaxed slightly. This type of discussion was exactly why he liked having his family close by.

"Who with?" Tripp asked, not a trace of teasing on his face.

"Whitney Wilde." Jeremiah cleared his throat.

"My wedding photographer?" Tripp's eyebrows shot sky-high. "Holy stars in heaven." He looked at Liam, who already knew this information. "I miss a ton by not being here."

"I told you that."

"There wasn't a ranch out here," Tripp said.

"You have a great house," Liam said. "Beautiful land."

"I miss being here too," Rhett said.

Jeremiah listened to his brothers lament how they'd like to spend more time at Seven Sons, where they'd all come originally to heal and hide. Jeremiah thought he'd do that forever, but none of the others.

"How's the therapy going?" Liam asked, and that brought the focus back to Jeremiah.

"Good," he said. "Really good."

"Good enough to ask out a woman," Tripp said. "I'm still a bit stunned by that."

"Maybe he sees all of us happily married and wants that too." Rhett watched Jeremiah, who refused to look at him.

He'd always wanted to get married. Always. Out of all of the brothers, he'd been the first one to propose. It had taken a year to plan the wedding, and while everyone else dated, none of them bought diamonds.

So yes, seeing three of his brothers happily married might have spurred him toward a different path than he'd been on a year ago. Being so close to Liam and Callie may have turned him toward therapy so he could overcome some issues so he could get back to the altar.

"Is that what you want?" Liam asked. "To get married?"

"I don't know," Jeremiah said.

"You said you'd never do that again," Tripp said.

"I know what I said." He also didn't want to be alone forever. And one thing he'd learned in January after Skyler had moved out for school, after Liam had married Callie and moved next door, after Wyatt started spending time with a mystery woman, was that Jeremiah didn't do well alone.

"Being married is great," Liam said.

"So great," Tripp agreed.

Jeremiah finally looked at Rhett, and it was clear he sure did like being married too. The bottomless pit that Jeremiah had sealed four years ago opened, and the pain went on and on. And on. He felt like he might drown in it, and taking a breath hurt his chest and spiraled through his lower back.

He really wanted to be married and had for a long, long time. Jeremiah was made to be married, as he experienced most things with a great deal of passion, from being frustrated with pests in the corn fields to loving a woman and wanting to dedicate his life to taking care of her.

Maybe you should just marry Whitney, he thought.

"Guys," Rhett said. "He's not ready for that."

"Why not?"

"He's...improving—"

"He needs more time."

"I'm not broken," Jeremiah said amidst all the other talking, but no one heard him. At least they acted like they didn't.

"Once he's healed, he'll be fine."

"Maybe dating will heal him."

"Maybe it'll just break him further."

Jeremiah couldn't take any more of the bickering, of the speculating about how he felt, and he really, really hated that they all thought he was still damaged. Even if he was.

He got up and walked out of the living room, Wyatt and Tripp still arguing about how whole Jeremiah was.

Broken echoed through his mind, almost drowning out Rhett calling after him. He simply increased his speed and made it to his bedroom despite Rhett following him.

"Jeremiah," he said again as Jeremiah went into his bedroom. He closed the door and leaned against it, his chest heaving.

Rhett wasn't giving up, and he knocked on the door. Jeremiah stepped away from it, and when Rhett opened the door, he could still hear the other brothers squabbling. "I'm sorry," he said. "I didn't think it would delve into that."

Jeremiah took off his cowboy hat and hung it on the hook on the wall beside the bed. He didn't know what to say. He took a moment to breathe, and then he turned back to Rhett. "I've always wanted to get married."

"I know that."

"I'm so lonely."

Pure compassion crossed Rhett's face, and he hurried across the expansive master bedroom and drew Jeremiah into a tight, brotherly hug. Jeremiah clung to him too, glad he had this special bond with his older brother.

They'd done everything together growing up, and Jeremiah had always looked to Rhett as an example. He loved his brother with his whole soul, though he could've done without the family meeting to discuss his broken heart.

"Go with your heart," Rhett said, his voice quiet and somewhat choked. "You'll make the right decision."

"My history disagrees," he said, stepping back from his brother. "In fact, I trust my heart the very least when it comes to making decisions." The problem was, his head didn't do a great job either. Everything felt so tangled.

Rhett's phone rang, and he looked down. "It's Evelyn."

"Answer it."

He did, turning and moving toward the door. "Hey, baby," he said. "Everything okay?" He left the room, and Jeremiah went to close the door again. He couldn't let go of the idea of just going whole-hog and getting hitched.

After all, three of his brothers had made a fake marriage into something wonderful and lasting.

Maybe he could too.

8

Whitney celebrated her nephew getting his driver's license, shot her seniors, and obsessed over what to do with her hair on Friday night—when Jeremiah would arrive to whisk her off to a romantic dinner. He hadn't said where they were going earlier in the week, and Whitney had experimented with her hair down, curled just-so. She felt like she was going to church. So she'd pulled it up on top of her head and made the ponytail straight as a stick. But she felt too much like a cheerleader, and that wasn't working for her.

She'd bunned it and twirled it and sculpted it messily, but that all felt like she was trying too hard.

Jeremiah had called and said he'd like to take her to Sevano's, a super upscale restaurant in the newer part of Three Rivers's Main Street. Whitney had changed her outfit four times since that phone call, and she'd texted non-stop with Jeremiah the previous night to find out what he would be wearing.

Clothes? he'd answered, and Whitney had panicked as she stared at the phone.

Now is not the time for your teasing, she'd said.

I'm not teasing, he'd responded. *So like jeans and a shirt? My cowboy hat?*

Of course, men had things so much easier than women when it came to things like this. Whitney wanted to know what color his shirt would be, and he'd said he'd just pull out the cleanest one.

But she needed to *know.* She could then decide if she wanted to match him or if she wanted to go with a contrasting color.

But he wouldn't tell her.

She looked good in pink and red, what with her tan complexion and dark hair. And her bright red lips.

She added the final touch of that and checked to make sure her bright pink blouse lay flat in all the right places. She thought for a moment of Dalton getting ready for his date too and quickly tapped out a *Good luck tonight!* message to him.

You too, he sent back. *Details over lunch tomorrow?*

Whitney smiled and answered with, *If I don't have another date,* adding a winking emoji to her text before sending it.

She tugged on the end of her black skirt so it would brush the tops of her knees. She stepped into the tasteful pair of black heels—no pantyhose—and drew in a long breath before pushing it all out again.

"All right," she said to her empty house. "I'm ready."

Not two seconds later, her doorbell rang. As if he was a guard cat with the ferocity of a tiger, Jones meowed and looked over his shoulder at her. "Go get it," she told the cat, who of course, did no such thing.

Whitney had to answer the door herself, which she did to find Jeremiah standing there with a dashing smile on his face. She couldn't move. He really was the most handsome man in the entire world, with those broad shoulders, covered in a red, white, and blue plaid shirt. The sleeves were short and his biceps strained against the fabric. His cowboy hat had been switched from the normal dark charcoal one he wore around the ranch to a pristine, white one that looked amazing against his tan face. The silver in his sideburns made her fingers twitch to touch it, and she let her eyes travel down his jean-clad legs to a pretty pair of cowboy boots with white and yellow stitching on them.

"Wow," she said, only realizing after she'd spoken that she'd actually vocalized anything.

"No kidding," he said. "Look at you, Miss Whitney."

"Oh, you're going to pull out the Texas accent," she said, flirting shamelessly. "And the manners. I see how it is."

"My momma would be mortified if I abandoned my manners now." He offered her his arm, not even trying to come inside her house, and Whitney grabbed her purse from the couch beside her. She tucked her phone into the pocket and linked her arm through his.

"How was your week?" he asked.

"Oh, you know all about it already," she said. "I've told you everything over the last couple of days." It felt like it had been a lot longer since she'd seen him, but it really had only been three days.

"Well, Skyler came home on Wednesday, and he already has a date tonight," Jeremiah said as they went down the front steps. "So that made me realize how slow I've been."

Whitney glanced at him as surprise ran through her. She hadn't been expecting him to talk about his prior relationships tonight, on their first date. "Oh?" she asked, deciding that would be safe.

"Yeah," he said. "You're the first woman I've been out with in town."

"Oh, I'm aware," she said. "The women of this town like to talk about you Walkers, you know. Especially now that a few of you are married."

Jeremiah just led her around the front of his truck and opened the door for her. He didn't close the door right away, and his gaze burned into hers. "What?" she asked.

"Nothing." He backed up, closed the door, and started around the front of the truck. It looked like he was muttering to himself, and Whitney's nerves started jumping around in her veins.

Jeremiah got behind the wheel and glanced over at her. "Do you ride, Whitney?"

"Didn't we talk about this once?"

"I'm not sure," he said, flipping the truck into gear and backing up. "Did we?"

"I can't remember either," she said. "I mean, I ride a little bit. Not a ton, and not for a few years." She watched his profile, admiring his long, sloped nose and strong jaw. "I'd like to go with you, if you're offering."

"Just around my ranch," he said. "It doesn't have to be a big thing. Then we can stop whenever we want."

"And you can make me dinner afterward." The perfect date came together in her mind, down to the brownie baked in the cast iron skillet he'd scoop vanilla bean ice cream onto and they'd share. Maybe he'd kiss her after that too....

He shook his head, chuckling. "You're really hung up on that, aren't you?"

"I feel like I missed out last time," she said. "For a really dumb reason." She turned away from him, wanting to talk about something else. "What was the name of your horse again? Pretzel?"

"Stonestepper," he said. "Pretzel is Liam's."

"You guys don't share?"

"No," Jeremiah said. "I mean, I can ride any horse, but when I go riding, I ride Stony."

"Oh, so you're the horse whisperer?"

"I talk to the horses, sure," he said, and Whitney

turned back to him, expecting him to laugh. He didn't. "They're great listeners," he continued. "But they didn't have any strategies for how to deal with certain things." He shrugged with one sexy shoulder. "So that's why I started going to Dr. Wagstaff."

"Because the horses couldn't teach you how to meditate?"

"Right," he said.

Whitney watched him make turns and head down Main Street. She loved the old buildings, the way everything was kept clean, and how the city put up flags and banners to celebrate city events and wreaths for Christmas.

"Are you going to tell me why you didn't date?" she asked. "And why you're seeing Doctor Wagstaff?"

"Those are really personal questions," Jeremiah said.

"I know," Whitney said. "I told you about my no-good boyfriend that I kept going back to. That was personal too. That's how we get to know each other, Jeremiah."

"Well, they are the same reason...." He turned into the parking lot at Sevano's. A long hiss came out of his mouth. "Almost four years ago, my fiancée left me standing at the altar." He released the steering wheel and looked at her. Whitney saw a dozen emotions running through those eyes she liked so much.

"Just standing there, by myself. In front of everyone I knew, everyone I loved." Pain filled every word. "I felt like an idiot. So foolish. Why couldn't I see that she didn't love me? Didn't want to marry me?"

"I'm so sorry," Whitney said, because she couldn't imagine not being able to walk down the aisle toward Jeremiah. He called to every one of her cells, and they were all screaming at her to lean a little closer, take a little deeper breath, commit every single thing about him to memory.

Jeremiah shook his head, breaking their eye contact. "So Rhett bought the ranch—he'd just gone through a bad break-up too—and we moved here. Started fresh. Didn't date."

"Rhett obviously dated," Whitney said. "And Liam, and Tripp."

"Well, there *was* a pact," Jeremiah said.

Whitney smiled, because she could just see Jeremiah's face when he found out the pact only meant something to him. And while she didn't want to be on the receiving end of his anger, he sure was attractive when he was passionate about something.

"Anyway, I'm doing a little better now," he said. "Not as good as—" He cut off, his eyes widening as he met Whitney's.

"Not as good as what?" she asked.

"Let's talk inside," he said evasively.

Whitney wanted to demand that he tell her now, but she watched him slide out of the truck and round the front again. This time, he didn't mutter to himself. He opened her door and offered her his hand.

"You're very mysterious, Mister Walker," she said, to which he finally laughed. Whitney liked the deep, rich sound of that, and she felt like a princess as she walked into the restaurant with him and they were promptly whisked back to a private booth in the corner.

"Have you ever eaten here?" he asked.

"Once," she said. "For my parents' fiftieth wedding anniversary."

"They must've gotten married real young," he said.

"Momma was only twenty," she said. "She claims the Texas air keeps her young, but it's really the Botox." Whitney whispered the last few words and smiled at Jeremiah.

"My parents got married young too," he said. "All of us boys are a real disappointment to her. Well, I mean, Rhett and the twins are married now. So not all of us. But you should've heard her talk a year or so ago. It was like we'd failed completely by not marrying and having loads of babies." He lifted his water glass to his lips, his face slowly turning a shade of red.

"Wow," Whitney said. "You're really not great at this dating thing." She giggled. "Though we've been out once before, and you didn't bring up marriage and babies and past relationships and all of that."

"Too much?" he asked.

"No," Whitney said quickly. "I mean, no."

The waiter arrived and they put in their drink orders. Jeremiah looked back at Whitney, another dose of anxiety in his expression. "Okay, I have something really crazy to talk to you about."

"I like crazy. Remember the oddball thing?"

Jeremiah shook his head. "That was a compliment."

"I know." Whitney reached across the table and covered his hands with hers. Fireworks exploded up her arms, and she pulled in a breath at how electric everything with him felt. He seemed likewise as stunned by her touch, and she started to pull away.

His fingers tightened and held onto hers. "It's more of a favor."

"A favor?"

"An insane favor." He let go of her hands and sat back as the waiter arrived with their drinks. "Do you know what you'd like?" he asked, looking from Jeremiah to Whitney.

She knew Julius Barnaby and had for years. He owned part of Sevano's, but not many people knew that. She'd gone to a few local business owners meetings for a year or two with her father, and she'd seen him and Karl Brinkerton, who owned the other part of Sevano's, at the meetings.

"We need a minute still," Jeremiah said. "I should probably look at the menu." He picked up his and glanced at it. Whitney needed time with the menu too, and it was more like a book and she'd only been here once.

"I'll circle back." Julius knocked on the table a couple of times and walked away. She and Jeremiah studied the menu, and when Julius returned, she was ready with her order.

"Prime rib," she said, handing the menu back. She went through ordering her sides, and Julius turned to Jeremiah.

"Same," he said, giving back the menu.

Whitney grew warm from head to toe, and she ducked her head, glad she'd just showered and let her hair fall down her back. She'd clipped back the front of her hair, but plenty still spilled over her shoulders.

"Okay, so we'll have a few minutes," he said. "I feel like I should tell you before you eat too much."

Whitney squirmed, glancing out into the rest of the restaurant, but with the limited view, her gaze gravitated back to Jeremiah.

"Okay, this is stupid." He lowered his head, the brim of his cowboy hat obscuring his face.

"Just say it," Whitney said. "I mean, what's the worst that can happen?" She thought about her pseudonym and how she'd feel if Jeremiah knew she was Lake Winters. It would be very, very hard to tell him that, and her imagination started running through a dozen different scenarios for what kind of favor Jeremiah Walker would require of her.

The man was a billionaire. He could buy anything he wanted, anytime he wanted it, including two incredibly expensive prime rib dinners at the most expensive restaurant in six counties.

"You're freaking me out," she said.

Jeremiah lifted his eyes to hers. "I want you to marry me," he said.

Whitney opened her mouth to respond, but the words had rendered her speechless. Her brain struggled to catch up, but all she could think was that oxygen was the wrong thing to breathe, and now she was slowly suffocating, the gorgeous Jeremiah Walker in front of her, waiting for her to say something.

9

Jeremiah's pulse raced like it was trying to win the Kentucky Derby. Whitney looked like he'd hit her with that same cast iron skillet he'd dropped the first time he'd met her. Her beauty stunned him as much now as it had then.

"I'm sorry," he said. "Let me frame this a little better for you." His words ran now, rushing out of him in long sentences. "They think I'm broken. My brothers, I mean. And I'm not broken, at least, not as much as I used to be. And they called a family meeting because I had a date with you. A *date*." He scoffed and shook his head, realizing that Whitney's eyes continued to search his face, looking for answers he couldn't give. Might never be able to give.

"It wouldn't be real," he said. "But you could live at the ranch. Shoot all you want there. And I could show them I'm over Laura Ann." He took a big breath and glanced around, but no one sat anywhere near them. He'd specifically asked for the most private booth in the restaurant, and it seemed like he'd gotten it.

Whitney scoffed, folded her arms, and leaned back into the booth behind her. "I—I—"

"You have no words," he said. "And I *am* over Laura Ann. I am. I'm ready to be dating again. I really am. I just want to…accelerate things a little."

"I'll say," Whitney said. She couldn't seem to look anywhere but at him, and Jeremiah sure did like that. "What are you going to tell your brothers? They know we haven't been dating."

"We can plan it for a few months," he said weakly, hearing how stupid his plan sounded. He'd been thinking about Whitney and marriage and how their wedding would solve a lot of problems. Rhett, Liam, and Tripp would back off. Wyatt wouldn't call him broken anymore. His mother would be thrilled, and Jeremiah wouldn't be alone at the homestead once fall arrived.

He was getting a whole lot out of the arrangement, and he knew that. He'd offered for her to shoot at the ranch, but she hadn't jumped at the chance to be his bogus bride in exchange for access to shooting at Seven Sons.

Idiot, he chastised himself. But he hadn't been able to think of anything else in the two days since the family meeting. In fact, he'd been dreaming of Whitney in a long, white dress every time he slept.

"You want to plan our wedding to take place in a few months?" Whitney asked.

"It won't be real," Jeremiah said.

"And how long does it need to be?" she asked. "Why don't we just date and see if we want to get married? Dating can show your brothers the same thing." She sounded slightly hysterical, and Jeremiah's foolishness doubled.

"Forget it," he said.

"I'm...."

He held up both hands as if waving off the cavalry. "Forget it. Honest."

Thankfully, the waiter returned with two huge plates of the most delicious prime rib Jeremiah had ever seen, breaking the terrible, awkward moment. Whitney didn't say anything, but she picked up her silverware.

Jeremiah did the same, wishing he could tell Whitney how much he liked her, how beautiful she was, and that yes, he'd definitely like to keep dating her.

He said nothing, and Whitney finally asked, "Do you have a middle name?"

"Joseph," he said, the name sticking in his throat. After all, middle names should come before proposals, and he couldn't help feeling like the world's biggest tool. Even the prime rib tasted like dust, and Jeremiah wished he could go back in time and fix this date.

But if that were possible, he'd go back five years and

break up with Laura Ann instead of asking her to marry him.

———

*D*ID *people ever call you JJ?*

Jeremiah had gone to bed an hour before the text came in. He kept his phone on at night, though, especially now that Evelyn was within a month of her due date. Sometimes Orion had a horse he slept in the stables with, and he might need to get in touch with Jeremiah.

Maybe that was why he didn't sleep very deeply, though he knew it was because he was afraid to dream. Of course, he still dreamt, because even he couldn't go all the time. He caught cat naps in the hay loft that could be an hour, and he sometimes slept for thirty minutes after lunch.

No matter what, he was easily roused from sleep when his phone notified him of a new text, and he puzzled over the one from Whitney. *JJ? Why would they call me that?*

A slip of relief comforted him that she'd texted him. By the time they'd finished dinner, talking about mundane things, and he'd dropped her off back at her house, Jeremiah had convinced himself he'd never hear from her again. And next time he called? She wasn't going to answer.

But here she'd texted him.

Because of the Jeremiah Joseph. What a mouthful.

He smiled at the emoji that came in, because it was smiling. *My mother was very religious.*

Oh yeah? I don't think your brothers have overly religious names.

Micah is, Jeremiah sent back. Rhett's a family name. Tripp and Liam, well, I don't know about them. My daddy always wanted a son named Wyatt, it being so cowboy-ish and all. And Skyler is named after my uncle that died a couple of months before he was born.

He rolled his shoulders and laid back on the pillows. Why had he said all of that? Whitney didn't care about his brother's names. A sigh slipped out of his mouth, and his eyes drifted closed.

"You have no idea what you're doing," he muttered to himself. "A little help would be nice," he said to God. "I've messed up royally. Would it have killed You to let me know the idea was terrible *before* I proposed?"

He sat straight up, horror moving through him. "Oh my word. I *proposed* to her." A moan started somewhere down in his gut and rose through his chest. He didn't understand how he'd gotten himself into this situation. He was almost forty-three years old, for crying out loud. He should know better. So much better.

His phone chimed rapidly a few times in a row, but he took his time lifting the device so he could look at the screen.

Wow, great stories, Whitney said.

I'm not named after anything that I know of.

Anyway, I know it's late and you get up early. We'll talk tomorrow.

Jeremiah read the texts again and then again. He wanted to ask her to lunch tomorrow. Maybe he couldn't screw up lunch, and she'd said they could talk, which was also comforting.

Feeling like he had nothing left to lose, he tapped out a quick message. *Lunch tomorrow?*

Then, thinking quickly, he added, *I promise I won't propose again.*

Haha.

Maybe next time, you could at least get down on one knee.

Good-night.

Jeremiah chuckled slightly, then pulled in a breath. "Wait," he said. "Next time?" He'd never get to sleep now, but he plugged in his phone and laid back down. Surprisingly, he did fall asleep faster than he ever had, and he dreamt of Whitney Wilde and those pretty red lips as she walked down the aisle toward him, wearing a vibrant, white wedding dress.

The following day, he drove to town again. He parked in Whitney's driveway. He walked up to her front steps. He was not going to say a single thing about his brothers, or how broken he was, or why he'd vowed to never date and fall in love again.

Besides, he wasn't in love with Whitney. He had feelings for her, sure. But that was a lot different than being in love and attempting to build a life and a house and a family together. No wonder she'd looked at him like he'd grown four heads.

He hadn't lifted his hand to knock yet when the door opened. Whitney held onto the door and smiled at him. "You lost, cowboy?"

Jeremiah simply stared at her. Was she really going to just move past his blunder last night? Act like it hadn't happened? Why couldn't he do that as easily as she did?

"A little," he finally said. "See, I was lookin' for this place that has the best mac and cheese sliders in town. You heard of it?"

"I sure have." She reached for something and came up with her purse. "Let's go. I'll show you the way." She grinned with those lips and walked right by him, practically skipping down the steps.

Jeremiah turned and watched her, wondering if he could just move on too. Dr. Wagstaff seemed to think so, but something inside him told him to talk to Whitney and clear things up. He climbed into the truck with her and started it so the air conditioning would start to blow.

"Look, are we going to talk about what happened last night?" He twisted toward her and looked at her.

Whitney gazed steadily back, and Jeremiah had no idea what she was thinking. He knew he liked her. He knew she was beautiful. He knew she made him feel something he'd not felt in so long. Too long. Years.

"You said to forget about it," she said. "And I gave up a

lunch with my nephew, where he was going to tell me all about this date he had last night, to go to lunch with you. So let's go."

Still Jeremiah didn't put the truck in gear and move. "I don't want to keep you from Dalton."

"Oh, I'm going to buy him ice cream on Monday." Whitney waved her hand like the change in plans was no big deal.

"Whitney," he said, and the merriment slipped from her face.

She swallowed and looked away from him. "What do you want me to say?"

"I don't know," he said. "I'll just let it go."

"Oh, I know you, Jeremiah Walker. You can't let this go. You'll be thinking about it for weeks."

"I feel so stupid," he said. "I'm really sorry."

"Nothing to be sorry about," she said. "And honestly... I've been thinking about what you said last night, and, I don't know." She shrugged and rubbed her hands up and down her arms. "Maybe it's not a crazy idea. Maybe I just needed a night to sleep on it."

Jeremiah couldn't believe what he was hearing. "Are you serious?"

"I mean, you'd get to show your brothers you're not broken, and I'd get to shoot at the ranch...."

Jeremiah could only stare. "That's hardly a fair trade," Jeremiah said. "And you'd have to move to the ranch, and what will you tell your parents?" He shook his head. "No, it was some idiotic plan that I conjured up in my sleep-deprived mind. It's fine."

"I'm just saying maybe we should think about it," Whitney said. "Like you said, we could get married at the end of the summer. My parents wouldn't need to know anything about anything." She looked at him, an intense look on her face. "You aren't going to tell your brothers, are you?"

"That I concocted a completely insane plan to ask you be my fake wife to prove to them that I'm whole?" He gave her a dry laugh. "Of course I'm not going to tell them."

Whitney smiled at him, maybe a little more timidly than she had in the past. "Well, then, maybe we should talk more about it."

"Maybe," he said. "But I'm not up to it today. Can we just eat burgers and take a walk and talk about your cats?"

Whitney laughed, and Jeremiah put the truck in reverse. "Yes," she said. "That all sounds really nice."

"Great." Jeremiah was the king of putting hard things off until he could deal with them. Or until he was forced to deal with them. But right now, he really did just want lunch and easy conversation.

Plus, it was absolutely crazy that Whitney hadn't run for the border, that she'd texted him, and that she was even considering becoming his bogus bride.

10

Wyatt Walker's gut wouldn't settle down, no matter how many horses he rode for Ethan Greene. This went on for days before he finally turned right off River Road instead of continuing straight to go back to Seven Sons.

The sun wouldn't set for hours now that summer was dawning in northern Texas, and Wyatt hadn't seen Marcy Payne for several weeks. He liked her; she knew he liked her. He'd had several good indications that she liked him too—but her father was going through a lot of health problems, and Marcy's schedule and stress had exploded.

She was running Payne's Pest-free by herself these days, running her father to his multiple doctor's appointments, sometimes an hour away in Amarillo. She cooked for him. She sat with him after his chemotherapy treatments. She tended to his lawn.

Wyatt texted her about once a week, as he'd set an alarm on his phone. Not that he needed that. He thought about the blonde constantly. He wanted to take her to dinner. He wanted to help her with whatever she needed, from her own yardwork to picking up groceries for her and her father, to sitting with her while she sat with her daddy.

He wanted to hold her hand. He wanted to kiss her. He wanted her in his life. But he was willing to wait. He'd spent a couple of weeks with her in January, with nightly visits and dinners and laughter.

Then she'd tearfully told him about her father's colon cancer, and that she wouldn't be able to see him in the evenings anymore, and maybe once she could sleep more than a few hours at night, they could spend more time together.

He drove without thought, turning on the dirt road that led out to Marcy's hangar, knowing she'd be there. She didn't go to her father's until about seven, she'd said, because she had the workload of two people she was managing herself.

Wyatt had offered to help her, but she'd challenged him with a single word. "How?"

He hadn't known what to say. She claimed not to have the money to hire someone else, and where would she find a good pilot anyway? Wyatt couldn't fly a crop-duster, though he'd watched a few Internet videos as if he could learn that way.

He'd watched his brothers offer money to the women

in their lives, and while Liam and Callie had made things work between them, there had been quite a few rocky months. And Wyatt didn't know Marcy quite as well as Liam had known Callie Foster at the time he'd offered to buy her ranch but let her keep it.

So Wyatt hadn't offered Marcy a dime, though he had plenty of money to put someone on her payroll.

He realized he'd been sitting in his idling truck when Marcy opened the door and stepped outside. She crossed her arms and leaned against the doorframe, sexy and sweet in that military green jumpsuit she wore to fly, repair planes, and manage the crop-dusting business that rested solely on her shoulders.

Wyatt had seen her peel that jumpsuit off, his heart hammering in the back of his throat, to reveal a sexy yet sweet pair of cutoffs and tank top. She stepped out of her work boots and left them just inside the hangar, wearing flip flops home, and he liked watching her shed her mechanic's skin and become a whole new woman with just a few changes.

She lifted her hand and waved, and Wyatt got himself out of the truck. "Evening," Marcy said. "What brings you out this way?"

"I heard there was a party out here," he said, looking around and feeling flirtatious. He walked right up to Marcy and engulfed her in a hug. "And I miss you."

She giggled and settled right into his embrace, and

Wyatt couldn't help thinking how perfectly she fit in his arms. "There's no party out here, cowboy."

"Must've gotten bad directions." He stepped back and grinned at her. "Are you nearly done? What's on the docket for tonight?"

Weariness filled Marcy's eyes though she wore a smile. "Picking up dinner for Daddy. It's romantic comedy night."

Wyatt wanted to invite himself along, because he knew Marcy wouldn't do it. He bit back the words. She'd received him well, and he didn't want to push her into a place she didn't want to be.

She turned back to the hangar. "It's too dang hot already." She went inside, holding the door for him to follow her. Wyatt ducked his head and did, wondering why he hadn't gone home to shower the smell of horses off his shoulders before he'd stopped by to see her.

But if he'd done that, Marcy would've likely been gone, off to movie night with her sick and dying father. Guilt moved through Wyatt, as he shouldn't be frustrated that Marcy didn't have time for him. She was dealing with so much, and he should've brought her dinner instead of just showing up and hoping for more than she could give.

"How about I bring you guys dinner one night this week?" he asked, stepping onto that tender ground between them.

Marcy turned back to him, her blue eyes searching his. "You know what? That would be great."

A grin burst onto Wyatt's face. "Awesome. I can stop and bring you something tonight, if you'd like." He glanced at the desk in her office, which was a complete mess, with folders and papers and old to-go coffee cups littering every available inch of the surface.

Marcy let out a long exhale as she sat down. She ran her hands through her hair and gathered it into a ponytail, securing it with a band from her wrist. Just that simple action made Wyatt's throat dry up and his mind blank. A woman had not affected him like this in years. In fact, Wyatt had never met a woman like Marcy Payne, and he'd known a lot of women on the rodeo circuit.

As if he needed to be reminded of his time in the saddle, his lower back gave him a twinge of pain, which radiated down both of his legs. He reached for the desk—well, a lunge would probably be a more accurate description of what he did—dislodging a couple of folders and knocking a thankfully empty coffee cup to the floor.

"Sorry," he said quickly, easing into a bend to pick up the cardboard cup.

"Are you okay?"

"Fine," he said, staying down and stretching his back for as long as he dared. Standing was hard on Wyatt, though he could walk and ride and most everything else without too many issues.

"I have a couple of things to do before I'm done," she said. "Do you want to stay? Then you can grab dinner and bring it over."

"Sure thing," Wyatt said, tossing the cup in the trashcan and looking at the chair he'd waited in previously. It was covered with a pile of dirty rags.

"I can—"

"I got it," Wyatt said. "Want me to throw these in the washing machine?"

"Do you know how to run a washing machine?" Her eyes sparkled with that tease he'd seen in January.

"Of course," he said. "I lived on my own for a lot of years, sweetheart." He kicked a grin in her direction, scooped the mechanic rags off the chair, and left the office. He'd spent enough time in the hangar to know where the laundry facilities were, and he dumped the rags in the machine. Another pile waited there, and he added those too. He walked the shop, picking up every dirty rag he saw, before returning to the laundry room and starting the load.

He reached into the cabinet above the machine and pulled out two garbage bags. Maybe Marcy would be embarrassed if he started cleaning up, but maybe she'd be grateful too. And Wyatt could sit with her or do something, and while both were good options, he didn't want her to feel rushed or like he didn't want to help.

He filled the first bag with trash from the shop itself, emptying the various trashcans around the hangar and picking up the remains of what she'd been eating. He made a mental note of the chocolate covered pretzel bags, the empty bags of cheddar and sour cream potato chips, and the sleeves of saltine crackers.

At least he knew what to get her now should he find himself wanting to give her something she liked. And he did. He wanted her to be thinking about him as much as he did her. He wondered if she did as he took the trash out to the big bin on the north side of the building.

Marcy was absolutely right about the heat this week, as it seemed like the devil himself had breathed over the whole state of Texas and heated it unnaturally. Still, he stayed outside for a moment and took a deep breath of the dusty air. It was extremely quiet out here, with the highway a ways off and only scrub brush out here.

Eventually, he returned to the hangar and Marcy's office, where he started picking up her empty coffee cups and emptying the trash beside the coffee pot on the small counter to the side of her desk.

"You don't have to clean up," she said.

"I want to." He gave her another smile, finished the chore, and took the garbage back outside. By then, the rags were done, and he moved them into the dryer. Satisfied, he returned to Marcy's office and eased himself into the chair in front of her desk. A sigh came out of his mouth and his back and shoulders tightened to a point past comfortable and then relaxed.

He looked up, his eyes immediately finding Marcy's. She saw something in his movement, he knew, but she didn't ask if he was okay again. "Thanks for cleaning up."

"I said I'd help you anyway I could," he said. "How are things going?" He saw the panic before she shuttered it behind her stoic mask. He wished he had a magic button that would erase that look from her eyes, that feeling from her life.

"Things are going," she said.

"Is it business? Or your daddy?"

"Things here are good," she said. "Great." She closed a folder and tossed it on top of a nearby pile. "It's Daddy." That was all she said.

Wyatt didn't ask anything else. Marcy's hurt and pain radiated through the room, and the only sound in the room was her sniffing and reaching for a tissue. She kept her head down while she wiped her eyes and nose, and Wyatt had no idea what to do. He didn't want to crowd her behind the desk, and besides, he struggled to control his own emotions.

"I'm real sorry, sweetheart," he finally said, his voice tight and maybe a touch too high.

Her eyes lifted, and she smiled through the tears. He got up then, moving around the desk, and crouching in front of her. He took both of her hands in his. "I don't think it's a secret how I feel about you," he said, almost a whisper. "You call me, say what you need, and I'll do it."

"I know." She leaned into him and cried into his shoulder. Wyatt wrapped his arms around her and held her until she quieted, thanking the Good Lord above that he'd followed his gut and made that turn.

Of course, now his back was screaming at him that this

position was not acceptable. He employed every muscle in his core, but he started trembling after half a minute.

Marcy pulled away, and Wyatt stood up quickly, stifling the groan threatening to come out of his mouth. Holding that back caused almost as much pain as the compromising position, and he took a stilted step back.

Thankfully, he had his own truck, stocked heavily with painkillers, and he'd swallow four as soon as he settled behind the steering wheel.

Marcy took her time wiping her eyes, and she stood up too. Their eyes met, and she gave him another small smile. "I can tell something's wrong with you, Wyatt."

He sure did like the way she said his name in her Texas twang, and he smiled through his own pain. He didn't want his brothers to know about his injuries and constant pain. With his job at Bowman's Breeds, he could stop by the physical therapist and his doctor without anyone knowing.

But maybe it was time to tell someone.

"I suffered several injuries during my time in the rodeo," he said. "I have chronic back pain now, and I go to physical therapy twice a week for strength analysis." He watched her reaction, the sympathy rolling across her face. "I work with a trainer five days a week for core strengthening and all of that. It's manageable, most of the time."

"I can't even imagine," Marcy said.

"I'm glad you don't have to," he said. "I haven't told

anyone about it. Not my brothers or anything. So I'd appreciate it if you kept it to yourself."

"Of course," she said. "I'm glad you told me, because you're kind of, you know, perfect."

Wyatt chuckled, ducking his head. "I'm not anywhere close to perfect, sweetheart."

"That might be true," she said. "You like the barbecue at Duck's instead of the stand out east."

"Duck's is right in town," he said, glad her face had brightened, and the fun, flirty woman he liked so much had returned. Of course, he liked Marcy no matter what, and he was actually thrilled she'd broken down in front of him. It meant she trusted him. And he'd shared something important with her too.

So maybe they could have a real relationship in the future.

"Okay," he said. "What am I picking up? And you better text me your address, because I've never been to your place."

11

Marcy Payne couldn't help the irregular way her heart beat in her chest. She had no control over what her pulse did, right?

But Wyatt Walker made everything inside her sing, from her hair follicles all the way down to her pinky toenails. Just the rumble of that big truck he drove had her breath hitching. She'd gone out to greet him when he hadn't come in right away, and only mild embarrassment remained after she'd practically soaked his shirt with her tears.

But people got to cry over cancer, didn't they? The Lord knew Marcy had shed plenty of tears. She was the oldest Payne sibling and cousin in the Three Rivers area, and she was expected to hold everything together. She only wet her pillow in the middle of the night, when there was no one else around to see the carnage. Well, no one except Robot, at least. And her hamster didn't care if she cried or not.

She pulled onto the highway first, Wyatt's beast of a truck behind her. She'd get on ahead to Daddy's and make sure there wasn't a pile of dishes in the sink or any disgusting smells wafting from the bathroom. Wyatt would be several minutes behind her with the Italian food she'd ordered on her phone.

Marcy had come to rely on so many things she'd never even heard of since her father's diagnosis. Grocery delivery, online shopping, and meal delivery. Of everything she'd done, tapping a few times and having dinner show up twenty minutes later was the most magical.

Tonight, she'd tapped the carry-out button, as Wyatt would stop by for the food. Sudden nerves hit her, and she glanced in her rear-view mirror. The man had never met her father. "This could be a bad idea," she muttered to herself. She had plenty of cousins to help with Daddy, and a couple of them might actually be at the house.

She picked up her phone, though she normally had a firm commitment to driving hands-free. Desperate times and all that. She swiped and tapped without swerving off the highway, tucking the phone against her ear a moment later and listening to the line ring.

"Heya, Marce," her cousin said.

"Alyssa, hey," she drawled. "Listen, where are you right now?"

"Sitting with LJ," she said. "We're waiting for Remmy to be done with swimming lessons."

"So you're not at my dad's?"

"No, I left Savannah there, but she had to get to work by six."

Relief cascaded through Marcy with more force than she thought possible.

"Is he okay?" Alyssa asked.

"Oh, yeah," Marcy said. "Yes, sorry, I should've led with that."

"My heart might be thumpin' a little right now," Alyssa said, the line on her end scratching just a bit. "Just a minute, baby. Momma's on the phone."

"I'll let you go," Marcy said, not wanting to be drawn into a long conversation with her cousin. "I'll see you later."

"Helen and Gerty from down the street brought y'all a pie," Alyssa said. "I hope your daddy saved you some." She laughed, and Marcy put in the obligatory chuckle.

"Okay, thanks, Alyssa."

"And that other widower down the street, he stopped by earlier too. Somethin' about turning on the irrigation water."

"Daddy knows how," Marcy said, working hard to keep the impatience out of her voice.

"Do you think he's strong enough?"

"If he's not, I'll have someone come do it." Marcy thought of the impressive muscles in the man currently following her back into town. Wyatt Walker could easily get the irrigation water running again for them, and Marcy would like to see those muscles in action.

Heat filled her face, and she cleared her throat. "I'm pulling up now, Liss. I have to go." A tiny fib. Surely the Lord understood and excused little lies in trying times, didn't He?

She should've known better than to call her cousin anyway. In the past, she'd have known when the swimming lessons were. Who was playing soccer at what time and in what park. She'd have known Alyssa had taken the morning shift and Savannah would be over in the afternoon.

But Marcy now operated on whatever fire was burning the brightest and the most out of control. She worked on putting that one out before it turned everything to ash, and then she focused on the next issue.

At least she could still work, which honestly, had been her saving grace these past four months. That, and Wyatt Walker, if she was going to be completely honest. And after that little lie about pulling up to Daddy's when she'd just passed the city limit sign, Marcy figured she might as well be totally truthful.

Wyatt had seemed to know exactly when to text her. Exactly when to show up outside the hangar, usually with a box of doughnuts or her favorite coconut diet cola, ice cold, and that cowboy swagger. That sexy smile. His friendship and support.

Marcy had learned a lot about swallowing her pride in the last several weeks as well. She'd made some mistakes in her work, and it was much easier and quicker to say, "I'm sorry, Mister Reinhold. I'll get that fixed right away, sir," than it was to argue, get angry, or try to figure out why she'd dusted the wrong field when she'd been doing it right for five years.

She wasn't terribly aged yet, but she felt like her thirty-eight-year-old brain had doubled its years, and if she didn't write something down, it didn't get remembered.

She now lived in the Before the Diagnosis, and the After the Diagnosis. Before, she was fun, carefree, flying planes all over the panhandle, making sure every farm and ranch that had hired her got exactly what they'd paid for.

Fertilizers in the spring. Pest control all summer and fall.

She got to work on airplanes when she wasn't flying them, and fry potatoes while her father tried to get her to dance in the kitchen, and laugh when her younger brothers brought their wives and girlfriends to watch the Thursday night comedy they all loved.

After, on Thursdays, they all settled down to watch television together, but only those who hadn't had a sniffle or a scratchy throat in over a week. They laughed, sure, but it didn't have the same joy in it.

After, Daddy wasn't dancing anywhere. Sometimes he was so sick right after a chemotherapy treatment that he couldn't make it to the bathroom on time.

After, Marcy had gained ten pounds with her lack of dancing and cooking, coupled with the stress of running the crop-dusting business completely on her own and providing for Daddy's health needs. The plan had always been for her to take over Payne's Pest-free, but she'd only just begun learning what she needed to know when Daddy had been diagnosed.

But that was in the Before, and she lived in the After now. Marcy knew it did no good to wish for the life she'd had Before. Wishing never really worked anyway, not for her, and not in this situation.

She pulled into her father's driveway, noting the black cat with white paws had been left outside. Or maybe she'd escaped. No matter what, Tails had come back, and Marcy reached down to pick up the cat as she walked by.

"Daddy," she said upon entering the house. "I'm home." She wasn't sure why she felt like she needed to announce her arrival, as he sat only a few feet away and had known she was home the moment the door opened. Maybe earlier, as her ancient truck had quite the growly motor.

"Baby doll," he said, his voice weak and hoarse. He still wore a smile though, and the fiercest wave of love sang through her. "How are the planes?"

"Still flyin'," she said, their little way of saying everything was fine at work. Everything was fine with Marcy. "My friend stopped by tonight, and I sent him to get dinner. He should be here with it in a few minutes."

Daddy said nothing, just kept rocking himself back and forth, back and forth. Marcy ducked into the kitchen at the back of the house and washed her hands, running her still-wet hands over her face and through her hair. There were dishes here, but nothing to be embarrassed about. She picked up the mail and leafed through it. Nothing interesting.

She dashed down the hall to check on the toilet paper situation in the bathroom. Check. Everything here was fine, good, fit for company.

"Gerty brought a pie," her dad said as she re-entered the living room.

"I saw it," Marcy said, though she'd actually missed the pie in the kitchen.

"Savannah told me I couldn't eat any. Too much sugar."

"Well, she's right," Marcy said, bending to drop a kiss on her father's forehead. "And you should tell your girl-friend to stop bringing you sugary, fatty foods. Doesn't she know you have cancer?" She giggled, because laughter—while it didn't cure everything—definitely helped keep both of their spirits high.

Daddy laughed too, shaking his head. "If she wants to bring us pecan pie, I'm not going to tell her no." He also didn't deny that widowed Gertrude Morris was his girl-friend. In fact, he had taken her out a time or two, in the Before.

"I'm not givin' you any," Marcy said. "No matter how

many times you ask." She kicked off her flip flops and sank onto the couch, a sigh leaking from her mouth before she could pull it back in. She enjoyed ten seconds of relaxation before the doorbell rang, causing her to shoot right back to her feet.

"That'll be Wyatt. You be nice now, you hear?" She didn't wait for Daddy to answer before she opened the door.

The scent of marinara sauce and garlic bread hit her nose, and her mouth watered. Or maybe that was from the sight of the delectable man carrying the two bags of food. "C'mon in," she managed to say, glad she could interact with Wyatt without making a fool of herself.

He stepped inside, where Marcy took one of the bags of food. The one with the bread, she thought, as the warm, yeasty scent of it tantalized her. "Daddy, this is my friend, Wyatt Walker. Wyatt, my father, Martin Payne."

Wyatt said, "Nice to meet you, sir." He reached out his free hand for Daddy to shake. He couldn't quite lift his arm that high, and Wyatt had to bend lower. Awkwardness descended on the room, and Marcy dealt with it by walking into the kitchen. Male voices met her ears, but she busied herself with getting out plates and silverware. A few moments later, Wyatt joined her.

They worked together to get the food out and on plates, and Marcy took her dad's to him in the living room, getting the TV tray situated and everything nice and steady in its place. "Water, Daddy?" she asked. "Sweet tea?"

"Both, please," he rasped, and Marcy took an extra moment to look at him. His eyes looked clear today, and he seemed plenty alert. Maybe she was worried about nothing, though the first few days after a chemo treatment were the worst.

Back in the kitchen, she filled a few glasses with ice cubes. "Sweet tea, Wyatt? Water?"

"Tea, please," he said. "What did your dad want?"

"Both." She poured the tea and he took a glass to the water dispenser in the door of the fridge. The ease with which he just stepped right in to help her made her heart soften even more toward him, and she took the full glass from him and returned to the living room.

Too much heat in the kitchen anyway.

Wyatt followed with their drinks, which he sat on the end table, and then he went back into the kitchen, returning with their food a moment later.

Daddy had the TV on, but the volume was almost all the way down. Marcy would go nuts if someone didn't say something soon, but she couldn't think of a single thing.

Thankfully, Wyatt said, "Wow, this is great. Reminds me of a little Italian place I ate at in Calgary once."

How he knew that magic word, Marcy wasn't sure. But Momma had been from Calgary, and her father's entire soul had just lit up. He started talking, and Marcy didn't say a single word during dinner—just what she'd wanted.

Wyatt laughed and chatted like he and her father were old friends. Marcy took their plates back into the kitchen, pure exhaustion moving through her. She rolled her shoulders and stretched her neck; her eyes closed as they were starting to sting.

"I'm gonna head out," Wyatt said softly, his hand sliding down her arm to hold hers.

Thrills and chills shot to her elbow, her shoulder, down her back. "Okay," she managed to say. "Thank you so much, Wyatt. You saved me tonight."

"You call me with anything you need now, okay?" He looked at her earnestly, and anyone would agree with him when he wore such a fiercely lovable look.

"I will," she promised, though should she need help, she had a plethora of blood kin to call on. But she'd want to call Wyatt—and maybe, just maybe, she would.

He swept his lips across her forehead and said, "All right, then. See you later, Miss Marcy." He walked back into the living room and said good-bye to her father. Then he was out the front door and gone. Marcy gave herself a few seconds to sigh in happiness and daydream about what her life would've been like with Wyatt in it Before.

Five seconds, then ten.

Then she shut down the thoughts, because she needed to focus on what was happening right here, right now, and no amount of daydreaming about a handsome rodeo cowboy was going to erase her situation at hand.

"Sugar," Daddy called. "What about that pie...?"

12

Skyler Walker flew from the saddle, barely feeling the hard earth beneath his cowboy boots as he ran toward the calf he'd just roped. In the back of his ears, he could hear Wyatt yelling at him, but the words were nonsense.

He wrapped his arms around the cow and hefted him right up into the air. Then down. Rope out, wrap, wrap, tie, hands up!

Skyler stood up, his grin splitting the whole world around him.

Wyatt whistled through his teeth, and Skyler turned toward his older brother. "Time?"

"Six-point-three," the rodeo champion said.

He bent to release the calf, who ran off immediately. He gathered the reins of his horse and walked toward Wyatt. "I so coulda made it." Skyler's heart bobbed against the back of his tongue, his adrenaline clear up in the stratosphere.

"It's a good time," Wyatt said. "I mean, it's not championship time. But it's real good for someone who hasn't ridden in five months."

"I ride in Amarillo," Skyler said, climbing up on the fence and sitting next to his brother. "Whew. It sure is hot, ain't it?"

"That it is." Wyatt gazed out across the corral he and Skyler had been running rodeo trials in, a faraway look on his face. He blinked, his attention coming back to Skyler, who was starting to feel more relaxed after that last run. "Do you like college?"

"You know what? It's not bad," he said. "I mean, I'm not living in a dorm with a bunch of other people, and I eat a lot better than everyone there." He chuckled, glad he'd missed that phase of life where he counted every penny and ate only boxed pasta and wheat crackers. "Lotsa girls."

"Oh, boy." Wyatt rolled his eyes. "Do they know you're thirty-five-years-old?"

"You know, age doesn't come up as much as you might think it does."

"You have gray hair."

"I'm distinguished," he said, laughing. After all, that was Skyler's solution to everything: laugh. Make a joke. Stand out, but keep the spotlight on someone else. Then he didn't have to share anything real with anyone, even his brothers. He didn't have to talk about how deeply his complete failure as a mechanic and business owner had scarred him. He didn't even have to think about it.

He danced, and laughed, and bought fresh fruit smoothies for everyone. If Skyler Walker was anything, it was the life of the party. Always.

But in his private, quiet moments...he barely recognized himself or his life anymore. He still wasn't sure if that was a good thing or a bad one.

And this moment was too quiet. "Are you going to come to the summer dance this weekend?" he asked.

"Absolutely not," Wyatt said.

"Why not?" Skyler looked at him. "There are some older cowboys like us that go."

"Y'all have fun then."

Skyler smiled, because smiling over the top of pain had become second nature. "You don't want to go because you're hung up on Marcy."

"I'm not 'hung up' on her." Wyatt scoffed. "I like her, and as soon as she has space in her life, I'm going to be in it."

"You sound awfully sure of that."

"I am sure of that," he said, looking at Skyler. "Don't tell me you don't have one woman in Amarillo you thought seriously about."

"Maybe one or two," Skyler said with a shrug. He didn't want to get married, and he was fine without a steady girlfriend. He knew how to get invited to the parties and events, and he knew he had a certain charm and charisma that drew people to him. After a couple of weeks, his place was *the place* to be, and he didn't even have to leave the apartment. He didn't have to clean up afterward either, because he had plenty of money for a housekeeper, for food, for replacement dishes if his got broken.

Not that he was throwing keggers out of the apartment he'd rented in Amarillo. But he rolled out of bed thirty minutes before class, brushed his teeth, and left the mess to Geraldine. Done.

"One or two," Wyatt said, shaking his head. "Did you date them at the same time?"

"I don't date anyone," Skyler said. "A date here and one there isn't dating."

"Well, at least we agree on that."

"Hey, listening to you and Jeremiah pine after your women is enough for me."

"I do not pine," Wyatt said. "And Jeremiah says nothing."

"Why do you think that is?" Skyler looked at Wyatt, moving into his serious mode. When it came to his brothers, he was fiercely protective, and he'd do anything for them. "How's he really doing?"

"He's dating Whitney Wilde, and he sure does like her."

"He doesn't bring her around the ranch."

"Would you?" Wyatt chuckled. "I mean, I'm planning

to keep Marcy away for as long as possible, especially when everyone is here. We're *loud*, Sky."

Skyler tipped his head back and laughed, and sure enough, the booming sound went right up into the atmosphere. "I guess we are."

"Plus, he works a ton."

"Less now, I think," Skyler said. "He actually does seem like he's making some good progress now that he's seeing that counselor."

"He sure does."

Skyler let the conversation lull again, because he'd been toying with the idea of contacting the same doctor Jeremiah had been seeing. Maybe he could move past some of the emotional blocks he felt in his soul too. Or maybe they were fine.

His phone rang, and he pulled it from his back pocket. "It's Bennett."

"Oh, your boyfriend," Wyatt teased, but Skyler just rolled his eyes as he swiped on the call.

"Hey, Ben. What's up?"

"I just tried Wyatt, and he's not answering. Can you tell him the puppies are ready to be picked up?"

Skyler swung toward Wyatt. "He's right here." He moved the phone away from his mouth. "The puppies are ready."

"Oh, let's go."

"We're on our way out."

Bennett asked, "Are you going to the dance this weekend?"

"Thinking about it," Skyler said, a familiar tactic for him. He never committed to something first. Maybe there would be something better he should be doing, and he didn't want to be roped into one thing too soon.

Wyatt swung down from the fence, and Skyler followed him. He led his horse toward the stables while Bennett said, "I'm going just to see. Me and JD, if you want to hang out with us, watch from the sidelines for the first little bit."

"I'll probably be there," he said.

"See you in a minute," Bennett said, and Skyler hung up so he could brush down Fixed Ticket and put him back in his stall. He gave him a big bucket of oats, just like he promised if the horse would slip back into the rodeo champion he'd been, and he cupped his hands on both sides of the horse's nose.

"Good boy, Ticket," he said. "See you tomorrow." He did love living here at Seven Sons. It was like God Himself had reached down from heaven and touched the land with the tip of his finger. There was just something special about it. Healing. Restorative.

He and Wyatt went next door, because Jeremiah could often be found catnapping in the loft, and sure enough, he poked his head over the railing after the door had slammed shut.

"Your dogs are ready to be picked up," Wyatt said. "Wanna go?"

"Yes." Jeremiah climbed down the ladder and dusted bits of straw from his shoulders. "We have everything, right?"

"We have bowls, collars, and leashes," Wyatt said. "Bennett said you'd get a bag of food for him when you picked him up. Then you can get more when you know what kind he's been eating."

"I think I'm going to put him on a raw diet," Jeremiah said.

"Of course you are," Skyler said, a blip of true happiness stealing through him. "I could've called that."

"What in the world is that?" Wyatt asked.

"You know, real food," Jeremiah said as they made their way toward the homestead. "Those bagged dog foods have so much grain in them. They're not good for your canine."

"Ooh, canine," Skyler joked, elbowing Jeremiah in the ribs. Sometimes he felt decades younger than his more stoic older brother, especially since Jeremiah's wedding fiasco a few years ago. Skyler wanted to tell him if he just pushed it all away and surrounded himself with other people all the time, he'd be fine.

But Jeremiah had gone to the right while Skyler had taken a complete left after a devastating setback. And the one time Skyler had called being stood up at the altar a "setback" Jeremiah had clocked him right in the mouth. So all things considering, Jeremiah was definitely doing better.

"I don't want to drive," Jeremiah said.

"Me either," Wyatt said quickly, before Skyler even knew what was happening. He looked back and forth between his two brothers.

"Fine," he said. "You guys are such babies."

"It's a long way to Three Rivers Ranch," Jeremiah said, yawning. "I'm tired." He went up the steps to the back deck first, and Skyler waited to go last. His brothers would wash up and then they'd go.

Jeremiah was right, and over an hour later, Skyler finally made the turn from asphalt to dirt to get to the ranch. Bennett lived in one of the neat, little cabins behind the barns and stables and other outbuildings, but they didn't need to go romping around the ranch to find him.

They weren't the only ones there to pick up their puppy, and Bennett had the little rascals in a pen on the front lawn of the sprawling homestead of the ranch. Across the street from it sat a second homestead, and while Skyler had been out to Three Rivers once before, he had the strong thought that the brothers needed to do that at Seven Sons.

He was going to school for accounting, to be able to manage the ranch's finances. He shouldn't have to live with Jeremiah forever, especially if anything happened with Jeremiah and Whitney. He couldn't really imagine Jeremiah risking his heart and agreeing to another wedding, but Skyler had thought he could fix cars. So anything was possible.

About ten kids laughed and squealed as they played with the puppies on the grass. Skyler smiled at their exuberance while Wyatt and Jeremiah started talking to Bennett about business. Money and paperwork were exchanged, and Jeremiah bent to clip on one collar, then another.

He was beaming like the moon when he straightened, and Skyler couldn't help smiling too. Jeremiah had been through a lot, and Skyler knew the power of having a constant companion, a good friend, to greet him when he walked through the door. Not only that, but these dogs would go everywhere with Jeremiah. He'd train them to herd cattle, and they'd be his shadows for the rest of their lives. Skyler was actually a little jealous of Jeremiah, not for the first time in his life.

Jeremiah had been a god in high school. Rhett was the oldest, but Rhett was a bit quieter, a bit more academic. Jeremiah had been the athlete in the family, popular and kind despite it, and Skyler had looked up to him more than he'd ever admitted to anyone, ever.

"Ready?" Jeremiah asked, holding both leashes in one hand.

"That was a long drive for five minutes of pick-up," Skyler complained. "You're buying me dinner."

"Pick the place," Jeremiah said. "As long as we can order now and pick-up when we get there, or drive through somewhere." He gazed down lovingly at his two new cattle pups. "They can't wait in the car."

Skyler nodded at Wyatt. "Call Spears. You know what I like."

"Oh, boy," Wyatt muttered under his breath, but he tapped before he lifted the phone to his ear. Skyler knew Spears wasn't Jeremiah's favorite—maybe that was why he'd picked the teriyaki bowl specialists?—but he'd survive.

"Brown rice for me," he said as Wyatt started to order, and Skyler made a fake gagging noise.

"All right, guys," Jeremiah said, lifting both puppies into his arms to put them in the back seat with him. He completely ignored Skyler's teasing about his taste for brown rice. "You'll have to learn how to jump into the truck real soon. But for now, you can ride right here with me." He grinned at Skyler and added, "Close the door for me, would you?"

Skyler did, shaking his head though he was secretly glad his brother had so much joy streaming from him.

He'd forgotten what it felt to have that in his life, and a keen sense of mourning moved through him as he opened the driver's door and got behind the wheel. Soon enough, he'd be at the dance, and he wouldn't have to be reminded of how empty his life was.

13

"Oh, my goodness, look at them." Whitney crouched down and let Jeremiah's new puppies jump at her face and lick her.

"Guys," he said sternly, tugging on their leashes. "Stop it. That's impolite."

But Whitney didn't mind. Three weeks had passed since Jeremiah had talked to her about marrying him to prove a point to his brothers, but he hadn't brought it up again. Not one time. Whitney almost had a couple of times—he'd said they could talk about it—but in the end, she'd chickened out.

"What are their names?" she asked.

"This one with the white patch around her eye is Willow. This fine fellow is Winston." He pulled the puppy away from one of Whitney's sneakers. "He's a wily one, but really smart."

"They're so dang cute." She scooped Willow into her arms and let the puppy lick her face again, despite Jeremiah's protests. She laughed at the squirming puppy flesh, the way the tail kept whacking the back of the couch. "C'mon in. You want to put them in the backyard?"

"It's fenced?"

"All the way," she said, though she'd already confirmed this fact for him on the phone earlier.

Whitney wasn't complaining about the last three weeks. She and Jeremiah had spent a lot of time together, especially on the weekends. He wasn't afraid to take her out, and he held her hand as they went for early-morning walks, before the sun heated the day too much.

She stifled a yawn as he released the puppies from their leashes. Winston ran right outside, nearly tumbling down the steps, while Willow approached more cautiously. Jeremiah turned back to her, all smiles, but even Whitney wasn't expecting him to sweep his arm around her and ask, "They're great, right? I mean, just great."

Whitney giggled and grabbed onto his impressive biceps as her balance tipped. "They really are. I give you a week before they can shake, roll over, speak, and herd a couple thousand head of cattle." She liked the way the heat of his body melted into hers, and wow, he smelled like pine trees and spicy soap, with maybe a hint of mint.

Her eyes automatically dropped to his mouth, and she

forced them upward again, only to find Jeremiah looking at her lips too.

And suddenly, she wanted to kiss him very, very badly. Well, maybe she'd been thinking about doing that for at least a couple of weeks now, but while they spent a lot of time together, not much of it was in complete privacy.

Jeremiah cleared his throat and stepped back, releasing her and turning to face the backyard. "Are we still going hiking?"

"Yes," she said. "Yeah." She tucked her hair behind her ear and looked around for her shoes, though they weren't in the kitchen. "You wanna fill up the backpacks?"

"Yes," he said. He got busy at the sink while she went into the living room and started lacing up her hiking boots. Jeremiah had picked up his puppies last night, and he'd called with a laugh in his voice while one of the pups yipped in the background.

They seemed to be able to get ready at the same time now, and he went into the backyard to get his dogs while she took the backpacks out to her grandfather's truck. He brought the dogs right into the cab with them, something that surprised her. "You don't make them ride in the back?"

"I'm scared one of them will fall out," he admitted. "I'm going to wait until they're a little older."

She fired up the engine and backed out of the driveway. "So are we ever going to talk about, you know, the proposal thing?"

"Why don't you talk about it?" he asked.

"Okay, so it's almost June," she said. "We've been dating for a month."

"Have we?"

Whitney whipped her attention to him. "We haven't? Are you seeing someone else?"

"No," he said. "No, nothing like that."

"Then why wouldn't we be seeing each other?"

"I don't know," he muttered, focusing out his window. "I just hadn't thought about it."

"You're a bad liar," she said. "You think more than any person I know." She made a turn to go east, into the hillier parts of the panhandle, if any of it could be considered hilly. She and Jeremiah had hiked out here for several mornings, but one of the trails didn't allow dogs. She drove on to the second one, expecting Jeremiah to say something.

She'd parked before he said, "I've thought a lot about it."

"And?"

"And honestly, I think it's still a good idea." He got out of the truck and focused on clipping the leashes to the dogs' collars. "Down," he said. "Come on, guys. Down."

Both dogs did what he said, and Jeremiah closed the door and stepped to the back of the truck. Whitney got out and put her water pack on too, watching Jeremiah the whole time. He seemed perfectly relaxed, which was a bit different than she'd seen in the past. She could always tell how he really felt by the tenseness in his jaw, but now...no tension.

He glanced over at her, and Whitney quickly ducked her head. "You want me to take one of them?" she asked.

"No, I want them to walk on the leash together." He shouldered his pack too and went to the end of the tailgate. He extended his hand toward her, and she easily slipped her fingers into his.

"I'd do it," Whitney said. "And not just because I booked a wedding that would be perfect at Seven Sons."

Jeremiah chuckled, his hand tightening against hers. "That's the deal, and I won't even question you about it."

"I might bring in fake corn stalks and stuff. It's an October wedding."

"Love, we'll have plenty of corn stalks in October."

"Pumpkins?"

"I've already planted them."

Whitney thought about what kind of baby shoots she could do on the ranch, but that would require divulging her secret, and she wasn't sure she wanted to do that. "Let's talk about specifics. I'd live at the ranch...don't you have two brothers who live there?"

"My bedroom is massive," he said. "Like, huge. You could sleep in the closet and be fine."

Alarm pulled through Whitney. "The closet?"

"It's *huge*," he said.

"I think huge is a subjective word," she said. "I'll need to see this room and this closet."

"It's a suite," he said. "I mean, I could put a second bed in it and still have tons of space."

"And then we'd have to tell Wyatt and Skyler why there are two beds in the master *suite*." She enunciated the T heavily, but she didn't dare look at Jeremiah.

His dogs trotted along at his side, though every few feet, one tried to slow down and stop or rush ahead. He kept a steady hand on them, bringing them along with him, right where he wanted them.

"First off, Skyler will be back at college by the time we get married. And Wyatt...well, Wyatt minds his own business."

"Doesn't mean he's stupid."

"No, he is not stupid," Jeremiah mused, his head down. "Walk," he said to the dogs, and they obeyed him, for a moment at least. He repeated it a few times as they continued up the trail.

"How long do you think we need to be married?" she asked.

"I don't know," he said.

Whitney swallowed. She could sleep in a bed in Jeremiah's room if she had to. She'd only been inside the homestead at Seven Sons a time or two, and she certainly had no idea what lay down the hallway that veered left just before the kitchen. Maybe there was another bedroom there she could slip into after Wyatt thought she and Jeremiah had gone to bed.

"There's a place for my computer?" she asked.

"Big office at the front of the house."

"You'll let me bring my cats?"

"Of course."

"I can keep my house, for you know, after all of this ends?" Whitney tried to see the end of this. Would they break-up? Was she going to marry him, and then...*then what?* she asked herself. She'd been asking the same thing of the Lord, but she hadn't gotten an answer.

Well, she had, but she didn't dare admit to herself or anyone else that she could actually have a real relationship with Jeremiah. A real marriage. One that didn't have to end, and one where she could then sell her house and become a permanent part of Seven Sons Ranch.

Such thoughts were dangerous, and Whitney didn't dwell on them for long.

"Yes," he said quietly. "Keep your house."

"I can shoot on the ranch?"

"That's part of the deal."

She stepped in front of him, needing to see his eyes when she asked this next thing. "And us, Jeremiah?"

"Us?"

She squeezed his hand with both of hers. "What happens to us? What's the end of this?" She looked around, but she couldn't enjoy the splendor of these hills. Mania rose within her, and she half-laughed and half-scoffed. "I mean, what do you see happening to us? Me and you." She swallowed, her mouth so dry. "I like you."

"I like you too," he said, not bothering to correct his

dogs as they strained against their leashes. "I don't know what will happen with us, honestly."

"I don't like that answer."

"I don't have another one." He exhaled and shook his head. "It's a crazy plan. I don't know all the steps. I don't know the end from the beginning."

Whitney couldn't help hoping that they could fall in love for real. She did like Jeremiah, and other than Blake, he was the only man in the past decade that had intrigued her at all.

But he didn't know about Lake Winters, and she wasn't anywhere near ready to tell him. *He'd keep your secret*, she told herself, but she still didn't open her mouth to tell him.

No, when she opened her mouth again, she said, "So we'll sleep in the same room, but we'll not be sleeping together. Do I have that right?"

"Yes," he said, his voice tight and low. "I'm not going to take advantage of you. I...I...I'm not even sure I'm ready to kiss you."

"Maybe if you talked about your ex-fiancée, you'd be able to move forward," she said. Her heart thrashed in her chest, because she'd been secretly hoping to share a kiss with him at the summit. She saw that possibility disappearing into the rising sunlight.

"I do talk about her," he said. "With Doctor Wagstaff."

"What if I wanted to know about her?" She nudged him. "If I'm your wife and all."

That jaw jumped, and Whitney didn't like it. Not one little bit.

She didn't push Jeremiah, because she'd learned that he'd talk eventually. This time, it took him all the way until they'd reached the top of the little hill before he said, "Her name was Laura Ann Palmer. We were together for three years, the last one of that engaged." He let go of her hand and took the dogs over to the edge of the trail, his breath lifting his shoulders up and down, up and down.

"I loved her," he said. "I loved her so much. I wanted to be married so badly." His head dropped, and Whitney wasn't sure if she should approach him or not. He faced her, the sunlight glorious on his face. "I didn't see what I should've seen."

"This happened in Austin?"

"Yes."

"Does she still live there?"

"I have no idea where she is," he said. "She left the golf course where we were getting married, and I don't know which direction she went in. I spoke to her once, and Rhett bought the ranch, and my life is here now."

Whitney smiled. "I'm glad it is."

"Me too," he said, coming toward her. He paused just outside of her reach. "I'm glad I'm here, and I really don't want our first kiss to happen at our fake wedding."

Whitney's eyes widened. "Me either."

Jeremiah's gaze dropped to Whitney's mouth, and he moved. Acted. Took her right into his arms, swept his cowboy hat off his head, and lowered his lips to brush hers. Oh, he was a tease, testing, but barely.

She pulled in a breath, steadied herself with her hands on his shoulders, and leaned into him. He kissed her again, really making the connection this time, and Whitney knew then that she never wanted to kiss another man.

He may not have kissed a woman in almost four years, but he certainly hadn't forgotten how. Oh, no, he had not.

Whitney could not get enough of him. Could not get close enough. Could not stop kissing him.

14

Jeremiah's senses heightened, and the scent of Whitney's perfume was so strong. The silky smoothness of her skin beneath his fingers. The taste of the lemon drops she'd been sucking on during their hike.

He kissed her, and kissed her, and kissed her, his fear of her shoving him away disappearing after the first few seconds. She kissed him back, so he couldn't be doing too bad of a job. Right?

He finally regained control of himself—it had been a long time since he'd kissed a woman, and he'd forgotten how wonderful it could be—and pulled away. He sucked in the cool morning air, hotter than he'd ever been.

Probably not, but it sure felt like it.

"Wow," he said, opening his eyes and looking right at Whitney. Heat had crawled into her face, and she cleared her throat and tucked her hair behind her ear. "I mean... *wow*."

Whitney giggled and shook her head. "You just haven't kissed anyone in a long time."

That was totally true, but Jeremiah had never experienced this sprinting of his pulse in his chest. Even when Laura Ann had squealed, let him slip a diamond on her finger, and then she'd kissed him.

But even then, that pulse-pounding had been from his nerves, not because he'd just experienced the best kiss of his life. So much of the anger he'd been carrying with him simply disappeared, and he took Whitney's face in both of his hands again.

"I guess maybe I better kiss you again just to be sure." He touched his lips to hers again, more sure this time. But his passion didn't accelerate so fast he felt thrown out of his own mind, and he was able to go slower, explore deeper.

He pulled away again, still definitely in the wow-category. He drew her into his arms and held her, not caring that she pressed her cheek to his chest, so she'd know how she affected him.

Eventually, the sun's rays touched the top of the hill where they stood, and Whitney stepped away from him. He had so many other things to say, lots they needed to talk about, but he didn't know where to start.

"If we go now," she said. "We'll have time for a quick breakfast." Whitney's eyebrows lifted. "You in?"

"Breakfast with you? Always." He smiled as he took her hand and started back down the trail. "And I don't want you badgering me about a proposal. A man likes things to be special."

A peal of laughter filled the sky, and Jeremiah chuckled too. He whistled for the puppies to come to him, which surprisingly they did. He stooped to pick up the leashes, then re-centered his hand in hers.

"Just because this might not be entirely real doesn't meant it can't look like it," he said.

"What do you mean?"

"Do you want to tell your parents that you're marrying me to prove to my brothers I'm not broken?" The sting of what Wyatt had said months ago barely shocked Jeremiah anymore. Kissing Whitney had healed him much more than he'd been able to anticipate.

"No," Whitney said.

"Yeah, because when they ask you why you'd do that, I don't think 'so I can shoot at the ranch when I want to' would go over very well with them."

Whitney nodded, her eyes trained on the ground as they navigated a rocky patch in the path. "So it looks real on the outside."

"It *has* to look real on the outside," he confirmed. "And in that case, maybe I'll just wait another couple of weeks, propose, and say we want a fast wedding. Then my brothers don't have to know. The secret is really a secret."

"Our secret," Whitney said. "That way, it's easier to tell the same lie to everyone."

Lie. Jeremiah didn't like the sound of that. No, he hadn't exactly been on his knees a whole lot over the past few years, but he didn't want to lie either. That certainly wouldn't get him into God's good graces.

"It's not a lie," he said. "We're getting married. No one will ask why."

"Really?" She glanced at him. "Your brothers won't be surprised?"

"Maybe that I got engaged again at all," he said. "I've always said I wouldn't." He paused, tugging on the leashes to get the puppies to stop. "Maybe we should just run away to City Hall. Today." Though, in his mind, he knew they couldn't tie the knot today. Liam had told him he'd had to wait seventy-two hours from the time he got a marriage license to when the I-do's could happen.

"My mother will go ballistic," Whitney said. She pulled on his hand now. "Keep moving, cowboy. Daylight is burning, and I'm already going to be late."

"We don't have to go to breakfast," he said as he got his feet moving again.

"Yes, we do," she said. "We need to keep talking about the engagement and the wedding and the after-the-wedding."

"Oh?"

Whitney gave him a look out of the corner of her eye. "How long did it take Laura Ann to plan your wedding?"

Jeremiah sucked in a breath. "We were engaged for a little over a year," he finally said.

"And you want to wait a couple more weeks to propose and then get married in August. You're talking six weeks."

"We'll say that the only way I agreed to an engagement at all was to have it be really short." He liked the sound of that, but he couldn't believe he was talking about this.

"My mom will still go nuts," she said.

"I'll help with whatever," Jeremiah said. "Money, planning, food, whatever."

"Maybe I should text her right now and give her the heads up." She actually let go of his hand and slid her backpack off her shoulders, taking her phone out of the pocket while she kept pace with him.

Their conversation stalled, and Whitney didn't speak until they got back to her truck. Then she lifted her eyes from her device and asked, "What date are we looking at?"

Jeremiah's whole life flashed before his eyes in that moment, and he could not believe he was even considering getting married again. Especially because this one was fake. Fake! Why put himself through the trouble?

"How about August fourth?" she asked. "That's a Saturday, and then I can have the next couple of weeks off during the busiest time for produce." She smiled as she said it, her dark eyes twinkling at him.

"Will you still be expected to work at the store after we're married?" he asked.

"Probably," Whitney said. "And Jeremiah, don't think my family won't try to rope you into doing something too." She grinned and went back to her phone.

"Me?" he asked, putting the backpacks in the back of the truck and lifting the puppies into the cab. "What could I possibly do?"

"You don't know my mother very well if you have to ask that," Whitney said, and Jeremiah's anxiety rose a notch. No, he didn't know her mother all that well. Sure, he knew Molly; they'd talked plenty of times.

"Don't you sell your cattle for beef?" Whitney asked as she handed him the keys. "I need you to drive, cowboy. My mother wants me to call." She gave him a smile that looked absolutely gleeful and got in the passenger side.

Jeremiah stared at her as she lifted her phone to her ear. Then he rounded the truck and got behind the wheel. He couldn't believe she was going to let him drive what was now her most prized possession—after her camera, of course.

Her grandfather's truck. He remembered the day she'd bought it, because she'd posted about it on social media, and he'd wished he'd been there to take it for its inaugural drive. Of course, Blake hadn't been in any of the pictures either, and Jeremiah wondered about that.

She only spoke with her mom for a few minutes, and she didn't give any details. She said things like, "We're not sure, Mom," and "I'll let you know as soon as I know," before hanging up.

"When did you get this truck?" he asked, the width of the steering wheel a bit awkward, as he wasn't used to it.

"I bought it the day after Blake said he needed to find himself in Chicago." She rolled her eyes. "Or wherever he went."

"You don't know where he went."

"I do not, and I don't care."

Jeremiah pulled up to the diner, though he much preferred the pancake house. But they were much busier, and while their service was fast, they could get coffee and doughnuts to go at the diner.

"So I suppose I'll have to start meeting the family," he said, his stomach filling with a bit of lead.

"I suppose," she said.

"I don't do well with the family," he said, glancing at her before getting out of the truck. He handed her the keys when they met at the hood, and she grasped his fingers.

"Jeremiah, you've already met all of them. This is not a big deal. I'm the one who has to meet your burly brothers. Six of them."

"Burly?" Jeremiah laughed, glad when Whitney did too.

"Oh, and I need a special meet and greet with Wyatt."

"Wyatt? Why?" He held the door open for her, the scent of frosting and cinnamon reminding him that he didn't normally hike before dawn.

"He's a *huge* rodeo champion, Jeremiah. And Dalton is obsessed with the rodeo."

Jeremiah chuckled. "Ah, I see. All right. I'll talk to him."

————

"Sit," he said a few days later. He pointed to the ground, expecting both dogs to obey him. They did, going right down, their doggy eyes looking up at him with the most pleading of expressions. He tore off a chunk of cheese and gave a bite to Willow first, then Winston.

He held out his hand, clearly showing them the treat they'd get if they listened. "Stay." He backed up a step and repeated the command. Willow whined, and Jeremiah already knew she was the more vocal of the brother-sister duo. "Stay," he told her again.

After several steps, he said, "Come on," and both dogs ran over to him, their claws slipping on the hardwood floor in the homestead.

He laughed as he gave them each another treat and then scrubbed behind their ears. He'd only had the puppies for five days, and they were already such good friends. He loved having their warm bodies next to his while he lounged on the couch in the evening, while he slept at night, and while he worked around the ranch.

He loved taking care of them, teaching them to walk on a leash by going the half-mile to the Shining Star Ranch and back every evening. Whitney had taken to joining him if she didn't have a shoot, which meant she'd come once.

Jeremiah needed to get to town tomorrow and buy her a ring, and pure dread filled him from top to bottom. His heart stalled for a moment, reminding him of everything that had happened once he'd gotten on the diamond path before.

But Whitney wasn't Laura Ann, and this wedding wasn't even real. He could do this. He would, if only to show Wyatt and Liam and anyone else who thought he was still too damaged to have a woman in his life exactly how wrong they were.

He felt better than ever, and he opened the door and said, "All right, guys. Time to get to work." While he made his way across the lawn to his office in the barn, his mind moved through alternate scenarios to him purchasing a ring for Whitney. She seemed like the type of woman who knew exactly what she wanted and where to find it.

Maybe we should go ring shopping together. He typed out the words and sent them to her. *Tomorrow?*

I have a shoot in the morning, a birthday party for my niece in the afternoon, and a shoot in the evening, she sent back. *Maybe after the morning shoot, before the party? But then you'd have to be prepared to come to the party with me. And that means meeting everyone at once.*

"Everyone at once," Jeremiah said, almost like a sinister echo. He looked up, wishing he had someone to talk things through with. Maybe meeting everyone at once was the way to do it. Like ripping off a Band-aid—get it all done quickly.

The ranch was always busy, but June seemed to be particularly so, especially after a wet spring like they'd just had. It felt like everything on the ranch grew in June, from the trees, to the bushes, to the undergrowth, to the crops and hay. Jeremiah had mowing to do, and baling to attend to, and inventory on their feed, hay bale rotation, the cleaning of another barn....

And Whitney had two shoots in one day. If she had time to go buy a ring before the birthday party and then attend it, so did he.

Tell me what time and where to pick you up, he said. And I'll be there.

I'm shooting downtown in the morning, she said. I can meet you at TRJ.

He puzzled over the letters, even going so far as to search for their meaning online. A horse snuffled on the other side of the wall, and Jeremiah knew he needed to pocket his phone and get to work.

"Oh, of course," he said when the Internet spat out the answer he needed. "Three Rivers Jewelers." His chest seized. His throat narrowed. He very nearly threw up.

He could *not* believe he was going to go buy a diamond ring and make Whitney his fiancée tomorrow.

"You need a better plan," he muttered to himself, recognizing that the nerves of proposing were different than the ones screaming at him about getting engaged again.

And he could only imagine what his brothers would say.

He'd just decided to call Rhett when his phone brightened with an incoming call. "Speak of the devil," he said in lieu of hello. "I was just about to—"

"Miah, sorry," Rhett said, his voice panicked. "Evelyn is going into labor. Can you please call everyone? I'll text you what room she's in when we get to the hospital."

"Yes," Jeremiah said, a new kind of anxiety moving through him now. "Go. We'll be there soon."

Rhett hung up without another word, and Jeremiah turned away from his work. He was not going to be sitting in a smelly, hot barn while his first nephew was born. Oh, no, he was not. He dialed Liam as he left the barn at a jog, almost forgetting to take the pups with him.

"Call Momma," Jeremiah said, scooping both wiggly dogs into his arms. "And then Tripp. Evelyn and Rhett are on their way to the hospital."

15

R hett did not like the panic running through his body. He told himself that plenty of men had made it through childbirth with their wives. But he really didn't like seeing Evelyn in pain. He hated that the hospital was fifteen minutes away, and he couldn't do anything about anything.

But drive faster. He could do that.

"Rhett," Evelyn said as he ran the stop sign at the end of the lane.

"You're in labor," he said. "There's no one coming." He accelerated on the highway, wishing he had a siren and a light to stick to the top of his truck. It was Friday morning, and plenty of people were on the roads as they went to work.

He wanted to lean on the horn, but Evelyn wouldn't

like that either. A groan tore from her throat, and Rhett went around the cars in front of them. "Hang on, baby," he said. A couple of people honked at him, but he didn't care. His pulse throbbed in the back of his throat.

Evelyn panted on the seat next to him, bracing herself against the dashboard.

"Okay?" he asked.

"Just get us there," she said through clenched teeth.

He was trying. It seemed to take forever—Evelyn had two more contractions, one of which made a cry fly from her throat—before Rhett pulled up to the emergency entrance. "Stay here," he said. "I'll be right back."

He dashed toward the entrance, where a row of empty wheelchairs waited. He grabbed one and hurried back outside, where he helped Evelyn out of the high truck and into the wheelchair. She kept both hands on her stomach as if she could hold back the pain that way. Another contraction hit her as Rhett wheeled her inside, and thankfully, someone had seen his mad grab of the wheelchair, because a man wearing a blue set of scrubs met him.

"My wife," Rhett said, his voice filled with air.

"How far apart are the contractions?" the man asked, taking over behind the chair. Rhett matched him stride for stride as they went through a set of double-wide doors. "Name and birthdate?"

"Evelyn Walker," Rhett said. "Birthday is February ninth...." His mind blanked on the year, and thankfully, Evelyn filled it in for him. "And the contractions were four minutes apart when we left the house, twenty minutes ago."

"They're three minutes, ten seconds," Evelyn gasped out. "And they last for just over a minute." She held up her phone. "I have an app I've been using to track it."

People seemed to come out of nowhere, and Rhett was separated from Evelyn. A dark-haired woman attached herself to Rhett, and she pulled him out of the stream of traffic in the emergency room. "Let's get her checked in down here," she said. "And then I'll tell you where they have her."

"I'm not going to miss it, am I?" Rhett asked. Evelyn disappeared into a room, and the curtain was closed behind her.

"No, sir," the woman said. "This will take five minutes. She might not even leave emergency before then."

Rhett reached up and took his cowboy hat off. He was suddenly so hot, and he turned toward the woman. "Okay, what do you need?"

"Insurance?" the woman asked.

"I'm with Texas State Police," he said.

She cocked one eyebrow, but Rhett wasn't going to explain to her what he did for a living. He could buy this hospital and not even use half the money he had in his bank account.

"What's your name?" she asked.

He went through the questions, and sure enough, she

let him go right as the curtain opened. Evelyn had changed into a gown, and she was laying in a bed now, which two people pushed from behind her head.

"We're going up to labor and delivery," a woman said. "She'll be in delivery room six, and then recovery room four-forty-seven, if you want to meet us up there."

"I can't just come with you?" he asked. "I can go into the delivery room, right?" The thought of missing the birth of his son had Rhett's cells vibrating in a very bad way.

"Sure," the man with them said. "James called her doctor, and he's on his way in."

"Great," Rhett said, his emotions fluctuating so much his head hurt. "Evvy? Hey, you okay?" He matched his pace to that of her bed, and he took her hand in his. She squeezed, and Rhett loved her more powerfully in that moment than any other leading up to this event.

He couldn't even fathom what she'd been through over the past nine months, and as she leaned her head back and groaned, Rhett just wanted all of this pain to end.

The hallways in the hospital were sterile and long. The elevator smelled like lighter fluid and bleach, and when Rhett stepped onto the fourth floor, he immediately wanted to leave.

The cry of a baby reached his ears, and pure joy filled him. "Almost there, Evvy."

She got pushed into delivery room six, and all kinds of things happened. She got hooked up to an IV and a pulse monitor. The emergency nurses left and two women in pink scrubs entered the room.

Jeannie and Deb introduced themselves, and they were much calmer with Evelyn. They took her blood pressure and temperature, and one of them took her phone and recorded the information from the app.

Another contraction came, and Deb leaned over Evelyn. "Are you doing an epidural?"

"Yes," Evelyn said.

The nurse nodded and stepped over to the phone. Rhett took her place, taking her hand so she'd know she wasn't alone. "You're doin' great, baby," he said. "The doctors are going to be here real soon." He sent up a prayer that what he'd said would actually come true, and relief filled him when Doctor Partridge walked in, a huge smile on his face.

"We're having a baby today," he said, and while Rhett had only met him a week ago, for a twenty-minute appointment, he liked the man a lot. He had a very good air about him, and Rhett thanked the Lord for good hospitals and good doctors as Doctor Partridge pulled a rolling stool over and sat in front of Evelyn. He checked her and said, "Oh, yes, this baby will be here soon. Epidural?"

"Yes," Deb said. "I called Doctor Swapp. He's two minutes out."

"He has ten," Doctor Partridge said. "And then the epidural won't do any good."

"It won't do any good?" Rhett repeated. "What does that mean?"

"It means your wife is very close to having your son," Doctor Partridge said. "And if she doesn't get the epidural in ten minutes, the drugs won't have time to do what they need to do anyway. The baby will be here already."

"Don't let me have the baby without drugs," Evelyn said. "Rhett."

But Rhett didn't know what to do. Thankfully, Doctor Partridge stood up and went to Evelyn's side. He spoke to her kindly, with plenty of encouragement, telling her that lots of women had babies naturally, but they'd do everything they could to get the epidural done on time. As if summoned by Rhett's desperation and fear, the anesthesiologist walked into the room.

"Ten minutes," Doctor Partridge said.

"We just need three," Doctor Swapp said. She went to Evelyn's side too and asked her if she wanted the epidural.

"Yes, please," Evelyn said, her voice full of pain and relief.

"When was the last contraction?" she asked.

"One minute," one of the nurses said. "They're coming fast, Doctor."

"Let's roll her."

Rhett stepped out of the way and watched as Evelyn got rolled onto her side and the epidural administered. He moved back to her side the moment he could, and everything accelerated from there.

Before he knew it, Doctor Partridge was telling Evelyn to push, and Rhett could barely breathe by the time the doctor said, "There you go, Evelyn. He's out." He said something to a nurse, who stepped in to do what he wanted.

And then Rhett saw his son. His baby. The tiny infant was passed from hands to hands, where one woman wiped his face, and then the baby cried.

Tears sprang to his eyes, and he didn't care who saw. The woman cooed at the baby, wrapped him in a blanket, and turned to Rhett. She handed him the infant and said, "Go show your wife."

The doctor still worked with Evelyn, but Rhett stepped closer to her head and said, "Evvy, he's perfect." The baby hadn't opened his eyes yet, and Rhett snuggled him right into Evelyn's chest as she wept.

He pressed his lips to her forehead. "You did it, baby." Pure love and joy filled him, and he felt about as close to heaven as he thought a person could feel.

"What are we going to name him?" she asked.

"Conrad," Rhett said. "Your momma's maiden name, right?"

"Conrad Rhett?" Evelyn looked up at him, and she was the most beautiful woman in the world.

"Yes," he whispered.

Evelyn kissed the infant, who made a soft grunting noise and seemed to snuggle right into his momma. "I'm sure the waiting room is full. You better go talk to them."

Rhett turned toward the door, and a nurse caught his eye. "She needs at least twenty minutes before she can have any visitors," she said. "We want to make sure she's warm enough. And we'll have to take the baby for a bath in about five minutes. If you want to come, you best be back by then."

"Five minutes," Rhett said. "I won't miss it."

16

Callie couldn't sit still, and she paced from Simone to where Liam stood with Tripp and Skyler. Wyatt was at Bowman's Breeds, which was much farther than Seven Sons, and he hadn't arrived yet.

Callie felt like her stomach had been hooked to a motor, and it was twisting, twisting, twisting with every moment that passed. Why hadn't someone come out yet? Was everything okay with the baby?

She wouldn't be able to live if it wasn't. In that moment, Callie was wildly reminded of how badly she wanted to be a mother. She and Liam had talked about starting their adoption file or going through the foster care parenting classes. But in the six months since they'd gotten married, they'd done neither.

Turning back to Simone, she walked toward her sister. "Do you think everything is okay?"

"It's been half an hour," Simone said. "Remember how long it took you to show up?"

She smiled, because while she'd lost her mother at a young age, Daddy had still told all of the girls many stories about them. "Sixteen hours."

"If we're here that long, I'll go crazy," Simone said.

Callie would too, because the last thirty minutes had felt like thirty hours.

Wyatt entered, his face frantic. "Well? Anything?"

Miah assured him that they hadn't heard anything yet, and Callie thought she might burst. Any moment now....

Just when she thought she couldn't wait for another second, Rhett came through the door, and he wore the widest smile on the planet. "It's a boy."

A cheer went up, because the Walkers didn't exactly mind being loud in public. Callie rushed forward with the rest of them to congratulate Rhett, who said Evelyn couldn't have visitors for another half an hour.

"What did you name him?" Wyatt asked.

"Conrad," he said, and Callie sucked in a breath. Conrad was her mama's maiden name. "And his middle name is Rhett."

Miah hugged Rhett for a long moment, and it was nice to see these tough cowboys exhibit some emotion. Who knew something that weighed less than eight pounds could do such a thing?

"They're giving him a bath in a minute," Rhett said. "And I don't want to miss it."

"Take some pictures," Liam said.

"You know what you should do?" Ivory said. "There's this lady who does newborn pictures. You should get some of Conrad. She puts them in vegetables and flowers and fruits and stuff."

"No way," Miah said. "They're not doing that."

"Why not?" Ivory asked, and Callie was actually impressed the woman dared to go toe-to-toe with the mighty Jeremiah Walker.

"Because those pictures are ridiculous," Miah said.

"Your girlfriend is here," Wyatt said.

Miah stepped out of the conversation and over to Whitney Wilde, and Callie couldn't help staring as he took her into his arms and kissed her.

Actually *kissed* her.

Good for him, Callie thought, and she did miss the talks they'd used to have. But he'd obviously found some way to move past Laura Ann, and he and Whitney made a cute couple. He turned back to the group with her, and while Rhett went back through door to return to Evelyn, Miah started making introductions.

Whitney had met a lot of the brothers before, and she'd taken Tripp's and Ivory's engagement pictures. Callie hadn't officially met her, so when Miah said, "Liam's wife, Callie Foster. Walker. Callie Walker." He chuckled. "That's still hard for me."

"Nice to meet you," Whitney said, but she looked like she was about to come apart at the seams. Her eyes kept darting around nervously, but she kept her grin in place. Miah would not leave her side, despite Callie's efforts to catch his eye.

She missed their friendship, but she returned to Liam's side. "How much longer until we can go back and see the baby?"

"Rhett said thirty minutes. It's been maybe five, sweetheart." He slid his arm around her and pulled her close. Callie wrapped her arms around him and let him hold her, comfort her.

"Liam, I want a baby," she whispered, and Liam brought his attention right back to her. His eyes searched hers, and Callie didn't know what else to say.

"On Monday, I'll find out what we need to do to get a profile at the adoption agency," he said. He touched his lips to her forehead, and Callie fell in love with him even more than she already was.

Her phone chimed, and then Liam's. All across the room, phones chimed. "Pictures," someone said, and Callie couldn't get her phone out fast enough.

Finally, after thirty long minutes, Rhett returned and he said, "Two people can go back at once. She wants Simone and Callie to come first. And we have to be quiet back there, so if you boys can't handle that, you can't come back." He actually looked like he meant it too, and Callie grinned at him. Already the overprotective husband and father.

With that, Callie linked arms with Simone and

followed Rhett. Down the hall, through the door, and she found her sister lying in a hospital bed, a baby cradled in her arms. A real baby. The most beautiful baby in the world.

"Oh." Callie paused, her hand fluttering up to her mouth as Simone moved forward. She should've stopped to get Daddy and Gran, but she reasoned she hadn't known how long the labor would be. She could bring them by tonight or tomorrow, when the waiting room was less crowded.

Simone leaned over and kissed Evelyn's forehead, and Evelyn passed her the baby. Simone wore a light that filled her whole face, and Callie knew exactly how she felt. She crossed the room and leaned over to hug Evelyn.

"Congratulations," she whispered. "He's just so beautiful, isn't he?" She peered down at the baby in Simone's arms. "I love him so much already." The baby didn't have a single wisp of hair on his head, and he looked so peaceful with his eyes closed and his body all bundled up.

"You want him?" Simone passed Conrad to Callie, and tears streamed down her face.

Simone put her arm around Callie. "Oh, honey."

Callie shook her head. "I'm fine," she whispered. "Honest, I am."

Monday couldn't come fast enough, and Callie hoped she could hold a baby of her own someday soon.

17

Because those pictures are ridiculous.

Whitney kept her smile in place as she met everyone in Jeremiah's family. That wasn't the hard part, for her, at least.

But the words he'd said to everyone about her baby photography cut through her over and over again.

Ridiculous, she thought. Her photography was *not* ridiculous, and yet, she felt like she could never tell Jeremiah now. She honestly had no plan for when to tell him, and things between them had been going so well.

But her anger simmered down low in her stomach, and she knew it wasn't going to go away. She couldn't deal with it with so many people around, and Jeremiah had a tight grip on her hand, almost like he needed her to stay close to maintain his own sanity. Whitney was willing to be that person for him, but she'd definitely have to tell him about Lake Winters before they got married.

Probably before they even got engaged. After all, he wouldn't say such hurtful things about her photography if he knew she was Lake Winters. That didn't really matter though. He'd still think them, and Whitney knew how he felt.

And if Evelyn hired her? How could Whitney expect to ask Evelyn and Rhett to keep her secret for her? They wouldn't, she knew that. So she'd just say she was busy if they called, though she hated that. She wanted to do the baby photography, and posing Jeremiah's nephew among fresh peas and carrots? That sounded like a dream come true for her.

A sigh passed through her whole body, and Jeremiah stepped forward when Callie and Simone returned. "I want to go," he said. "Will you wait for me?"

She nodded and faded into the background as he disappeared through the door with the twins. That was more than two people, but she couldn't imagine anyone telling those three Walker men that they couldn't be there.

Whitney sat down on a couch, surprised when Wyatt joined her, a long sigh spilling from his mouth. "Hey," he said, smiling at her.

"Hey." She smiled at him. He was handsome, as all the Walkers were, and he seemed to be very down-to-earth. "My nephew is big into the rodeo," she added.

"That so?" he asked, rubbing his hands together.

"I told him I might be able to introduce the two of you."

Wyatt looked weary for a moment, just a beat of time. "Does he ride?"

"Yeah, of course," she said.

"Bring 'im out to the ranch on Saturday or Sunday. I ride the most then."

"He will literally die," Whitney said with a smile.

Wyatt grinned at her. "I ain't nobody special, ma'am."

Oh, he could charm anyone with that cowboy accent, and Whitney shook her head. "Well, I think you've won a bunch of championships or something, so Dalton thinks you're special."

"How old is he?"

"Just turned sixteen. I taught him to drive."

"Wow." Wyatt's eyebrows went up. "Brave woman."

"More like trying to keep my sister from killing him." She laughed, glad when Wyatt did too. Jeremiah returned a couple of minutes later, and he asked if she wanted to go see the baby.

She shook her head. "Let your family do it. I need to get back to the store." She'd run out when Jeremiah had called, and Patsy said she'd finish her job. But she'd only been here for about forty minutes, and she might as well get back so the green beans got put in the right place.

Jeremiah walked her out to her truck and kissed her. Whitney enjoyed the taste of him, the slow, easy way he kissed her. He made her feel cherished, and loved, and absolutely beautiful.

If only he liked her pictures too.

"Tomorrow morning?" he asked, kissing her again. "What time?" But he kissed her before she could answer. The sun beat down on her, but she could barely feel it. Someone honked, and Jeremiah chuckled as he pulled away from her.

"Sorry," he murmured, still grinning. "What time should I meet you at the jeweler?"

"Shoot should be done by eight," she said.

"Well, they won't be open by then. Breakfast?"

"Pancake house," she said, putting one palm against his chest and pressing him back. Maybe by then she'd have found a way to tell him about Lake Winters.

"See you then," he said, falling back again. He turned and walked away, and Whitney went back to Wilde & Organic.

She found Patsy in the produce section with plenty of boxes to go. "I'm back," she said, tying on her apron. "Thanks for covering for me."

"How's Evelyn?" Patsy asked.

A bit of surprise trickled through Whitney. She hadn't known her sister and Evelyn Walker were friends at all. "I didn't see her," she said. "But the report is that everyone did great, and the baby is super cute." Whitney smiled, pulled on her gloves, and opened a box of cabbage. She wanted babies so badly, and she couldn't believe she'd wasted so much time on a man like Blake. He didn't really know her, and he'd never really supported her dreams.

Kind of like how Jeremiah thinks your baby photography is ridiculous. The annoying voice in her head wouldn't go away, and Whitney grew more agitated with every head of cabbage she stacked.

"How are things with you and Jeremiah?" Patsy asked.

Whitney blinked, trying to focus on the conversation and the work. Those thoughts were so dang loud in her head. "Okay," she said.

"Just okay?"

She glanced over to Patsy and then around the store. But they were still closed, and no one could overhear. "He hates the baby photography."

Patsy stalled in her arrangement of the tomatillos. "He said that to your face?"

"He doesn't know it's me."

"You haven't told him?"

No wonder Dalton didn't like talking to his mother. Everything was a question, and it was said in such a way that made Whitney feel like she'd never be able to do anything right. "No," she said. "When we got back together, I was hanging my spring photo up, and he made a comment about how weird it was. So I didn't say anything." She shrugged, broke down the box, and moved to the purple cauliflower. "I thought I'd, you know, eventually tell him. Today, he made another comment about how ridiculous it was when someone suggested Evelyn and Rhett hire me for newborn pictures."

"Oh, wow." Patsy wore a look of sympathy on her face. "What are you going to do?"

"I don't know." She stared at the vegetables and kept her hands busy to get them all in the right places. "I sure do like him."

"I can see that." Patsy nudged her, and Whitney found a smile on her face. "Maybe pray about it? See what you feel like is best." That was Patsy's answer for every-thing—pray about it.

Whitney didn't hate the advice, and she placed the last head of purple cauliflower on top of the pile and closed her eyes. *What should I do about Jeremiah?*

That was a very broad question, and Whitney would like a checklist, please and thank you. But no loud voices boomed through the store. No soft ones either. No impressions. No feelings. She opened her eyes and moved down to the yellow squash. She didn't have time for prayer right now anyway. The store would be open in twenty minutes, and she and Patsy would be lucky to have the produce section ready in time.

———

THE NEXT MORNING, Whitney tucked her camera into the protective bag and put it in the trunk of her car. She'd invested thousands in her photography gear, and she always took great care with it. She double-checked to make sure she'd taken off her strap and put her light meter in the backseat before she locked the car and crossed the street.

Jeremiah looked up from the bench in front of the pancake house as she approached, a smile blooming across his handsome face. Maybe his thoughts and opinions about the baby photography didn't matter. Maybe she'd never have to tell him.

Don't be stupid, she told herself. She was going to *marry this man.* Maybe it wouldn't be real at first, but what if the relationship could be? Would she have to constantly look over her shoulder to make sure he didn't see her editing the newborns? Lie to him about where she was going and who she was shooting?

Yeah, she couldn't keep the secret for forever. But as Jeremiah chuckled and swept her into his arms, she thought she certainly didn't need to tell him today. She accepted his kiss, not caring that they stood in front of the busiest place in town on a Saturday morning.

"I'm starving," he said. "I don't usually eat breakfast so late."

"It's barely after eight," she said.

"Yeah, and a lot of work on the ranch is done by dawn," he said. "It's so hot during the day."

Whitney just shook her head and climbed the steps to the pancake house with him. "I want to stop by the bakery after this too," she said. "I need to take something for my niece's party."

"I never say no to stopping at the bakery," he said.

He held up two fingers for the hostess, who promptly grabbed menus and said, "Follow me."

They'd only made it a few steps when Jeremiah stopped. "Squire," he said, glancing around at all the cowboys in the booth. He dropped Whitney's hand as the other cowboy rose to shake his. "You brought the whole crew."

"Just a few," the other cowboy said. He was closer to Whitney's age than Jeremiah's, though she probably had a year or two on Squire too. Whitney knew who he was, of course. Retired military hero. Had gone off to vet school and had just returned to run the biggest ranch in town. Everyone knew who the Ackermans were.

"I don't see you out on the weekends," Squire said, moving his gaze to Whitney.

"Yeah, well, I lose track of the days in the summer," Jeremiah said, grinning. "This is my girlfriend, Whitney Wilde."

"My pleasure, ma'am," Squire said, reaching for her hand.

"Nice to meet you too." Nerves fluttered through Whitney's stomach. This was what she'd imagined meeting his family to be like, but that had been easy. Jeremiah had stepped around Squire and was talking to another man, and it was clear Jeremiah had a second family unit in town she hadn't known about.

Squire turned back to the half-dozen cowboys

crammed in the booth. "He's talkin' to Pete Marshall. He runs Courage Reins out at the ranch. And we brought along some of our boys that have been workin' real hard this spring." He nodded to them and started rattling off names. Whitney knew a couple of them, but not all of them.

They tipped their hats and said, "Ma'am," over and over.

She knew Bennett Lancaster the best, as they were the same age and had gone to high school together. She knew Duke Somers too, and both of them watched her with a little too much interest.

"How long y'all been dating?" Bennett asked.

"Not long," Whitney hedged. "How do you guys know Jeremiah?"

"Oh, he attends all the ranch owner meetings in town," Squire said. "Pete and I go as much as we can. Jeremiah's always there."

"They're on Thursdays," Pete said. "You must be something special to get him off that ranch any other time." He grinned and lifted his coffee mug to his lips.

Heat rose through Whitney, and she really just wanted to go sit down. But Jeremiah just stood there, smiling around at everyone. She linked her arm through his and nudged him, and he finally looked at her.

"Oh, right, well, we're over here," he said, lifting his hand. "Good to see y'all." He finally continued through the restaurant to the table the hostess had laid their menus on. Whitney sat with her back to the table of cowboys, but the weight of their eyes still lingered on her shoulders. And it was heavy.

"Wow, ranch ownership meetings on Thursdays," she said as she unwrapped her silverware. "You're a man of many layers, Jeremiah Walker."

He burst out laughing, and Whitney sure did like the sound of that. She liked that *she* could make him laugh, and she wondered when the last time she'd felt so happy had been.

She didn't know, and she felt herself slipping further in love with the man across the table from her.

18

"Is that the one?" Jeremiah peered down at Whitney's left hand, where she wore a diamond the size of a baseball. Not really, but it was big. Huge. Way bigger than what he'd bought for Laura Ann all those years ago.

"I do love this one," she said. "But it's very expensive." She looked up at him. "We should get something fake. It's not like this will become an heirloom." She kept her voice low, as the saleswoman never seemed to go more than two feet from them.

Jeremiah didn't know what to say. True, their wedding wasn't entirely real. But his feelings for this woman were absolutely real. One-hundred percent real, and growing by the hour.

He'd thoroughly enjoyed breakfast, and Whitney knew her own mind, so the ring shopping hadn't taken long at all. She'd tried on four rings before this one, and the way she wouldn't take it off told him how she really felt.

"This one," he said to the saleswoman. "Can she wear it out?"

"Depends on the sizing," she said to Whitney. "How does it feel?"

"It's great," she said, holding her hand out to admire the ring.

Jeremiah moved down the counter with the woman and paid for the ring while someone else took it from Whitney to "make it shine." If it wasn't shining already, Jeremiah thought he must be blind.

His heart flopped around his chest, and he couldn't believe what was happening. The woman handed his card back to him, and he slid it back into his wallet. He'd just bought an engagement ring.

He looked at Whitney, almost feeling outside of his body. He'd felt like this before, too—once while he stood at the altar all dressed up for a wedding that wouldn't happen.

Then he found himself accepting the posh black bag with a little black box inside it. Whitney laced her arm through his, and they left the jewelry shop. Outside, Jeremiah sucked at the air, panic moving through him.

"Are you okay?" she asked.

He couldn't answer. His instinct was to run, and he crossed the street in front of the statue and headed into the bark park. On Saturday at this time, it wasn't terribly busy, because the sun had already baked the Texas Panhandle to a crisp.

Still, he found a shaded bench and practically fell onto it. "What am I doing?" he asked under his breath. *Is this the right thing to do?* he prayed. *Because I'll take this ring back right now. Just tell me what to do, Lord.*

Whitney appeared at his side, and she sat at the other end of the bench, plenty of space between them.

"I'm...." He didn't know what to say. "I maybe panicked a little back there."

Whitney looked at him, and her beauty struck him right between the eyes. She was kind, and faithful, and hard-working. That dark hair, and those red lips, and the eyes that devoured him every time he looked at her.

Jeremiah Walker had been in love before, and he knew he was swimming in very dangerous waters at the moment. He gripped the bag with the diamond ring in it as if pure pressure would keep him from falling in love with the woman beside him.

But in some ways, he already had.

His mind cleared, and he remembered how whole he'd felt this past week. How miserable he'd been without her at the beginning of the year.

"Whitney," he said, his voice even and calm. "I'm a little scared to say this, but...."

"Just say it," she said.

Jeremiah opened his mouth, completely unsure about what would come out. "Will you marry me?"

Hey, at least it wasn't *I'm falling in love with you.* He sure didn't want to say that while sitting in a smelly, hot dog park. No, that declaration should happen out on the ranch or in her grandfather's old truck. Somewhere that meant something.

A smile filled her whole face, and she nodded. "Yes, I'll marry you."

He fumbled with the bag and then the box while she slid closer to him and held out her left hand. With clarity, he slipped the ring on her finger and admired it.

His gaze switched to hers, and they leaned toward each other together, her touch almost explosive as he kissed her. He'd never felt anything like it, and he clung to her for an extra moment before pulling away.

"Okay," he said, blowing out his breath. "All right. We're engaged." A trickle of mania crept through him, and he knew he'd have to make the announcement at dinner tomorrow night. Maybe call a family meeting. Or maybe a text would be good enough.

"Are you ready for this afternoon?" Whitney asked, cuddling into his side.

"I honestly don't know," he said. "Let's go over the family again."

"We don't need to do that." She stood up and held out her hand. "It's too hot out here. Let's go back to my place. I can upload my pictures and you can take a nap before the party."

A nap sounded heavenly, and Jeremiah couldn't find

anything to argue about. They stopped by the bakery for a dozen of her niece's favorite doughnuts—raspberry fritters —and Jeremiah parked his truck behind Whitney's in her driveway.

He'd been to her house several times in the past, but never inside. She welcomed him in, as did her two cats. He wasn't entirely a feline person, and the cats seemed to be able to smell his puppies on him. But they didn't run and hide.

"Jones and Jess," she said, introducing them. "And Jeremiah. Lots of J's around here." She smiled and hooked her thumb down the hall. "My studio is down here. I'm just going to go get the pictures uploading."

"How long does that take?"

"Two seconds to start," she said. "About ten minutes or so to get them all imported. Help yourself to coffee or whatever in the kitchen."

He nodded, and she left, the cats stalking after her. Jones and Jess were definitely the aloof, snooty type of cat, and Jeremiah just shook his head at their retreating tails. There was no coffee in the kitchen, but plenty of light pouring in the back windows. Whitney had yellow curtains over the sink and along the widows that over-looked the backyard. A cat door had been installed right into the wall, and the only exit along the back of the house led into the garage.

Everything seemed bright and white, and Whitney didn't leave dirty dishes out, piles of mail, or anything she'd get to later. Everything was in its proper place, including a mail key that was attached to a keychain that looked like a five-year-old had made it.

"They probably did," Jeremiah said to himself, replacing the key in the also obviously homemade bowl on her kitchen counter. She'd put change in there too, and when she joined him in the kitchen, her keys went into the dark green ceramic as well.

"You didn't make coffee," she said.

"I drank a ton at the pancake house," he said. "I probably won't even be able to nap because of it." He slipped his arms around her waist. He suddenly didn't want to nap at all. "You have a nice place, Whitney."

She melted right into his arms. "Thank you. I love this house. It's not huge, but it's nice."

"Did you remodel it?"

"Nope, it came like this." She swayed with him, pressing her cheek against his.

Her house smelled like sugar and mint, as did Whitney herself. "I'm glad you have a nice place," he said. "When you move to the homestead after we're married, I can pay for it."

She pulled away. "You don't need to do that."

He searched her face. "You're going to keep the house, though, right?"

"Yes, we talked about that."

"Because the marriage isn't going to be real," he said, actually leaning closer to see how the words affected her.

She blinked quickly, almost a flinch. Could she *want* the marriage to be real? "Right. I'm going to keep the house so I can come back here after we...."

Jeremiah didn't finish her sentence either. He didn't want to break-up with this woman. He might not know everything about her yet, but what he did know was enough to know he wanted her in his life. He wanted to know more about her. He wanted to fall in love again.

And as if someone had entered his mind with a duster, all the cobwebs inside his head were suddenly gone. He gazed at Whitney and leaned down to kiss her. He kissed her, and kissed her, and kissed her, because he had a lot to say and no way to vocalize the words.

A few hours later, he let her lead him into another house, this one on the other side of town and with considerably more cars parked in front of it.

All evidence of their make-out session had been erased from his face. His cowboy hat perched neatly on his head, and he'd even caught forty minutes of sleep. Whitney had edited her pictures with the door closed, and Jeremiah hadn't minded the pure peace in her house. She had a nice couch that he thought he could take many naps on, and it had just been nice to be away from the ranch and in the presence of his fiancée.

His fiancée.

He couldn't believe those words, but he better get used to them, because one step through the front door of Whitney's brother's house, and Jeremiah would be enduring a lot of introductions.

The door opened up to one big room, and someone had pushed all the couches against the walls. A couple of tables had been set up next to the dining room table, and they filled the space in the dining room and living room. Adults stood in the kitchen, sat at the tables, or lingered on the couches.

Jeremiah froze, taking in all the chaos. He supposed his family could be a bit overwhelming too, especially when all the brothers were together, and especially now that they were starting to get married and have children too.

There were no babies here, though. All of the kids seemed to be older—maybe eight or nine years old and up. He reached for Whitney's hand, all of the names they'd talked about completely abandoning him.

Whitney dropped his hand to hug her sister, and then she stepped back. "Patsy, this is Jeremiah Walker."

No label. He couldn't help glancing at her left hand before looking into Patsy's face. She had the same light skin, same dark hair, but the similarities between her and Whitney stopped there. Patsy had a more square face, with lighter eyes and bushier eyebrows.

"Ma'am," Jeremiah said.

"Nice to meet you," Patsy said with a warm smile. "I

mean, I've met you around town, of course. The light parade." She cut a look to Whitney, who just smiled. So Jeremiah did too, and he asked her about her kids.

"Oh, Billie's over there, and Dalton is around somewhere. Probably in the backyard." She rolled her eyes, and Whitney said she'd make sure he came in for everything important.

They moved on, and Jeremiah met her brother, the one with the daughter turning seven. She, apparently, was the youngest of the nieces and nephews in the family, and Jeremiah wondered if Whitney wanted children. They hadn't quite talked that far ahead, and he realized how much he'd put the cart before the horse.

"My momma," Whitney said. "Molly. But you know her."

"That I do," Jeremiah said, sweeping his cowboy hat off his head. He felt sweaty and hot, and he sure hoped he didn't look it. "Good to see you again, ma'am."

Molly looked at Whitney and back to Jeremiah. "You two make a mighty fine couple," she said, smiling for all she was worth.

"Momma," Whitney warned, but Jeremiah had already put the ring on her finger.

"What?" Molly asked anyway, completely ignoring the danger in her daughter's voice. "You called the other day about a possible wedding date." She spoke the last two words as if they were scandalous.

Jeremiah looked at Whitney, who looked right back at

him. She had called her mother after the hike, and she was wearing the ring. Anyone could see it, if they only looked down a couple of feet.

They seemed to be able to communicate without words at all, and Whitney lifted her left hand so her momma didn't have to look anywhere but straight ahead. "He asked me to marry him this morning." Whitney squealed, and it sure sounded like she was excited. Positively *thrilled* to become his wife. "We're engaged!"

"Engaged. Oh, Dear Lord in Heaven." Molly reached for the countertop and braced herself against it. Her eyes filled with tears and she laughed as she hugged Whitney tight. Then she turned to Jeremiah, and he just kept his smile plastered on his face as she embraced him too.

"Oh, I can't even...this is so wonderful."

Guilt filled Jeremiah, and he hated that Molly Wilde didn't have the whole truth. But he hadn't lied. He had asked Whitney to marry him that morning, and she had said yes. They were engaged.

"Larry, get over here," Molly yelled over her shoulder. "Your daughter is engaged."

Those words stopped the whole party, all the chatter, everything. Everyone came over, and Whitney showed the ring to her siblings and in-laws as if they wouldn't believe it was true without diamond proof.

Everyone immediately looked at Jeremiah after that, and he held up his hands as if to say, *What choice did I have?*

He put his arm around her and pressed his lips to her cheek. She leaned into the pressure, and a collective, "Aw," went up from her family members.

And now that Whitney's whole family knew about the engagement, it wouldn't be long until his brothers did too. "Excuse me," he said, stepping over to a set of sliding glass doors and going outside.

He pulled out his phone and hesitated. Rhett had just had a baby yesterday, and Jeremiah didn't want to burden him with the task of spreading the word about his engagement. The twins had always buddied up, and Skyler and Micah had the youngest sibling bond. Wyatt was the odd man out in the group of seven brothers, and while he had a thing going with Marcy Payne, he denied he was dating her.

"Waiting to date her," he'd said. "When she's ready."

Jeremiah texted him, as he'd be the least likely to call and the most likely to have time to text everyone else.

Hey, he thumbed out. *I'm at a birthday party for Whitney's niece, but I wanted to tell the family something before they heard from someone else. Would you text or call around? I'll call Momma later, so don't tell her.*

He read over the text a couple of times and then sent it, his pulse ricocheting between his ribs. Drawing in a deep breath, he started typing again.

Tell em what? Wyatt asked.

I'm engaged. He stared at the words, still having a hard

time believing them. *Whitney and I are getting married in August.*

He sent the message zipping through cyberspace, and he turned to survey the lawn. A teenage boy laid in a free-standing hammock, and their eyes met.

"You must be Dalton," Jeremiah said as the teen took out his earbuds. "You're the smartest one in the family, you know that?"

A slow smile spread across Dalton's face, but he made no move to get out of the hammock. "You're Whitney's boyfriend."

"That's right," Jeremiah said. "Jeremiah Walker. I've heard a lot about you."

"Ditto," he said.

"Oh, and since I just told my brothers, and Whitney's inside relaying all the details of it, you should know, I'm your aunt's fiancé."

Dalton's eyes widened as pure shock crossed his face. "Really?"

"Really." Jeremiah chuckled, hoping the engagement between him and Whitney wasn't so ridiculous that even a teenager wouldn't believe it.

"Wow, that's great," Dalton said, getting out of the hammock. He was a skinny, tall kid, but he embraced Jeremiah like they'd be best of friends. "I knew she really liked you." He released Jeremiah and sat back in the hammock.

"Did you now?" Jeremiah pulled up a chair and sat down. "What exactly does your aunt Whitney tell you?"

19

Whitney ignored Jeremiah's third text, her stomach a writhing mess of snakes. Life had gone back to normal after a couple of days of holding out her hand, smiling, and saying she and Jeremiah were simply mad for each other and would be married in just a few weeks.

It was more like two months, but that hadn't stopped Momma from calling her four times a day and texting about every hour.

Jeremiah's texts were normally the balm to her weary soul, but not when she had a newborn shoot on her calendar she hadn't told him about. He literally never asked who she was shooting, though they had often agreed to meet after her shoots, so he sometimes asked her where.

And tonight, he wanted to take her to dinner afterward. She hadn't told him that her shoot was *after* dinner, nor that she was trying out some of the lighting techniques she'd learned in her workshop. She never shot indoors, and she didn't want him to show up at her house while she still had apples and pears on her dining room table.

She could move Bea and Wendall to earlier, use the natural light that spilled through her big back windows....

Whitney shook her head. No, she'd moved the couple and their eight-day-old newborn a couple of times already. She didn't want to lose the business, and there was no real reason she couldn't shoot them that evening.

Just Jeremiah.

And he did not like it when she didn't respond to his texts. She stewed as she sat at her computer, her mind going round and round itself. The machine in front of her chimed, and she looked to the bottom righthand corner to find someone had chatted her through her Lake Winters website.

Just had a baby a few days ago. Wondering what your schedule is like? Your website says you like babies to be less than ten days old.

Whitney's hopes shot up to the stars. Another baby! She hadn't had one for a month, and now she might have two in one week. She smiled, already planning the second baby's shoot.

She put her hands on the keyboard and typed. Younger is better, she said. They're more pliable and sleep longer. Do you have something in mind for flowers, vegetables, fruits...?

My husband is a real cowboy, the woman said, adding a smiley face. *He'd probably like more rustic stuff for our son.*

Whitney's heart began to pound. Can I get your name and phone number? Then we can chat easier.

She pressed her eyes closed, praying with everything she had that it was not *Evelyn Walker* on the other side of that screen. "Please, please," she muttered to herself.

The computer dinged, and Whitney's eyes flew open. Evelyn Walker and a phone number sat there.

Whitney fell back in her office chair, numbness spreading through her. At least Jeremiah's assessment of her work had fallen on deaf ears. She supposed she should be happy about that.

But would Evelyn keep her secret?

All of her other clients had, but they didn't have to potentially lie to their brother-in-law that they saw every week. Sometimes several times a week.

She didn't know what to do. Now she was avoiding two Walkers, and as another message from Evelyn came in, Whitney knew she couldn't just go silent. That would be bad for business, number one.

So she picked up her phone and keyed in Evelyn's number. "Is now a good time to talk?" she asked when the other woman picked up the line.

"Yes, the baby is asleep," she said.

"Will your husband come to the shoot?" Whitney asked.

"Yes," Evelyn said. "I'm actually hoping to do two...."

"Two shoots?"

"One here at our house, and one at my family ranch. That one would be fun with corn stalks and cattails and eggs. My sister has chickens that lay the most beautiful, blue eggs."

Whitney pressed her eyes closed, because the brown and blue and beautiful baby shoot materialized right in front of her eyes. "That would be lovely," she said through a closed throat. "Unfortunately, my schedule—"

"Oh, don't say no," Evelyn said, a plea of desperation in her voice. "I'll come anytime, anywhere. I love your photos, and this might be the only baby I get."

How in the world could Whitney say no to that?

She sighed and hoped she wasn't about to ruin everything. "Evelyn," she said evenly. "It's Whitney Wilde."

"I—what?"

"I'm Whitney Wilde. Lake Winters is a pseudonym I use exclusively for the infant photography. I don't want Jeremiah to know...yet." She drew in a deep, deep breath, trying to find what she wanted to say. "I mean, I'm going to tell him. I just haven't yet, and I want to be the one who does."

Evelyn said nothing, and Whitney cursed herself for using her real name before the disclosure forms were signed.

"Why haven't you told him?" Evelyn asked. "It's not a bad thing, right?"

"No," Whitney said. "He's...made some comments

about the baby photos I have hanging in the store, and well, he doesn't like them."

"That doesn't mean he won't like *you*."

"I know." Whitney pressed her eyes closed. She didn't want to talk about this, not with Evelyn Walker. She knew the woman, sure, but they weren't best friends. "What's your schedule like?"

"I'm wide open," Evelyn said. "Rhett and I can be discreet."

"Is there another road to your ranch?" Whitney asked. "Or will I have to drive right by Seven Sons to get there?"

"Oh, well, there's only the one road...."

Whitney clicked on her calendar, and it was as if the Lord Himself had turned on a spotlight. All she could see was Thursday, and she'd recently learned that Jeremiah had ranch ownership meetings on some Thursdays.

"I'll call you back," she said. "Okay? Five minutes. I'll call you back."

Evelyn protested, but Whitney hung up anyway. Her fingers flew across the screen as she said the shoot was an "experimental indoor shoot" at her house until nine, but he was welcome to stop by before then. *You'd have to leave at seven-thirty at the latest*, she said, and even that was cutting it close. But she'd practiced with the fruits already, and she could get the scene set up in thirty minutes.

I'll bring steak sandwiches and be gone on time, I promise, he said, and relief poured through Whitney. He didn't suspect anything. But she hated that she was even worried that he suspected something.

When's your next ranch owners meeting? she asked, her brain firing as it tried to come up with a reason why she needed to know.

Thursday, he said, and Whitney felt all the stars aligning.

"Thank you, Lord," she whispered. She ignored his next message and called Evelyn back. "Thursday morning," she said. "It's then or not at all. And I have disclosure forms you and anyone else there will have to sign." She changed her mind on the spot. "Actually, only you and your husband can be there."

"My sisters...."

Things spiraled in Whitney's mind. If all the Foster sisters knew...Jeremiah had told her he was good friends with Callie. No way Whitney could keep Lake Winters a secret from Jeremiah if she booked this shoot.

So she just needed to tell Jeremiah before Thursday.

"Everyone has to sign the form," Whitney said. "And two shoots will take all morning. How early is too early for you?"

"We can start whenever," Evelyn said. "I live on Quail Creek Road."

"I think we should start at the ranch," she said, thinking that Jeremiah would be at his ranch ownership meeting in the morning. "How about eight?"

"Eight is great."

"If you have ideas for what you'd like to do, text me some pictures."

"I'm so excited," Evelyn gushed, and Whitney smiled. She hung up and leaned back in her chair. She had the feeling that she was in very real trouble.

———

"Put that light over there." Whitney pointed to the kitchen countertop, and Dalton did what she said. Jeremiah had said Wyatt could come with him that night, and Whitney had immediately called Dalton to invite him to be her photography assistant.

Her nerves rioted, but she was going to tell Jeremiah she was Lake Winters. She was. She'd gone to Wilde & Organic and bought all the fruits she needed. She'd polished them up, and the ruby red skin on the apples gleamed under the lights.

Jeremiah would see the fruit. The lights. The baby blanket. All of it.

"I'm so excited," Dalton said. "I'm going to go comb my hair again."

Whitney shook her head and smiled. "You look fine, Dalt."

Her nephew scurried down the hall anyway, and Whitney turned in a circle in the kitchen. She was ready for this. There were dishes on the table, which she would clear and clean before the newborn and her parents showed up.

The doorbell rang, and Whitney drew in a deep breath and wiped her palms down her jeans. Dalton came barreling down the hall, his eyes wide. "He's here."

"He sure is." Whitney wished he wasn't so nervous, because she was feeding off of his anxiety. She stepped over to the door and opened it to find a pair of cowboys on her front steps. Their shoulders touched, and they both grinned at her.

"Heya," Wyatt said.

Jeremiah stepped inside and drew Whitney into his arms. He kissed her quickly, and they made room for Wyatt to come inside too.

"I won't kiss you," he joked, laughing. He handed a white bag that smelled like salt and steak to Jeremiah.

Heat ran through Whitney's face. "Wyatt, this is my nephew, Dalton. Dalt, come meet Wyatt Walker."

Her nephew took a step and nearly went down as he ran into the end table. His whole face turned bright red, and Whitney smothered a giggle. Jeremiah wore a playful smile, but thankfully, he didn't laugh either.

"Nice to meet you, Dalton," Wyatt said, and he definitely made his tone swagger a lot more than Whitney had ever heard it. "Where's your cowboy hat?"

Dalton extended his hand to shake Wyatt's, smiling for all he was worth. "I'm still savin' up for one," he said. "I think you have a new one coming out soon, right?"

"November," Wyatt said. "I can get you one."

"You can?" Dalton's voice pitched up to the ceiling. "That would be awesome."

Whitney tugged on Jeremiah's hand to get him to come into the kitchen with her. Dalton kept talking to Wyatt, and she was encouraged by his ability to get over his fear. "So I have something to tell you," she said, moving to stand next to the counter with all the photography props.

Jeremiah took in the scene before them. "What's all this?" He put the white bag of sandwiches on the table and looked at her.

She cleared her throat and pressed her fingertips together. "Jeremiah, I'm, uh, I take the baby photos I hang up in Wilde & Organic." She sucked in a breath and held it for a moment. "I'm Lake Winters."

His mouth opened and then shut again, his face draining of color. "You...."

"It's fine," she said. "I'm not upset or anything." She swept her hand over the fruit she'd carefully prepared. "But my shoot tonight is a cute little girl named Charity, and her parents wanted her posed in a basket of fruit."

Jeremiah searched her face, pure panic on his. Before he could say anything, Wyatt's loud laughter filled the room, and Dalton came into the kitchen. "He's so great, Aunt Whitney. Thank you so much." He opened the fridge and pulled out a couple of bottles of soda.

"Are we eating?" Wyatt asked, and Jeremiah ducked

his head and fell back a couple of steps. Wyatt opened the bag of sandwiches, his eyes glued to his brother.

Whitney turned away and got down glasses and a pitcher. She had bottled soda and water, but she suddenly felt like sweet tea. After all, it had helped soothe her nerves in the past, and she and Jeremiah couldn't have the talk they needed to have right now anyway.

20

Out of all the things Wyatt had to do as a rodeo champion, talking to kids was the easiest. Dalton clearly had stars in his eyes, and Wyatt wasn't going to rope them and pull them closer to earth. If he thought the rodeo life was one he wanted, well, nothing Wyatt said would change that anyway.

"Do you compete now?" he asked the teen.

"I've done the junior bull riding," he said, and Wyatt thought a kid as skinny as him would've been knocked off a bull by a stiff wind. "I placed first."

"That's great," Wyatt said, meaning it. "Do you do FFA or plan on doing agriculture, animal care...?"

"Do you think I should?"

"There are great scholarships in the junior rodeo," Wyatt said. "I got involved in it through my high school

FFA program. And I got my college paid for by winnin' bronc riding events."

Dalton's eyes widened, if that was even possible. "I'll have to find out for next year."

"You gonna be a sophomore?"

"Yeah."

"You should be able to qualify if you're winnin' bull riding on the junior circuit already." He lifted his soda bottle to his lips, noticing that Jeremiah and Whitney hadn't said two words. "If your grades are okay, at least."

He watched Dalton's face fall slightly. Jeremiah had mentioned that Dalton liked hanging out with Whitney because she didn't nag him the way her sister did. Wyatt understood that on a deep level, as he'd always seemed to be the third man on a three-man team. He'd come along right after the twins, and he never could quite get either of them to side with him, and Skyler and Micah had brought up the rear, and they were as inseparable as Liam and Tripp.

Stuck between them, with two older brothers who palled around, Wyatt had taken to animals more than his brothers. Sure, he had friends, but it wasn't a surprise to anyone when he rode the rodeo circuit and left home the moment he could turn pro.

He took a bite of his steak sandwich, the sauce Lowry's put on their meat something out of this world. He hadn't come to lecture Dalton, but no one else was talking.

"What's with the fruit, Whitney?" he asked, nodding to the spread on the kitchen counter.

"It's for my shoot tonight." She flashed him a tight smile, and Wyatt wanted to leave. At least give Whitney and Jeremiah the space they needed to talk. He picked up his sandwich and his bottle of soda. "I feel like eatin' outside."

"Wyatt," Jeremiah said, but Wyatt shook his head.

"Dalton, you want to join me?" He saw a cat paw a tiny bell on Whitney's back door. "Looks like that feline needs to go out too."

"C'mon, Jones," Dalton said, opening the door as he balanced his food and soda in his hands too.

"You don't need to leave," Whitney said.

"I like eating outside," Wyatt said, and he followed Dalton into the garage, where he took a hard left and went through another door to walk into the backyard. Whitney was either hiding some very green thumbs, or she paid someone to keep her yard an oasis of trees, bushes, flowers, and vegetables.

"Wow." Wyatt whistled as he sat at the outdoor table on the patio. "Look at this place. It's beautiful."

"Aunt Whitney shoots out here sometimes," Dalton said. "I take care of the yard for her. She pays me."

"You take care of this?" Wyatt knew enough to know the bushes had been shaped recently, that the cattails required a lot of tender care, and the fruit trees lining the back fence didn't just grow by themselves. "That's pretty amazing, Dalton."

"Yeah?"

"Yeah, I think I've killed every plant I've ever had." He chuckled as he took another bite of his sandwich. "What do you think was goin' on inside?"

"I don't know," he said. "Aunt Whitney was acting weird before y'all got here." He shrugged and picked up his sandwich. "Thanks for the food."

"Yeah, of course." Wyatt watched the boy for a moment. "You know there's a horse training facility out at Three Rivers Ranch, right?"

"Bowman's Breeds."

"You should come work out there," he said. "Ethan and Brynn are lookin' for people all the time."

"I applied," he said. "I had to be eighteen."

Wyatt nodded, though he didn't understand that rule. "Maybe I could talk to them. I work out there now."

Dalton looked at him for a moment. "You work out there?"

"Sure do."

"But aren't you, like, rich?"

Wyatt laughed, though he could see things from Dalton's perspective. In fact, one of the main reasons he'd loved the rodeo so much was because of the earnings potential. He'd been a millionaire by the time he turned twenty-two, and he didn't need his father's billions to be a billionaire.

"Yeah, but everything has a price," he said.

"What do you mean?"

As if answering, a twinge of pain moved through his back. "I mean, I'd be bored out of my mind without somethin' to fill the daylight." He put the last of his sandwich in his mouth and finished eating. "You should come out with me sometime. We'll see if we can't get Brynn to sign off on something for you to do. Even just feeding or saddling. It would be a job, and you'd like it."

"I would like that," Dalton said. "Thanks." He grinned from ear to ear. "And maybe my mom wouldn't be after me to work at the store so much." He chuckled, and Wyatt saw so much of himself in the teenager.

"And I've got rodeo equipment and horses at Seven Sons," he said. "Have your aunt bring you out next time she comes to see Jeremiah. We can do some training."

"Are you serious? Like for real, serious?" Dalton jumped to his feet and leaned into the table. "Really?"

Wyatt smiled and said, "Sit down, Dalton. How much can you lift?"

"Lift?"

"Rodeo cowboys have to be strong," he said. "I think you might wither away once fall comes." Wyatt chuckled so the teen would know he was kidding.

"I can get stronger."

Yeah, and Wyatt could make the pain in his back, shoulders, and neck go away. He just smiled and said, "I can take you to the gym; show you the workout I do." Of course, then he might have to admit to more than Marcy about his injuries. He'd just go slow, not do the moves full out. Dalton wouldn't even expect him to.

His phone rang, and speak of the devil, Marcy's name sat on the screen. "I gotta get this," he said to Dalton, swiping on the call. He didn't stand up and move away from the boy, because he didn't have anything to hide.

"Hey, sugar," he said.

"Wyatt Walker," she said, her voice full of mock irritation. "How many times have I told you not to call me sugar?"

"It'll have to be one more, baby." He grinned at Dalton, really enjoying this game he and Marcy were playing. Of course, he'd like to be on the court with her full-time, but she was still holding him at arm's length.

He could gallop out there for a while, though, and he honestly didn't mind. "What's up?"

"I'm wondering where you are and if you could bring dinner to Daddy's. I was supposed to make it, but he didn't get the ground beef out of the freezer. And then I thought I'd go get something, but I can't leave him here." Something moved on her end of the line, and when she spoke again, her voice was barely a whisper. "He's not doing so great tonight."

"What do you want?" Wyatt asked, already standing up. "I've got a friend with me, but I'm sure he can come along for a ride."

"Oh, I don't want to pull you from something."

Wyatt looked through the windows that showed him the dining room table. Jeremiah and Whitney seemed to be in quite the involved discussion, and Wyatt didn't even want to take his trash back inside. "You're not pulling me from anything, sweetheart. Tell me what you want, and I'll get it and be there in two shakes."

He nodded to Dalton, who picked up all their trash and led the way back into the garage. He put the garbage in a can there, and pressed a button to open the garage door. Wyatt listened as Marcy outlined what she wanted from JCW's, one of the best burger joints in town—in Wyatt's opinion. Not that he'd tried them all...yet.

"Mushroom Swiss," he repeated to her as he ducked under the still-rising door. "Bacon cheeseburger. Large cheese fries. Got it." He hung up and realized that he'd ridden to Whitney's with Jeremiah.

"I don't suppose you have a car and know how to drive?" He looked at Dalton, who pulled a set of keys from his front pocket. A grin filled Wyatt's face, and he said, "Great, our first stop is JCW's. My almost-girlfriend and her father need dinner. And I need ice cream."

Dalton laughed as they got into the car. Wyatt had to slide the passenger seat all the way back just to fold himself inside the tiny sedan. "What do you mean by almost-girlfriend?" Dalton asked. "Because I think I might have one of those too...."

Wyatt sure did like this kid, and he explained his situation with Marcy as he texted Jeremiah about where he was going and that he'd get a ride back to the ranch with Dalton.

His brother didn't answer, which was never a good sign. The man wore his phone, and he saw everything almost the moment it came in. Sure, he had some times where he was really busy around the ranch, but since he'd started delegating more to Orion, Dicky, and the other cowboys, Jeremiah could be found napping in the hay loft every single afternoon.

So it was very odd that he didn't at least read Wyatt's text, and he wondered what had gone south between Jeremiah and Whitney.

None of your business, he told himself, because he wouldn't want one of his brothers sticking his nose into a situation of Wyatt's that he was handling just fine on his own.

And that was why he didn't tell anyone about his injuries or medical troubles. *You're going to have to*, he told himself, not for the first time.

This past week, his doctor had told Wyatt he needed one more surgery to fix everything in his back. And he couldn't go through that alone. Not again. Jeremiah at the very least would need to know, as he and Wyatt lived together.

But for right now, he just wanted a peanut butter cup shake, Marcy's food, and the freedom to spend an hour with her. He hadn't kissed her yet, and that was why he wasn't really her boyfriend.

But maybe one day soon....

21

Jeremiah knew he was coming across as angry and frustrated. And he was—with himself. "I'm so sorry," he finally said. "I should've led with that." He held up his hands in surrender. He didn't want to fight with Whitney. But being honest and truthful was extremely important to him. Extremely. He had to be able to trust Whitney, and to find out she was a whole different persona?

He didn't know how to process it. He just kept looking at the shiny, red apples. "Why didn't you tell me?"

She shrugged. "I don't know. I don't tell anyone but my clients."

"We're getting married in six weeks," he said. "Were you ever going to say something?"

"Yes," she said. "I just...I don't know. I hardly do any newborns, so it hasn't been an issue until now." Her dark eyes flashed with fire too, and Jeremiah backed down again. This woman had him doing things he never thought he'd do, like swallowing his feelings and buying engagement rings.

Jeremiah nodded. He could accept that. "I'm very sensitive about this," he said, ignoring his phone as it chimed. Whoever had texted could wait.

"I know," Whitney said. "But I'm not Laura Ann, and you've told me to just tell you, and I did. Heck, I laid out the spread I'm going to be doing." Her phone rang, and she said, "It's Dalton. Just a sec."

Jeremiah picked up his phone and saw that Wyatt had texted. He was going to get Marcy and her father some dinner.

"Yes, all right," Whitney said. "Yeah, of course. Have fun." She hung up. "Dalton went with Wyatt." Her eyes glittered at him, and Jeremiah's pulse pounced through his veins.

"What's that look for?" he asked, smiling.

"I suddenly find myself in need of an assistant for my newborn shoot."

His eyebrows shot up. "Well, you better find one," he said.

"Jeremiah," she said, almost a whine. "*You* can do it."

"No way," he said. "I don't know what I'm doing."

"Dalton doesn't either. He was just going to help with the lights tonight. I'm doing a new technique I learned in my class, and I don't quite know what I'm doing."

He cocked his head at her, glad their first argument had been somewhat minor. His stomach was still a bit tight, but he didn't believe she'd deliberately kept something from him. "So if you have an assistant, you can blame them, is that it?"

"Ah, you're getting to know me so well." Whitney laughed, and Jeremiah stood when she did, helping her take plates and trash into the kitchen.

He snaked his arms around her from behind and pressed his lips to the back of her neck. "Sorry I'm a little intense. I don't try to be."

Whitney turned in his arms, clasping her fingers behind his neck. "I like how intense you are. But you can't just jump to conclusions."

"Agreed," he said. "I'll work on that." He'd been making a lot of progress in his feelings about marriage and love and Laura Ann. Even four months ago, if he'd have found out about Whitney and Lake Winters, he'd have taken one look at the apples and pears and stomped out the front door.

So he'd definitely taken some good steps forward.

"And I'll admit that one of the biggest reasons I told you was because Evelyn called and booked me for Thursday morning."

Jeremiah looked into her eyes, seeing the slight panic there. He tipped his head back and laughed, swaying with Whitney in her kitchen. "Well, I'll thank her then," he said. "You don't have to keep secrets from me, even if I wouldn't like them."

"You just...you said the photography was ridiculous."

Jeremiah stilled, understanding hitting him. "Oh, my goodness. Whitney, no." He ran his fingers through her hair, wishing he could take back the stupid and rude things he'd said. "I didn't...I'm so sorry."

She closed her eyes and leaned into his chest, but he thought that might be a tactic so he couldn't see her face. And he didn't like that. "I don't care what you do, baby," he said. "Honestly, I don't. Shoot zombie brides or babies and pumpkins. I don't care."

"You don't like the pictures, though," she whispered.

"I don't have to like them," he said, which he realized was the complete wrong thing to say. "I mean, of course I like them. I can see the artistic value in them."

Whitney sighed and stepped out of his arms. "I guess it's just like me liking asparagus and you not," she said.

"I happen to love asparagus," Jeremiah said. "But if you're talking something like Brussel sprouts, then yes, it's just like that."

She gave him a quick smile, but it was tired and not full of her usual life. "I get to boss you around tonight, cowboy," she said. "Consider it payback for saying the pictures were ridiculous."

"Whitney." He took her chin in one hand and looked at her. "I'm sorry."

She nodded as much as she was able, and said, "Thank you."

Jeremiah kissed her sweetly, because he wanted her to know he really meant the apology. Thankfully, that seemed to work, and she started directing him where to put the lights, the basket, and the fruit.

Before he knew it, the doorbell rang, and a couple came in carrying the cutest, most precious baby girl on the planet. Jeremiah's whole heart melted, and he was once again reminded of how much he wanted to be a husband and a father. The ache to be married and have those family things felt unending, and he smiled as Whitney took the baby and cooed at it.

She looked up, and their eyes met. The moment was magical and perfect, and Whitney's smile was pure and beautiful. "Jeremiah," she said. "This is Bea and Wendall Roop. And their sweet baby Charity."

The baby yawned, and Whitney sighed. "Yes, you are, sweet girl."

"Nice to meet you," Jeremiah said, stepping forward and shaking their hands. "We'll be in the dining room. Whitney's got a basket and fruit and everything. Do you want to come with me?" He turned and went into the dining room, Bea and Wendall right behind him. Whitney brought up the rear, some of the softness disappearing from her face. This was the businesswoman Jeremiah had seen before.

She handed the baby to Bea and started asking questions about what kind of fruit. Red apples or green. Yellow pears or white. Blanket or not. Large basket or small. The design was decided upon, and Jeremiah took up a position near the lights Whitney had put on the kitchen counter.

Bea swaddled the baby in a bright white blanket, and Whitney layered a piece of burlap around that, tucking the tiny girl into the basket.

And in that moment, Jeremiah knew exactly why Whitney loved her newborn photography. The spirit in her house was unlike anything Jeremiah had ever felt before, and he felt his whole heart open as if God had reached right down out of heaven and said, *Enough, Jeremiah. It's time to stop hurting. Stop resisting. Stop trying and just do it.*

He closed his eyes and let the feeling flow through him. He'd been alone for so long, even without the support of the Lord, and he knew now that he wasn't alone. Not even close to it.

He couldn't erase the smile from his face as he watched Whitney work, and he couldn't believe he'd told her the photographs were ridiculous or weird. They weren't. They were made of magic, and he really wanted her to take newborn pictures of their own baby.

Bea and Wendall smiled through the good-byes, and then Whitney closed the door. Jeremiah stood several paces away, marveling at her.

"Thank you," she said. "You were a great assistant."

"I'm in love with you," he blurted out.

Whitney physically fell back against the front door, her eyes widening. "What?"

"That was the most amazing thing on the planet," he said, taking a step toward her, needing to explain. "When Laura Ann left me at that altar, my relationship with God broke too." He drew in a shaky breath, not wanting to cry in front of her. Pure gratitude streamed through him.

"But watching you taking photos of that baby, so fresh from heaven...." He shook his head. "I can *feel* something, and that's huge. I haven't felt much for so, *so* long." He reached her and slid his hands up her arms.

"I'm not alone," he whispered. "God hasn't abandoned me, and I didn't know it until thirty minutes ago."

"Jeremiah," she said. "That's great. I'm so happy for you."

She didn't say that she loved him, but it didn't matter. She stretched up and kissed him, and Jeremiah could feel it in her touch. And that was enough.

June blazed by in perpetual heat. July dawned, and that meant there was only one more month until August. He was getting married then. He and Whitney got along great, and they spent time walking with the dogs around the ranch, eating brownies and ice cream out of personal-sized skillets, and collecting flowers for newborn shoots.

Whitney only did Conrad's, and Jeremiah wasn't there for it, as he had a ranch ownership meeting in town.

Just like the one he had today. But the pictures of his nephew were stunning, with a dark red bandana wrapped around the baby, rope, and just the hint of a spur in the corner. Whitney had put Conrad up on the bulletin board in Wilde & Organic, and Jeremiah loved seeing his nephew up there.

He loved that baby to the core, and he found himself frequenting the house on Quail Creek Road more and more often. In fact, Evelyn had invited him to stop by for lunch after his meeting that morning, and Jeremiah wasn't going to say no to a free meal and rocking a baby while he slept.

He pulled up to the IFA building and got out of the truck, whistling as he went. Happiness streamed through him the way sunshine filled the sky. He had no idea people could be this happy. Or maybe he did, but he never thought it would happen for him.

"Morning, Jeremiah," Garth Ahlstrom said, and Jeremiah grinned at him.

"Morning, Garth. How are the kids?"

"Fine, fine," he said, reaching for the door.

"Here for Squire again?"

"He and Kelly went on a cruise." Garth followed Jeremiah into the building, and they headed for the room in the back corner. Pete Marshall already sat there, as did Gavin Redd, who owned a place on the road that led west out of town. LeRoy Myers sat in a chair, sipping coffee while he chatted with Mike Lowry, who made the best steak sandwiches in the whole state of Texas. At least according to Wyatt, and Jeremiah had been impressed too.

Jeremiah took a seat next to Gavin and said hello. Garth crowded in on the other side, and a couple more people entered. Tammy Fullerton, who owned the apple orchards. Wade Rhinehart, who owned a ranch even farther south than Seven Sons. And Brit Bellamore, who lived and farmed next to the Rhinehart's.

Jeremiah knew everyone in the room, as they'd all been coming to meetings for as long as he had. "Where's Bear?" he asked, glancing around.

As if on cue, Bear Glover walked in, and he literally looked like a human version of his name. He had his phone at his ear, and he barked something and then hung up. His bright blue eyes blazed with fire, but it extinguished almost immediately as he surveyed the group.

"Morning all," he said.

"Morning," everyone chorused back. Squire Ackerman sometimes led the group on that month's topics. Sometimes Gavin did. Jeremiah had once, but he hadn't liked it. He'd rather just listen to the talk around the various ranches that surrounded Three Rivers, and give a little bit of opinion and input if he felt like he had something to share.

He'd heard about Payne's Pest-free at meetings like these, and he'd learned about a job opportunity for Wyatt at Bowman's Breeds. He'd found all the cowboys he needed to help at the Shining Star Ranch next door from the men and women in this room, and he sure did appreciate all of them.

Now that his emotions were back, Jeremiah had had a hard time controlling them.

"Who's up today?" Bear asked, collapsing into a nearby chair. "I'm out, because I've got grasshoppers from here to Oklahoma, and I'm in a bad mood."

"Grasshoppers?" Garth asked. "At Shiloh Ridge? That's odd, right?"

"We get them every few years," Bear said. "But usually not until August or September. I've got Marcy comin' every other day, but I've lost a lot of corn."

"Who else has grasshoppers?" Garth asked, and it seemed like maybe he'd lead them in today's discussion.

Jeremiah hadn't seen even one grasshopper, thankfully. He shook his head along with everyone else, and Bear looked even more disgruntled. "Great, it's just me."

"Well, you're at a higher elevation," Garth said. "Closer to water. Maybe that's why."

"Maybe."

Gavin raised his hand, and Garth nodded at him. "I heard the price of yearlings is going way up this year. My guy out of Kentucky is desperate for horses."

That was good news for Jeremiah, who had twenty-four horses and could probably spare a few—for the right price. Since he and his brothers had so much money from their inheritance, he never really worried about things like grasshoppers eating his crops or selling his horses when the market was high.

But he knew a lot of the people in this room did worry about those things, because they had to. The chatter went on, and Jeremiah enjoyed his ownership meetings immensely. The spirit felt familial to him, and he shook Gavin's hand as he got ready to leave.

"Heard you were seein' someone," Gavin said.

"Yeah," Jeremiah said. "Whitney Wilde. We're getting married in a couple of weeks." More like three and a half, but for Jeremiah, that couldn't come soon enough.

"Well, I can tell," Gavin said. "You seem so much happier."

Jeremiah smiled and nodded. "I *am* so much happier." And he really was—at least until he pulled through the gate at Seven Sons and found Whitney there with her mother, clipboard in hand.

And that certainly didn't make him *un*happy. It only reminded him that he and Whitney were getting married very, very soon and she still hadn't said she loved him.

He hadn't said it again either, because he didn't need to make things awkward between them when everything was going so well.

<h1 style="text-align:center">22</h1>

arcy Payne didn't like to deal with conflict. It actually made a knot appear in her stomach, and she felt like she was going to throw up.

Plane engines didn't argue about prices. They didn't text her and ask her to dinner. They didn't expect her to clean two houses, and make sure Daddy got to his doctor's appointments, and deal with grasshopper infestations.

She felt like the weight of the world rested on her shoulders, and she had absolutely no release.

She dusted Shiloh Ridge again and again. She asked neighbors for help if she couldn't get Daddy where he needed to go. She gave discounts when she didn't want to.

As for Wyatt Walker and his invitations to dinner... Marcy actually liked those. But they brought pressure to her life she hadn't wanted to deal with. That was why she'd told him seven months ago that she couldn't be in a relationship.

Yes, he'd backed off. He dropped by once or twice a month. She called him when she absolutely needed help, and he dropped everything and came, no questions asked. He laughed with her, talking when she didn't want to. He held her, seeming to be able to sense when she needed that and nothing else. He walked around the hangar and picked up trash after bringing her soda and a sandwich.

Marcy liked him a whole lot, but she knew she was holding him at a distance. He knew it too. She glanced at her phone, the blasted blue light still flashing. She'd seen the text as it had come in, so she hadn't swiped it open to actually read it.

She didn't need to.

My brother's wedding is next week. Want to go with me?

There might be more to the message, but Marcy didn't need to see it. A wedding. His brother's wedding.

Of course, the whole town knew Jeremiah Walker and Whitney Wilde were getting married. That made four Walker weddings in about sixteen months, and the single women of this town were growing restless. If any of them had eyes at all, they'd know Wyatt was interested in her, but Marcy stayed off the radar of most other women, thanks to her job.

And that was just fine with her.

But if she went to the wedding as Wyatt's date... everyone would know. "Would they though?" she asked herself, stepping up onto the stool so she could lean over the engine more easily. The wrench felt right in her hand, almost like an extension of her own appendages. Marcy loved fixing things and she loved flying.

But she couldn't fix her father's cancer, and she couldn't fix the situation that kept Wyatt out of her reach. Heck, she was *choosing* that.

The wedding was at Seven Sons Ranch, and Marcy could probably attend with little fanfare. Jeremiah's social circle included ranch owners and not many others—Wyatt was the social butterfly in the Walker family—and surely the guest list would be small.

Marcy straightened, the scent of hot metal and grease thick in her nose. One of her favorite smells, actually. She wiped her hands on a blue rag and tossed it on the ground. Wyatt himself would probably pick it up later and launder it for her. A wisp of guilt pulled through her. She couldn't keep accepting his help, calling him whenever she didn't want to go pick up food, and letting him hold her hand if she wasn't going to at least *try* to make something out of their slow relationship.

She'd given very little back to him, and she wondered why he still came around. "You told him," she said to the plane in front of her. "I mean, I told him I wasn't in a place where I could have a real relationship."

The plane, of course, did not answer her. She really just needed some validation, but she hated talking about the same things over and over with her cousins. She'd told them about Wyatt, and no one blamed her for holding him back while they all dealt with her father's illness.

When is the wedding? she typed out.

Saturday, Wyatt's response came in lightning fast, which meant he'd been waiting for her to respond.

And you can respond to his texts, she told herself. No one wanted to feel like they were being ignored, and if she didn't want to talk to him anymore, she should just tell him.

This Saturday?

That's right. Three o'clock. Dinner afterward. We can skip that if you want.

Marcy rolled her neck, trying to find a reason why she couldn't go. She'd still be able to make her morning dusts, and Daddy could be alone for a few hours in the afternoon.

You can't miss the family dinner after the wedding, she sent him.

Yeah, you're probably right. But you can. I just don't want to sit by myself.

Marcy loved it when Wyatt showed his vulnerability. When she'd first met him, he'd been so aloof. Almost removed from normal humans, because he was a huge rodeo superstar. Even now, people asked for his autograph, and everyone looked his way wherever he went. He didn't even seem to notice, but Marcy did, because if word got out about them attending the wedding together, they'd be looking at her too.

He still had sponsors, and his line of cowboy hats and boots would be out close to Christmas. He was a living legend, and Marcy honestly didn't know what he saw in her. Small-town, Plain Jane, with a wrench perpetually in her hand.

I barely own a dress. She sent the text, knowing it was the weakest excuse on the planet. Unfortunately, it was also the best one she had.

I've seen you wear at least four different dresses, he messaged back. Can I call you?

Marcy's pulse pumped a little harder. If he called, she wouldn't be able to say no. He probably knew that. After all, it wasn't the first time Wyatt Walker had spoken, and the man had a voice made of gold and honey.

She did him one better—she called him.

"Heya," he said, perfectly at ease. "So tell me what's really goin' on."

At least he didn't beat around the bush. "I'm just...." She had no idea what to say, and Wyatt didn't jump in to offer her a reason.

"It's three hours, Marce."

Oh, so he was going to play unfair with the nickname.

"I know you don't want a boyfriend. I'm fine with that.

Come to the wedding with me, and I won't talk to you for a month. I'll leave you alone."

The thought of that sent Marcy into a tailspin, and absolutely nothing made sense. She wanted him to call and come by, but she was upset when he called and came by? She couldn't have it both ways, and she found herself saying, "I can come to the wedding."

"Thank you," he said softly, and Marcy wondered if there was more to him not wanting to sit alone.

"What's goin' on with you?" she asked. "You exist in your own world—the Wyatt Walker Show. You can't sit with your family at a wedding?"

"Yeah, I don't know."

"But you do know." If she had to admit hard things, so did he.

"I need another surgery," he said. "Next month. My doctors are optimistic and positive, but I'm...scared."

And Marcy was a puddle of goo now. The man held serious power over her, and she wanted to be his soft place to fall. She turned toward the hangar doors, where huge windows let in sunlight and heat. She was glad this place was air conditioned and heated, so she could work day or night.

"I haven't told anyone about anything," he said. "Just you. So, please, just like the last time I told you about my health, keep it between us."

"I haven't told anyone."

"I know that, sweetheart, and I appreciate it."

She turned away from the windows. "Well, what are you going to tell them when you go in for surgery?"

"I have time. I'm going to wait until after the wedding." He pulled in a breath, and it sounded sharp through the line. "And sugar, if you need a new dress for the wedding, go get one. I'll pay for it."

Marcy smiled and shook her head, a giggle coming out of her mouth. "You don't need to buy me a dress."

She could hear the smile in his voice when he said, "Yeah, but I would."

And she knew he would. Warmth filled her from head to toe, and she bent to pick up the rag she'd tossed to the floor earlier. "You know, I'm going to be doing maintenance on all the planes for the rest of the day...."

"Oh, I see how it is," he teased.

"I'm just saying, if you got off early...."

Wyatt laughed, and Marcy liked their relationship better when it was built on him bringing her snacks in the afternoon. Serious things like weddings and surgeries overwhelmed her pretty easily.

"Well, I might drop by," he said. "Thanks for calling, I have to run."

"'Bye." Marcy hung up, knowing Wyatt didn't run anywhere these days. Too much jarring in his spine, and she wondered what this next surgery would be. She hadn't even thought to ask.

What's the surgery? she texted him instead.

He didn't answer right away, and the ball in Marcy's

stomach rolled. So that was how that felt—and it wasn't good.

She also didn't quite know what it meant. What she did know was that she better figure out what she wanted when it came to Wyatt Walker, or either she was going to lose her heart, or he was. And she didn't want to be the cause of any more pain for the handsome cowboy.

23

After lunch on the day of his wedding, Jeremiah dressed carefully, making sure each piece was in the proper place. Last time, he'd had his father there with him. And Rhett.

Today, he did everything alone, the door to his master suite locked. No one came knocking. No one texted him. The ranch was set for a wedding in the backyard, as he'd watched the party supply men set up the tent, chairs, and altar that morning.

There would be no steps to climb this time. Nowhere to hide if Whitney didn't show up.

But she was already on the property, as she'd arrived with her mother an hour ago. Her sister had then come, and surprisingly, Callie had gone upstairs, where Jeremiah assumed Whitney had taken over one of the unused bedrooms so she could get ready.

He stepped over to the mirror and set his cowboy hat in place. It was a brand-new one he'd bought only days ago, specifically for his wedding. He'd kept nothing from last time, and he hadn't owned a hat this nice since standing at the altar years ago.

His heart beat irregularly, and everything went white. He reached for the countertop in the bathroom, grounding himself against the cold granite. "It's okay," he whispered to himself. He looked up and into his own eyes. "You love her."

But he still had the same old pesky problem that had been the root of his issue at the last wedding too. Did the woman he was about to marry love him?

He still didn't know.

"Doesn't matter," he told his reflection. "That was the deal anyway. She's not your wife. She's your bogus bride."

With the pep talk finished, he left the bathroom and the master suite. He found Rhett and Tripp in the kitchen, looking for something to eat.

"Dinner is literally in less than an hour," Jeremiah said.

Rhett whistled in response, scanning Jeremiah in his tuxedo. "Wow, brother. You look amazing." He took him into a brotherly embrace and clapped him on the back. "Are you ready to do this again?"

"I think I might throw up," Jeremiah said, not wanting to admit any weakness but feeling safe to do so with Rhett and Tripp. "Where is everyone else?"

"Wyatt and Skyler and Micah are getting dressed in his room," Tripp said. "Liam's outside checking on something Callie asked him to, which Whitney had asked about...I don't know."

Whitney had procured a small wedding cake. He knew she had a bouquet and flowers for the men too. He'd paid to have their dinner catered, and all the food waited in a low oven or in the fridge. The table was already set. Every little piece seemed to be in place, and it felt like the ranch itself was holding its breath.

The front door opened at the same time Wyatt, Skyler, and Micah came down the hall, and noise started to fill the homestead. Jeremiah shook Whitney's brothers' hands and told them they could wait here, in the air conditioning, or go outside to the tent.

They went outside, and Jeremiah opened the fridge too, needing something to quell the nerves in his stomach. Liam came inside. Jeremiah ate nothing. His brothers talked around him. He felt like he was floating somewhere outside his body, though he was aware of Rhett's concerned eyes darting toward him every few seconds.

The minutes ticked by, and more guests filled the chairs outside. Evelyn's father and grandmother. Wyatt ducked out the door with the words, "Marcy's here," falling from his lips. Skyler and Micah went to sit by Simone.

Whitney's mother came downstairs with Callie, and they both hugged Jeremiah.

"You've got this," Callie whispered to him. "Don't be nervous. She's going to show up."

Jeremiah nodded, though he thought he might actually be more nervous about the fact that Whitney would be there than that she wouldn't.

This was about to be very real, and all of his reasons for wanting this felt childish and stupid.

He turned toward the stairs to go tell Whitney this was a dumb idea. He'd proven to his family what he'd wanted to. They didn't have to actually say I-do. She didn't need to move in here. They could just go back to normal.

Normal.

Even as he thought it, he knew he'd never go back to who he was before. He'd changed so much in the past seven months, and he wouldn't even know the man who'd held her hand at the New Year's Eve parade so long ago.

"Time to go outside," Rhett said, touching Jeremiah's elbow. He turned toward his oldest brother, almost pleading with him to call the whole thing off.

"I can see the panic," Rhett said. "What's going on?"

Jeremiah swallowed, but the lump in his throat did not go down. "I don't think she loves me."

Even if the marriage wasn't real, he still wanted to be loved. He wanted to be married too. He'd shatter if this didn't happen today, and Jeremiah had no idea where he'd be then.

"I've seen her look at you," Rhett said. "When she

didn't know anyone was watching. Trust me when I say she's in love with you."

The back door opened, and Whitney's mother said, "Jeremiah? Are you coming? It's time to start."

He nodded at Rhett, his resolve gluing itself back together. He knew the lifetime of pain which could come from having someone refuse to come to the altar, and he wouldn't do that to Whitney—or her family.

He tugged on the end of his tuxedo jacket and turned toward the back door. He took his place at the altar, all those eyes on him again.

Then the back door opened, and everyone turned and stood up. They all looked at Whitney now, and Jeremiah couldn't tear his eyes from her either. She wore a beautiful white dress that hugged every curve in lace and beads. Her lips matched the red roses in her bouquet, and she kept her eyes on his as her father walked her across the deck, down the steps, and up the aisle that had been created under the big, white tent in the backyard.

"Live well," her father said to Jeremiah as he tucked Whitney's hand through Jeremiah's arm.

He leaned down and pressed a kiss to her temple, the motion natural and wonderful. Whitney smiled, actually smiled, and faced the pastor.

This is not fake, Jeremiah thought as he did the same. Please don't let this be fake for her either.

She squeezed his hand. He squeezed back.

"We're gathered here today on this beautiful ranch to

celebrate something just as beautiful," Pastor Daniels said, beaming at Whitney and then Jeremiah. "What a blessing love is, in all its forms."

He continued to talk, and Jeremiah actually liked what he said about relationships and love and building a lifetime of trust and respect.

But now that he stood here, at this altar, with Whitney at his side, he just wanted to rush to the end before she realized what a terrible mistake she'd made.

The I-do couldn't come fast enough.

24

Skyler Walker almost scoffed out loud when Pastor Daniels said, "Love can heal all wounds."

The man had clearly never been through anything all that hard. Not that Skyler wanted him to experience the scarring things of the world. But he wouldn't say such ridiculous things if he'd had even a taste of the trials Skyler had.

He crossed his arms, hoping the pressure against his chest would keep the guttural responses he had inside. Dormant. Silent.

Because love did not heal all wounds. Sometimes love was messy and complicated, and it could carve out a heart and leave it for dead on the side of the hot, Texas highway. Sometimes love wasn't enough, as Skyler had learned when he'd lost his mechanic shop and his girlfriend in a matter of days. Sometimes love was a cruel mistress that made a person do things they didn't understand, even going back to a situation over and over again that wasn't healthy for them.

"Always turn to each other," the preacher said. "Work through your own problems, and be sure to involve God."

Skyler could've scoffed there too. He could've stood up and yelled, "Where was God last year, huh?"

He stayed in his seat, his brain overheating with the length of this pastor's speech. He hadn't lived in Three Rivers for very long, and he'd skipped church as much as possible. It was a lot harder to do so here, when all of his brothers went every week and questioned him when he didn't.

In Amarillo, he hadn't had to answer to anyone, and he wondered, not for the first time, why he'd come back to the ranch for the summer. He wasn't getting any younger, and he could've just stayed at the university to get things done more quickly.

At the same time, Skyler knew why he'd come back to the ranch—he still had a hard time thinking of Seven Sons as home—and it was because he didn't particularly like college. Going to class wasn't hard; it was just boring. Maintaining his fun, party persona wasn't hard; it was just exhausting.

He couldn't believe he was thirty-five-years-old and still had zero purpose for his life. None. Nothing.

In a lot of ways, he wished he were more like Jeremiah. Skyler admired his brother immensely for what he was doing at the moment. It couldn't have been easy for Jeremiah to get dressed and stand at that altar again. But he'd done it.

Skyler had run from a lot of things in his past, and he wasn't willing to face them again. He shifted in his seat and glanced at Micah. He and Skyler had been close growing up, and close through adulthood too.

He'd told Micah in confidence that he couldn't imagine getting married, and Micah had actually agreed. Apparently, he had a woman in Temple that was making life very difficult for him, but he hadn't been ready to share any details.

Skyler wouldn't pry either. That was just how their relationship worked. He thought of the family meetings, and he secretly disliked those too. Skyler had done almost everything he could to stop being a Walker, and yet, he felt a sense of brotherhood and unity at this wedding that he couldn't explain away. He also couldn't turn his back on it.

So he watched, and he listened, and he wished with everything inside him that he could find the root of his issues and pluck it out of himself.

He simply didn't know how.

25

Micah Walker's mind would not stop revolving. He barely heard what the pastor was saying, though the speech on love was obviously moving. His mother wept in the row in front of him, and beside him, the gorgeous Simone Foster touched her eyes a time or two as well.

Micah himself was too hot to be wearing a suit. He needed a plan to make a clean exit from Temple. His semi-girlfriend there, Stephanie Sawyers, had roped him back into her life time and time again. No matter what he said, she had a solution.

"So look at those around you," the pastor said. Micah couldn't remember his name. He looked at Skyler, who looked angry and mournful at the same time. He turned toward Simone, her lovely lashes holding a teardrop or two.

Instinctively, and with his heart pounding loudly in his ears now, he reached over and took her hand in his. She smiled and ducked her chin, her fingers sliding between his easily. She squeezed, and Micah's brain quieted. Everything in front of him became crystal clear.

He needed to get out of Temple as quickly as possible. He needed to make a clean break with Stephanie. He needed to come to Seven Sons Ranch.

And Simone?

So what if she's part of the reason?

And his brain started around the merry-go-round again.

He hadn't spoken to her since January, when they'd worked on her cabin together. And those had been a couple of good weeks, without stress and a cramped chest and the possibility of having to deal with a woman who never listened to him.

He couldn't wait for this wedding to end so he could call Stephanie. And he wouldn't listen to her this time. He'd simply say they were over, and he was sorry if that upset her, but he was moving to Three Rivers by next weekend.

Next weekend.

A light entered his mind, and he knew he needed to do exactly that. And to do it, he'd need help. Good thing he had six brothers, each of them completely willing to come to his aid.

Well, Jeremiah would be on his honeymoon, but the

other five would come. They'd clean out his house, his carpentry shop, all of it. They'd get the trucks he needed, and buy him a new bed for the homestead, and keep Stephanie at bay.

He just had to tell them the truth. Tell them everything, which he hadn't done yet.

The truth was, he'd enjoyed some space from his large family these past ten years. He'd needed it. But he wasn't sure he did anymore.

"I do," Whitney said, and Micah smiled.

"And do you, Jeremiah Joseph Walker, take Whitney Ann Wilde, to be your lawfully wedded wife, to love and cherish, for now and throughout all time?"

"I do," Jeremiah said loudly, and Micah felt like cheering. He'd done it.

Jeremiah took Whitney into his arms and kissed her, and Micah stood up and cheered along with everyone else. The happy couple turned toward their family and lifted their joined hands, and he knew in that moment he'd never be happy with Stephanie.

Perhaps he'd known that all along. He wasn't sure why he'd allowed her to have so much power over him, or what about her drew him to her so powerfully.

A clean break, he thought as Jeremiah quieted the crowd. "All right, y'all," he said. "Give me ten minutes to get dinner laid out, and then we'll eat." He and Whitney walked down the aisle and up the steps to the deck, more applause surrounding them.

Micah turned to Simone. "Well," he said. "That's that."

"I'm so happy for them," she said. "They're so *good* together, you know?" She gazed toward the homestead, where the last of Whitney's wedding dress disappeared.

"Good together," Micah repeated, thinking it an interesting word choice. He would've said "perfect for each other" or "cute together."

"I don't care if he needs ten minutes," Skyler said on Micah's other side. "It's a thousand degrees out here, and I'm melting." He walked away, but Micah was content to let him go.

"He doesn't really like weddings," Micah said, the echo of Skyler's confession about never wanting to get married still loud in Micah's ears. He hadn't worked real hard at finding someone to settle down with. He wasn't like Rhett and Jeremiah, who both wanted the wife, the kids, the house, the dogs and horses, all of it. Perfect small-town Texas life.

But the last few years, Micah had learned how lonely his life was. Especially with almost all the brothers here at Seven Sons. He felt...left out. Left behind. And he didn't have anything keeping him anywhere else.

"How can you not like weddings?" Simone asked.

Micah chuckled. "Well, not everyone does."

Simone actually turned away from the homestead. "I need to run home and get my gift."

"Gift?" Micah didn't want to be left alone either. "I'll drive you."

Simone looked at him, curiosity on her face. "All right," she said.

Relief washed through Micah. They walked around the house to all the cars parked out front, and Micah stalled. "Uh, I can't get out."

"Let's walk then."

"It'll take longer than ten minutes." And it was boiling hot outside.

"You're right." Simone hesitated in the shade of the huge oak tree. "We can go later." She met his eye again. "When are you moving here? Or is that not happening?" She tucked her hands in the pockets of her dress, and Micah got the hint.

Not moving here? Not interested.

"I'm moving in next weekend," he said boldly.

Simone's eyebrows went up. "Wow, I hadn't heard that."

"Yeah, well, you're the first person I've told." He inched closer to her and casually put his arm around her waist. She simply looked at him, but the sparks between them were just as hot now as they'd been when they got in that paint fight in her cabin months and months ago.

"How's the new cabin?" he asked as he removed his arm and held the swing for her. She sat down, and Micah joined her.

"It's great," Simone said. "I love it."

He carefully reached for her hand, lacing their fingers together again. "Are you seeing anyone?"

Another heated moment passed between them, and Simone slowly shook her head.

Micah grinned, though he did still have some loose ends to tie up. And they needed to be tied quickly.

"Well—"

"Micah, we're eating," Tripp called from the front porch. "Have you seen Simone?"

"She's right here." Micah stood up and helped Simone out of the swing too. "We're comin'." He ignored Tripp's interested look as he climbed the steps, Simone a few paces behind him. "Sorry. Lost track of time."

He clapped Tripp on the shoulder as he passed, still grinning for all he was worth. He'd tell his brother everything at the family meeting that night. No need to have to say things twice, especially when all that had happened was a little hand-holding.

26

Whitney's dress swished around the kitchen at Seven Sons, and she couldn't erase the smile from her face. The Walker brothers weren't quiet, and her family didn't hold back either.

Tripp returned to the kitchen, with Simone and Micah right behind him. Whitney wasn't an expert on either of them, but even she could sense the sparks between them. Wyatt Walker sat on the couch with a pretty blonde woman that had grown up in Three Rivers with Whitney—Marcy Payne.

They weren't touching, but he'd brought the woman to his brother's wedding. That said something to her. All of Jeremiah's other brothers—except Skyler—were married, and they mingled with their spouses, talking to her parents or her siblings.

Dalton hovered close to her, a semi-worried look on his

face. Whitney knew he was worried she'd disappear from his life now that she'd married Jeremiah. And the truth was, she was going to leave Texas for the next two weeks.

She wished she felt bad about it, but a lot of produce came on in August, and she didn't feel bad about missing the extra hours in the store. Michael had hired another woman to do Whitney's job, and he'd move her to another position once she and Jeremiah returned from New York City.

Her stomach wobbled as her mother enveloped her in a hug. "Congratulations, dear," she said. "He's simply wonderful. Perfect for you."

"Thank you, Momma." Whitney smiled at her, tears pricking her eyes. She could never tell her mother that the wedding wasn't real. The fact was, it felt very real to her. She hadn't told him she loved him, and she wasn't sure how to say the words.

She'd only said them to one other man before, and he'd left for farrier school the following day.

Jeremiah had never given her any reason to doubt him and hearing him say he loved her had been absolutely wonderful. Talking to him about her infant photography had been so much better than keeping secrets from him.

The fact was, Whitney could see her whole life in front of her, with Jeremiah Walker at her side.

She looked around the homestead, realizing in that moment that she was going to live there. She'd not moved in any of her things yet, and Jeremiah hadn't asked her about them.

"Ready?" he asked, coming to her side.

"You're in charge of the meal." She grinned at him, glad when he leaned down and kissed her quickly. That felt real, as did his hand in hers. Why, then, did she still feel like his bogus bride? Like they'd somehow tricked everyone in the room into coming to celebrate with them when they shouldn't have?

"All right," Jeremiah said loudly, whistling through his teeth in a shrill, piercing way. Everyone quieted, and he put his arm around Whitney's waist, tucking her right into his side. "Dinner is ready. Let's eat."

"I'll say the family prayer," Rhett said. All the men took off their cowboy hats, and Whitney took a moment to take in all of them hatless while Rhett started the prayer. Then she closed her eyes and thought of where she and Jeremiah would be in just a few short hours.

Across the country.

Alone.

In a huge penthouse suite overlooking Central Park. Jeremiah had shown her the apartment he'd rented for two weeks, and she'd simply stared at the pictures. She couldn't even imagine what the space would be like in real life.

"Amen," Rhett said, and the room erupted with the word.

Surprisingly, Jeremiah did go through all the food he'd

laid out on the huge island in the kitchen homestead. It was pretty self-explanatory. Chicken drumettes. Hot rolls. Vegetables in a cup with ranch on the bottom. Fruit salad with vanilla lime custard. Tiny little bundt cakes for everyone.

He led her through the line of food first, and they sat at the huge table that stretched in front of the windows. It wouldn't hold them all, but seven couples could fit. Someone had set up more tables, and they'd definitely have enough room for everyone.

Whitney smiled and ate, chatted with Jeremiah's brothers, her parents, her siblings. Everyone seemed so happy, and before she knew it, Jeremiah was leaning over to her. "We have to leave for the airport in twenty minutes. Do you want to go change?"

She turned toward him, her eyes widening. "Twenty minutes?"

"Your bags are in the bedroom," he said, those dark, deep eyes devouring her. For all she knew, he'd chartered a flight to New York City. He might even own a plane she didn't know about. Jeremiah was full of surprises, as Whitney had learned over the last several weeks.

"Yes." She stood up. "I better go change."

"Yes, go, baby," her mother said, standing too. "We'll make sure everything is cleaned up here before we go."

Whitney smiled and went through the kitchen and down the hall. Halfway toward Jeremiah's bedroom, she realized she wasn't alone. Her husband walked right behind her, reaching past her to the doorknob to open the door for her.

She said nothing as he waited for her to step into the room in front of him, and a thrill ran down her arms when the door clicked closed behind both of them.

"Let me help you," he murmured, reaching for the zipper on the back of her dress. The moment between them was intimate and sweet and exciting all at the same time, and with the release of the zipper, Whitney felt like she could breathe again.

She turned into him, and he took her easily into his arms and kissed her.

"Jeremiah," she breathed, pulling away enough to get his name out.

"Mm?" He touched his mouth to her neck, sweeping a kiss up to her ear.

"I love you." The words might have trembled as they left her mouth, but that could've been from the sensual way he was kissing her.

He pulled away, his eyes locking onto hers. He searched, and searched, and searched for something on her face. She didn't know what.

She saw love in his face. Disbelief. Hope. Fear.

"Say something," she finally said, giving a half-giggle, half-scoff along with the words.

"I'm just...processing."

"What's there to process?" she asked. "I'm in love with

you, and we're married. I'm actually hoping we can stay that way. None of this bogus bride stuff."

He fell back a step as if he didn't like what she was saying. He took off his cowboy hat and tossed it onto his bed. She noticed that he hadn't bought in another bed, the way he'd said he would.

"Are you serious?"

"Do you think I would say such things if I wasn't?" Whitney stepped back into his arms. "Why can't you just kiss me again?" She wanted to do a whole lot more than just kiss him, but they now needed to leave for the airport in fifteen minutes.

"I can." He kissed her again, moving slower this time, as if her touch would tell him the truth. He pulled away quickly. "I love you, too."

"I know that." She pressed into him as her dress started to slip off her shoulders. Anxiety blipped through her, as she'd never been with a man before, and both of their families were only a short walk away.

She kissed him, pleased when he responded eagerly, kissing her more roughly than before. He laid her down on the bed, and she gasped. "Jeremiah," she said, her voice mostly air.

He didn't respond; he just kissed her again. He pulled away a moment later, his breathing ragged. "We need to change and go." He backed up and shrugged out of his tuxedo jacket.

He kept his back to her, and she slipped out of her

dress and into a pair of jeans and a flowered blouse while he pulled a polo over his head and stepped into a pair of jeans too.

She might have snuck a peek at him, finding those bare, wide shoulders beyond sexy.

He tossed his clothes on the bed, pulled on a pair of cowboy boots, and reached for their suitcases, which stood ready next to the dresser.

Whitney said, "I'll be out in a minute," and went into the huge master bathroom while he left the bedroom. She looked at herself in the mirror, and she looked like she was afraid of her own shadow.

"What have you done?"

She hadn't given much thought to what would happen after the I-do. They'd talked about separate beds so long ago, and then not again, and Whitney hadn't been prepared to fall in love with Jeremiah Walker.

But now that she had, she had to face the idea of sleeping with him.

With trembling fingers, she pulled her lipstick from her purse and slicked on another layer of the perfectly red color. Feeling more like herself, she tucked the tube back into the right pocket and left the bathroom.

"Help me," she prayed, not sure how to articulate much more than that.

———

A COUPLE OF HOURS LATER, Jeremiah gestured for her to go up the steps to the jet first. "I can't believe you," she said. "Is this your plane?"

"No," he said. "I just paid to use it for our flights."

"Who's is it?"

"A friend of Liam's," Jeremiah said. "Some big producer out of Hollywood. He works on the same team as Liam. I guess he's his boss or something."

"Wow." Whitney stepped onto the plane to the smile of an attendant and the pilot.

"Welcome," the woman said. "I'm Stacy, and I'll be taking care of you today."

"George King," the man said. "I'll be flying you to JFK. My co-pilot is running through the final checks now."

Whitney peeked into the cockpit to find another dark-haired man there. Then she turned to the rest of the plane, and it wasn't anything like she'd seen before. No rows and rows of seats, as many as could fit. No, the space spread out before them, with chairs lining the window and facing inward. A slim table sat in front of the chairs, with an aisle between them. A few seats faced the front in the back, where a closed door stood between those.

The attendant took the bags from Jeremiah, which were much bigger than carry-ons, and opened a cupboard by the entrance. The bags rolled right inside, and she said, "Take a seat anywhere. I'll be right there to take your drink order. We have snacks as well, and I'll bring the basket."

Whitney didn't know where to sit. It felt very odd to

be on an airplane and not be cramming herself between two strangers. Jeremiah put his hand on the small of her back and guided her further onto the plane, where they took a seat on the left side.

"Coffee for me, please," he said when Stacy arrived with a basket of granola bars, small bags of potato crisps, packages of cookies, bananas, apples, and beef jerky. "Cream and sugar." He looked at Whitney, who took a couple of bags of crisps though she'd just eaten plenty to last her the rest of the day.

"Ginger ale," she said.

Stacy smiled and walked back to the front of the plane. George locked the door into place and stepped into the tiny cockpit. Stacy returned with their drinks and started going through the safety procedures.

"We're second in line," George said over the intercom system. "We should be wheels-up in ten minutes. Buckle in, everyone."

Whitney took a sip of her ginger ale and buckled her seat belt. Her cup of soda sat down into the table, and Stacy left it there as she headed back up front and turned the corner. She must've had a seat there, because she didn't come back.

Jeremiah put his arm around Whitney's shoulders, and she leaned into him as he pressed his lips to her forehead. "It's not a bad flight," he said. "A couple of hours."

"We'll be in the air for two hours and fourteen minutes today, folks," the pilot said as if Jeremiah had summoned him to report the flight time. "And the weather in New York City right now is looking clear and warm, with a high temperature of eighty-three-degrees."

"That's downright cool," Whitney joked, and Jeremiah chuckled.

They said nothing as the plane took off, but Whitney could sense some of Jeremiah's own anxiety. They hadn't finished climbing before he unlatched his seatbelt and said, "Come with me."

"Where?" Whitney couldn't fathom what he could possibly show her at the moment.

He just grinned down at her and extended his hand toward her. She slid to the gap in the table and stood up, placing her hand in his.

"Stacy, we'll be in the back," he said.

"Yes, sir." Her voice came from around the corner.

He led Whitney down the aisle, opened the door, and took her inside a room. Not just any room.

A bedroom.

"Oh, my goodness." Whitney pressed her free palm to her heartbeat. "This is insane."

"I guess the guy who owns this jet flies from LA to London quite often, and he likes to go overnight." Jeremiah released her hand and turned back to her, something new in his eyes.

She could still see the love he had for her. But he possessed a new edge now. A hungrier edge.

"We've got a couple of hours to kill," he said. "And we're alone."

Her pulse zipped around her body, and everything inside her turned hot. "You want to...?"

"Can we?" He didn't touch her, and Whitney appreciated that.

She looked at the huge bed that took up almost the entire room. Shelves stuck out of the walls near the headboard, with small lamps there. All the shades in this part of the plane were pulled down, and Whitney wondered how sound-proof the room was.

"It's okay," Jeremiah said. "I know we haven't talked about this at all."

Whitney looked back at him, and everything nervous inside her calmed. She took one step toward him and kissed him, cradling his face in both of her hands. "I want to."

"You do?"

Oh, she definitely did. Instead of answering, she kissed Jeremiah again, excited and yes, a little scared, of being intimate with him. But she loved him, and he loved her, and they *were* married.

So this time, when Jeremiah laid her on the bed and kissed her, she didn't whisper his name. She wanted to make love with her husband, and she did exactly that.

27

Jeremiah loved the shape of Whitney's mouth against his. He'd never been with a woman, but he seemed to know what to do, and he and Whitney stayed in the bedroom on the plane until the pilot said, "We're making our initial descent into New York City, and we should have you on the ground in, oh, about twenty-five minutes."

"We should get up," he murmured to Whitney, who lay in his arms. He played with the ends of her hair, the sweet scent of her perfume making his head swim all over again.

"Mm," she said. "Do we have to?"

He chuckled. "I think so, sweetheart." He rolled away from her and sat up. "It'll be dark when we land. We'll go straight to the apartment unless you want to go see Times Square or something. I hear it's beautiful at night."

"We'll have plenty of nights to do that," she said, also moving behind him.

Jeremiah dressed quickly, turning just as Whitney finished too. Their eyes met, and a measure of shyness moved through him. He couldn't help smiling at his wife—his *wife!*—before he put his cowboy hat back on his head.

"Are you going to wear that all over the city?" she asked, nodding to the hat.

"You don't think I should?"

"I think you'll stick out like a sore thumb." She wrapped her arms around him, and Jeremiah gazed down at her.

"When did you know you were in love with me?" he asked.

The flirty smile on her face faltered slightly. "Uh, let's see. I'm not a hundred-percent sure."

"I fell in love with you when I saw you taking those infant pictures for the first time. You know, the little girl with the apples?"

Whitney gazed up at him, tipping up on her toes to touch her lips to his. "I know. You told me."

"So it was after that for you?" Jeremiah wasn't sure why he needed to know.

"Yeah."

"How long after?"

"Not long."

"And you didn't say anything?"

"Time to buckle up, folks," the pilot said. "Stacy, secure the cabin."

Whitney didn't answer as he reached for the doorknob and opened the door. They sat in the back row of seats and put on their seatbelts, no sign of their drinks from earlier, the snack basket, or Stacy.

Jeremiah leaned his head back and closed his eyes, happier than he'd ever been in his life. He was married to a woman who loved him. *Finally*, he thought. *Thank you, God. Thank you so much.*

And for the first time in over four years, Jeremiah felt completely healed. He felt whole. He absolutely was not broken.

"Look at that," Whitney said, her voice full of awe. "I need to photograph that building."

"We can come back tomorrow with your camera." Jeremiah had never seen skyscrapers like the ones in New York. He'd never seen a park as expansive and beautiful as Central Park, which he had a birds-eye view of from an entire wall of windows in the apartment he'd rented.

He'd thought he'd hate the hustle and bustle of the city, but it held a vibrancy that he really thrived on. He loved the bright lights at night. The constant motion of people. The noise in the subway and on the streets and in the small restaurants.

He and Whitney had gone to a couple of Broadway shows. They'd gone up to the top of the Empire State Building. They'd ridden a ferry out to the Statue of Liberty and toured Ellis Island.

He'd eaten foods he'd never known existed, and now they were on a walking architecture tour, and Whitney had a glow about her that made Jeremiah fall in love with her all over again every time he looked at her.

He loved spending time with her. They'd talked about anything and everything in the past couple of weeks, and a large part of him didn't want to return to Three Rivers. Then they'd have to go back to their real lives, with schedules and responsibilities.

He liked kissing her when he woke up. Making love to her whenever they wanted to sneak back to the apartment, be that in the middle of the day, at night after a full day of sightseeing, or sharing their love before they even got out of bed for the day.

He'd told her he wanted to be a father with a desperation he didn't know how to contain, and she'd said she wanted children too. Some of their conversations probably should've been had before their nuptials, but Jeremiah hadn't dared bring them up when his goal for the wedding had started out with him showing Wyatt and the rest of his brothers that he wasn't broken.

Everything had changed since that moment in the master bedroom at the homestead, when Whitney had confessed her love for him. The holes in Jeremiah's heart had been plugged, and he'd had no idea the joy other people had been feeling all this time.

"We're heading over to 42nd Street now," their guide said, and Jeremiah turned toward her voice. He wanted to bring Whitney back to this place, using that plane, every year on their anniversary, and he'd mention it to her tonight over dinner.

Someone said, "Yeehaw," as they passed, and Jeremiah touched the brim of his hat. He didn't care what anyone thought about him, and he loved being a cowboy. He had felt completely out of his element the first couple of days he and Whitney had been in the city, but no one had demanded to see his passport to be in New York—even if it did feel like he'd entered a completely new country.

They went inside the Daily News Building, and Whitney gasped at the huge world globe there. Jeremiah was impressed himself, and he wanted to visit a different US city every other month. He had plenty of money. Why couldn't he?

He knew that was his vacation brain, and that he had a ton of responsibility as the only Walker brother who seemed remotely interested at staying at Seven Sons Ranch.

"This is incredible," Whitney said, and Jeremiah could only agree.

"You're incredible," he whispered as the tour guide moved them over to something else. He trailed behind the other four people in their group, and Whitney rewarded him with a kiss next to that amazing globe.

"Where should we visit next?" he asked. "I heard Chicago has some amazing architecture too."

"That would be fun," she said. "Seattle. I've always wanted to go there."

"I can make that happen."

"You can make anything happen," she said with a smile. "I also want to go to a National Park. Yellowstone. Yosemite. Something like that."

"Do you like camping?"

"Um."

Jeremiah chuckled, because he already knew the answer to that question. Whitney didn't take forever in the bathroom in the morning before they left the apartment, but she wasn't in and out either. The first morning they'd been in the city, Jeremiah had marveled at her as she'd traced that red, red lipstick over her lips.

Then he proceeded to kiss it all off, so she had to redo it before they could go. She didn't seem to mind, and Jeremiah was operating all on the vibes he got from her. She told him what she wanted, and he did his best to oblige.

The tour continued, and when it ended, he asked the tour guide for the best restaurant nearby. They ended up at Bobby Flay's restaurant, which apparently was a TV chef Jeremiah needed to watch. He liked cooking, and he figured he could expand his horizons a little bit.

"So New York every August," he said. "For our anniversary."

"Yeah?" Whitney looked at him. "You think so?"

"Definitely. This is awesome. And there's so much more to do we haven't done yet." He lifted his water to his lips. New York restaurants didn't seem to know what sweet tea was—and their water tasted a little funny to him too. "We didn't even go down to Brooklyn, and we go home tomorrow."

She groaned. "Don't remind me. I don't want to go back to real life."

Jeremiah didn't either, but his phone flashed with a call. "It's Wyatt. Can I?"

"Of course."

He picked up the phone and swiped on the call. "Heya," he said, Wyatt's preferred greeting.

"What time will you be home tomorrow?" he asked.

"Uh, let's see." Jeremiah leaned back in his chair, almost dislodging a tray of drinks a waitress carried. He immediately straightened, forgetting how close together everything was in New York City. "I think we leave here at ten-thirty. So we'll be back on the ground in Texas about noon. Home an hour after that."

"So we can have a family meeting tomorrow night." He wasn't asking, but Jeremiah agreed anyway.

"About what?" he added.

"I just have something to tell everyone," Wyatt said. "See you tomorrow."

Jeremiah hung up and relayed the conversation to Whitney. "What do you think he has to say?"

"Well, he's been seeing Marcy Payne," Whitney said. "Maybe he's going to announce an engagement."

"Maybe," Jeremiah said, but he didn't think that was it at all.

They finished dinner and went back to the apartment. The following day, they packed up and went to the airport, where the jet he'd borrowed waited for them. Jeremiah didn't even ask for coffee this time; he simply took Whitney into the bedroom at the back of the plane.

By the time they walked into the homestead at Seven Sons, everyone was there. In the middle of the day.

"There they are," Rhett said, jumping up to welcome Jeremiah and Whitney home. Jeremiah actually felt like he needed a nap, but he could never leave food and dishes out and go to sleep.

The remains of lunch sat on the counter and table, and Jeremiah glanced around. "What's going on?"

Wyatt stood up from the couch, where he'd clearly been waiting for Jeremiah and Whitney. He winced, the pain clear on his face. He took a very pronounced, limping step. "I have some news for y'all."

28

Wyatt had been hiding his injuries from his family for far too long. When he didn't try to, everyone saw him. Tripp actually scooted to the edge of the couch and reached for Wyatt, as if he needed someone to hold onto.

Maybe he did.

"I have to have another back surgery in a couple of weeks," Wyatt said, his mouth so sticky and so dry. "I live in a state of constant pain, from knee injuries, back injuries, a separated shoulder that doesn't play nice sometimes."

He cleared his throat as his brothers' expressions turned from concerned to horrified. "I'm fine. I don't need a bunch of pity." That only made the injuries worse. "But I retired, because there was no way I could physically

continue in the rodeo." And it hadn't been an easy decision, even then.

"I don't need to be babied. I've been takin' care of myself
just fine for a while. I just wanted y'all to know. I've already
called Momma and told her. I'll be taking a few months off at
Bowman Breeds. Dalton's going to be picking up some of my
slack, and Ethan said I could come back whenever I'm able."

Oh, he hated those words. He hated feeling weak. He
hated the way his back spasmed, almost making him fall
down. He sank onto the couch next to Tripp, who simply
stared at him. "There. Now you know."

No one said anything.

Finally, Liam said, "What can we do, Wyatt?"

"Nothing," he said. "The injuries are injuries. They
don't get that much better. The doc says this next surgery
is going to be the last. There's not much more they can do
for me. I go to physical therapy a few times a week, and I
ice it, take painkillers, heat sometimes, whatever I can to
make it through the day."

And he was mighty tired right now. Fighting pain was
no laughing matter, and it was never easy.

"I'm so sorry," Callie said, the rest of the Foster sisters
following suit. His brothers started talking too, about who
could bring food to the homestead, and who could make
sure Wyatt got to his doctor's appointments.

He held up his hand, and they all silenced. He liked
that power, but he hated he had to be the one to share this

news. "Nothing needs to change. The nurses in the hospital are like slave drivers. I'll come home good as new. Besides, I, uh, already hired someone to look after me."

"Who?" Skyler demanded at the same time Rhett and Tripp did.

"I live here," Jeremiah said. "You don't need to hire a nurse."

"She's not a nurse," Wyatt said.

"You're not making sense," Liam said. "He's not making sense."

"Let him talk."

"I am letting him talk. He said he hired a nurse."

"No, he said he hired someone to help."

"Let him talk!"

"He's not talking."

"We just want to help you, Wyatt."

He closed his eyes, the noise his brothers and sisters-in-law could make absolutely overwhelming. At the same time, he could feel the love they had for him, and he really appreciated it.

"I guess I'm not paying her," he said, and that got most of them to settle down. "I just asked her if she'd come to the ranch and take me on walks. Visit me in the hospital and all that."

"Oh, it's a woman."

"I'll take you on a walk," Jeremiah said. "The dogs will need to go every day."

"It's Marcy Payne," Whitney said, and that got everyone to shut up. Every eye zeroed in on him.

"Is she right?" Rhett asked, clearly surprised.

"Yes," Wyatt said, deciding not to hide his feelings for the pretty blonde woman he'd been sneaking around to see for eight months now. "And we're not seeing each other. I just *wish* I was her boyfriend." He chuckled and shook his head. "She's dealing with a lot of family stuff at the moment."

"So are you," Tripp said.

"Yeah, well, she said she'd come make me walk and visit me in the hospital and all that." Wyatt puffed out his chest, immediately regretting it when a flash of pain stole down his spine. "And I don't need you guys butting into my business with her."

"We would never do that," Liam said, grinning around at the other brothers.

Skyler particularly wore a devilish smile. "When's the surgery?"

"August thirtieth," he said.

"So I'll still be here."

"If you even *look* at Marcy wrong, I will hunt you down in Amarillo and make sure all of your young, hip friends know how old you are."

Skyler burst out laughing, as did a few other brothers, and Wyatt couldn't help grinning too. The moment sobered, and he surveyed this crowd that was his family.

Six brothers. Four of them married, with wives now. One new baby. Hopefully more on the way.

"So that's my news." He nodded as appreciation and love moved through him. Sure, they were noisy and pushy and stuck their noses where they didn't belong. But they were family, and he sure did love them. "Who else has something to say?"

Everyone looked around at the others, and finally Liam said, "Callie and I have finalized our adoption paperwork. Now it's just a waiting game."

"Waiting for what?" Evelyn asked. "And that's so great. Congratulations, you guys."

"Now we just wait for a birth mom to pick our profile," Callie said, her hands twisting around themselves. "Our case worker said it could be a day to forever."

"Oh, it won't be forever," Tripp said, standing up and hugging his brother. "We'll pray for you guys. And you, Wyatt."

Murmurs of agreement went up, and Wyatt nodded his thanks for the prayers. He hadn't dared ask the Lord to heal him, because he thought if he had to continue his life with the physical pain, at least he wouldn't also know that God had heard his prayers and ignored them.

———

The weeks passed, and Wyatt only had one mishap where he forgot Jeremiah had gotten married. He'd gone into the master only wearing a pair of basketball shorts, saying, "Hey, I need to borrow—" before he'd realized his brother's wife was still lying in bed.

"Sorry," he'd said, blitzing his way out of the room as fast as his injuries would allow him. He hadn't seen anything. Whitney had laughed about it with him. But Wyatt didn't forget again.

Thankfully, Micah had moved in while Jeremiah and Whitney were on their honeymoon, and Wyatt had someone else to hang out with at night when the newly married couple retired early to their bedroom. Without Micah, Wyatt would've gone crazy—much the same way Jeremiah had way back in January when he was alone in the huge homestead at the ranch.

The night before his surgery, his father called him. "How are you, son?"

"Actually okay," Wyatt said. "I've had surgeries before."

"I know, but your mother and I worry about you. We always have."

"I know that, Daddy." Wyatt sighed and made sure the AC was still blowing. He'd just pulled into the driveway at Seven Sons, and the next time he left, it would be for the hospital, not the stables he'd fallen in love with.

"Jeremiah is taking you in the morning?"

"Oh, they're all coming," he said with a sigh. "We can't even fit in one vehicle, but Micah says he's driving his king cab too." Wyatt chuckled and added, "Maybe you could tell them it's not necessary?"

"I'm not going to do that," Daddy said. "We worked and worked with you boys to make sure you knew how important each other were. That you'd have friends come and go, but your family would always be around. Remember how many football games you went to for Jeremiah?"

Boy, did he ever. "I know, Daddy. I just hate the spectacle."

His father laughed, and Wyatt wished he was there with him so he could have one more hug before he went under the knife. "Son, you rode bulls for a living. With cameras on you constantly. You live for a show."

"Not this kind," Wyatt said darkly.

"Momma says she has a good feeling about it."

"I love you guys," Wyatt said.

"And we love you. Have one of the brothers call us."

"I will." The call ended, and Wyatt stayed in his seat, gazing at the huge oak tree in the front yard. The sunshine drifted through the air lazily, and he wanted to be with Marcy. But she'd taken on five new clients for the fall dustings, and he hadn't been able to see her much around the hangar.

He called her, wondering if she was on the ground or not. "Heya, Wyatt," she said, her voice full of exhaustion.

"Are you flying?"

"Just landed. Gotta get cleaned up and get over to Daddy's."

He wanted to offer to help, but he really just wanted to hear her voice and then go spend the evening with his family. Jeremiah had promised him a "last meal" of creamy mushroom pasta with steak, and Wyatt's mouth watered just thinking about it.

"I miss you," he said, wishing he wasn't quite so vulnerable with this woman.

"Surgery tomorrow," she said in response, and Wyatt hadn't gotten Marcy during one of her sentimental times.

"Yeah," he said. "Bright and early. I should be awake well before you finish dusting."

"I'll come by in the evening," she said, a plan they'd already talked about.

"Great." Wyatt knew when to end a conversation with her, and it was time. "See you then."

"Wyatt," she said, and he paused mid-reach for the end call button on his infotainment screen. "What are you doing tonight?"

"Eating dinner with my family."

"Do you have a minute to stop by?"

"You're in a rush, aren't you?" He'd played by her rules. He only stopped by periodically, and he'd told her if she came to the wedding, he wouldn't talk to her for a month. But then she'd invited him to her hangar, and they'd spent the rest of the afternoon talking.

He'd wanted to kiss her. Badly.

She hadn't been in the right place, and he could feel it. And she hadn't cut off communication with him after the wedding.

"I just want to give you a good luck hug," she said.

That was all the encouragement Wyatt needed. "I'm on my way," he said, flipping the truck into reverse. The call with Marcy ended, and he immediately called Jeremiah. "I'm going to be a little late tonight," he said. "I'm stopping by Marcy's for a minute."

"Take your time," Jeremiah said, and that right there proved how much he'd changed since marrying Whitney. He was still Jeremiah, but a less intense, less angry version of the man he'd been for the past four years.

Wyatt didn't blame him, and it sure was nice to see his brother whole again. Now, if he could just get himself whole too, Wyatt would like that.

29

arcy's stomach swooped when Wyatt Walker walked through the door. She was always a little self-conscious around him, as she smelled constantly of grease and metal, her hair never looked nice when he came by, and she was utterly exhausted. That meant she'd have no defense against his strong arms, brilliant smile, and Texas rodeo twang.

Sure enough, when he said, "Heya, Marce," she dang near swooned at his feet.

"Hey."

"You okay?"

She was the one who was supposed to ask him that. Not the other way around. "I'm just tired." She tossed the blue rag she'd been using to dry her hands into the sink and turned fully toward him. "How are you?"

"It's so good to see you." He took her right into his

arms, and Marcy clung to him. He was powerful, and strong, and kind, and good, and Marcy really wished she had time every evening to see him, spend time with him, get to know him, kiss him....

"Good to see you too, Wyatt."

He stepped back and straightened, a flash of pain moving across his face so quickly she almost didn't see it. "How's your daddy tonight?"

"I think he's okay." Marcy hadn't heard anything to the contrary from her cousin. "What's Jeremiah making for dinner?"

"Creamy mushroom pasta with steak," Wyatt said with a grin. "My favorite food."

"Oh, wow." Marcy giggled. "I don't even think I could boil the water to make pasta."

Wyatt chuckled with her, and she liked that she had strengths and weaknesses—some of which were not very traditional for women—and that he didn't try to change them about her. He didn't suggest she take some cooking classes, the way her last boyfriend did. He hadn't once mentioned that she might try a different brand of soap to really get the grease out from under her fingernails.

He liked her how she was, and Marcy thought that was the sexiest thing about the man.

"You want to sit in my office?" She knew standing was hard for him sometimes, and she started toward the tiny office in the corner.

He moved with her, and Marcy practically collapsed

into the chair behind the desk. "I'm surprised you can eat tonight with the surgery tomorrow."

"They said before eight," he said. "No eating or drinking after that. No breakfast tomorrow."

She nodded, suddenly ready to leave. She got up and opened the mini fridge on the counter next to the open door. "Well, I have one of your favorite sodas left." She took it out and extended it toward him.

Wyatt stood up, a new edge in his eyes that had Marcy's heart beat dancing in the back of her throat. "Marce." He took a step toward her, penetrating her personal space. This office was so tiny, and he was so big.

He reached up and ran his fingers down the side of her face in a tender gesture she hadn't anticipated such a rough and tough cowboy like him could do. The cold can of soda pressed between them, and he took it from her and set it on top of the fridge.

"I want to kiss you," he whispered, and Marcy really had no objections. Other than the fact that a kiss would mean they were serious. Dating, even. And she hadn't wanted that.

Had she?

Her brain misfired, and Wyatt swept his other arm around her waist. "Can I kiss you, sugar?"

Marcy didn't even remember thinking the word, but "Yes," came out of her mouth. Wyatt's lips touched hers, and fire sparked in every cell of her body. Strange, that had never happened before, and Marcy had dated several men over the years.

Wyatt kissed her like no one ever had before, and Marcy simply did her best to keep up. He backed her into the wall, a growl coming from his throat. He deepened the kiss, and Marcy had no objections.

None at all.

———

THE NEXT EVENING, Marcy's stomach writhed as she entered the hospital. She hated this place, and she didn't have time to be there. But she'd promised Wyatt, and she didn't want to let him down.

At the same time, the whole reason she hadn't gotten involved in a real relationship with him was precisely because of situations like this.

But that kiss.... Her blood heated just thinking about the kiss they'd shared in her office the previous afternoon. He'd left soon after that, and she'd stayed in her office chair until her legs felt strong enough to support her weight.

But something had been bothering her all day. She didn't have time to nurse two men back to full health, maintain the planes, and do all of the crop dusting herself. She barely had time to do one of those things, and she felt stretched thin in a half-dozen ways.

She stalled outside the room where the lady at the

information desk had told her Wyatt would be, and sure enough, she heard his voice coming from inside. He sounded in good spirits as he spoke with another man. The cadence and tone of his voice suggested a brother, and Marcy found Skyler there when she finally dared to peek around the corner.

He sat in the only other chair in the room, facing the door. And he'd seen her.

She ducked back into the hallway, unsure about why she felt like she'd been caught. Her heart pounded, though, and she didn't hear Skyler approach over the hammering of it in her ears.

"You can go on in," he said. "I've got to get goin'."

"Oh, I'm—" She cut off as Skyler walked away, nothing else to say, obviously.

Marcy clutched the six-pack of soda she'd brought for Wyatt and entered the room.

"Heya, baby," he said easily, that smile so genuine on his face. But he looked tired, washed out, half of the man he'd been last night. He made no effort to move or stretch to touch her. He didn't reach for her, and the whole place smelled sterile and like death.

Her stomach revolted and tears sprang to her eyes. "How did it go?"

"The doctors said they did the best they could." Wyatt looked disappointed, and she liked that he didn't hide his true emotions from her.

"I'm sorry," she said.

"Not your fault."

She set the soda on the rolling tray in front of him. "Wyatt," she said, not really sure why everything inside her had started to tremble. Her thoughts tangled, like they'd been doing all day. "I'm not...I can't do this."

"Do what?"

"This." She gestured between the two of them. "I'm barely hanging on as it is, and my daddy is still so sick, and I can't nurse you back to health too."

"You don't have to," he said. "I have a huge family to do that." He still didn't reach for her, and she hated that more than anything.

"I'm sorry," she said, the tears falling down her face now. "I shouldn't have kissed you last night."

"Hey," he said, earnest and panicked now. "It's fine. I know where we are. You don't have to do anything you don't want to. Or can't do."

She nodded, sniffling and hating how every hole in her face seemed to be leaking. "I have to go. I'm so sorry."

"Marcy," he said after her, but she turned and walked away, much the same way Skyler had.

Every step shattered something new inside her, and she found herself running down the hall. Running away from Wyatt's calls for her to come back.

She wasn't strong enough for this, and she couldn't shoulder more than she already was.

So she ran, and she ran fast.

30

Whitney rolled over to find Jeremiah's side of the bed empty. Unsurprising. The man came to bed late and got up early, and Whitney would find him in the kitchen, bent over his phone or a puzzle book.

She'd run her fingers up his arm and along his shoulder, and he'd kiss her good morning. Whitney loved their routine, and the scent of coffee that hung in the air told her that it was in full swing already.

Wyatt was sometimes in the kitchen too, but more often than not, Liam or Tripp had come to get him for the gym or a physical therapy appointment. The first few weeks after his back surgery had been rough, his physical agony only enhanced by Marcy Payne's sudden departure from his life.

Whitney hated seeing him sitting alone in the kitchen or sleeping on the couch. She imagined him to be Jeremiah, after she'd stopped talking to him last January. She had to talk herself off the ledge at times like that, because she'd completely turned her life around in the last nine months.

She was married now, for crying out loud. Her life wasn't anything like she'd envisioned it would be when she'd set her New Year's resolutions.

She finally pulled herself from bed when she was in danger of being late for work at Wilde & Organic. She'd have to skip whatever Jeremiah had made for breakfast and drive straight to the store. After dressing quickly, she headed down the hall.

"Morning," Jeremiah said from the kitchen counter. He stood this morning, his coffee cup in his hand. "You're going to be late."

"I know." She grabbed her keys from the bowl on the built-in desk and kissed him quickly. She couldn't believe how completely she loved him, and she took a moment to marvel at her feelings. Maybe they were still new. Maybe she didn't understand them all. But she sure did like living here with him, wandering the ranch in the afternoon after her shift, and swaying with him in that swing under the oak tree.

Jeremiah did not take on a job at Wilde & Organic. He did go with her to her parents' house for meals and family activities, and he blended in effortlessly with her siblings and their spouses. The nieces and nephews loved him on-sight, of course, because he was tall and sarcastic, with that cowboy hat.

Dalton loved Seven Sons Ranch, and he came a couple of times a week to sit with Wyatt or take him on a walk. He kept Wyatt up-to-date on the happenings at Bowman's Breeds, though he'd gone to part-time work when school started.

Halloween came and went, and the Christmas festivities picked up around town, and around the ranch. Whitney woke up one morning, absolutely sure she was pregnant when she realized that she still hadn't started her period.

Excitement moved through her, and she pressed her palm flat against her stomach, wishing Jeremiah was in bed with her so she could tell him.

"I should do something special," she said to herself, and she sat up to start planning. The bakery at Wilde & Organic made a fantastic vegan chocolate cake, but she wasn't sure Jeremiah would be impressed by that.

But he loved everything at the bakery on Main Street, and Whitney called over there. "I need something for my husband," she said.

"Okay," the girl said. "Can you be more specific?"

"Can you make a cake that says surprise or something?" After all, Whitney didn't know if she was having a boy or a girl, and she wanted to take a pregnancy test to really be sure she was pregnant.

"Is it his birthday?"

"No," Whitney said. She wasn't going to tell this girl her news before she told her husband. She couldn't believe she was pregnant. Her mother would cry for days. "Just something that says surprise, but nothing with balloons or birthday stuff."

"Okay," the girl said. "Flavor of cake?"

"What are my choices?" Whitney continued to ask questions and get her cake ordered, and by the time she hung up, she was frustrated. Probably not as much as the girl taking her order, but still. Who knew there were so many different flavors of fillings and frostings? She'd just wanted a cake, for crying out loud.

She jumped into the shower, thinking of showing up that night with the cake, ready to tell Jeremiah that he was going to be a father. They'd talked about having kids, and he wanted as many as they could have. He was great with kids, and he wanted nothing more than to be a husband and father.

Whitney wept with gratitude for the life growing inside her, and thankfully, the hot water washed the evidence of her tears from her face.

She felt fine as she drove to work. As she stocked the produce section with her sister. As she went through her paperwork and then left the store. The cake wouldn't be ready until one, so she ran by her house.

The place didn't feel like anyone lived there, and she stepped just inside the front door and stalled. She'd loved this house the moment she'd parked in front of it several years ago. She loved the yellow siding, and the huge porch. She'd like the built-in cat door by the back door, and the airy, bright kitchen.

She'd moved her computer to the homestead on the ranch, taking the office that apparently Liam and Tripp had once shared. She still had plenty of business, and now that fall was in full swing, she'd started booking seniors who wanted fall foliage in their pictures instead of spring blooms.

And Christmas in Texas seemed to be a popular time to get married, as Whitney had three in the seven-day period surrounding the holiday. And one of them was right here at Seven Sons Ranch. Her first wedding at the ranch she now called home.

She understood on a different level why Jeremiah didn't want to open the ranch up as a wedding venue. This land possessed something sacred, almost like it had a spirit of its own. Yes, the windmill was amazing, the huge barn with the American flag, the hay bales, the pumpkins, the old corn stalks now that the fields had been harvested.

Whitney loved the horses, the chickens, the goats, all of it. She loved the cattle dog that lived part-time on the ranch and part-time with Rhett and Evelyn. She loved Jeremiah's beehives, and the cowboy cabins on the west side, and all the trees.

So she'd only booked one wedding here, and she was willing to play things by ear to see how they went.

Most of her furniture was still in the house, and after

she'd sent a text to Jeremiah saying she had some errands to run, Whitney curled into the couch, set an alarm on her phone, and put her hands on her stomach again. If she still lived here, her cats would've joined her, Jones settling on her hip while Jess would keep her feet warm.

She dozed, a sure sign she was pregnant, and stayed on the couch for several minutes after her alarm went off. Then she remembered the test she'd bought at the store that morning—at the self-checkout counter—and hurried into the bathroom to see if her suspicions were right.

If they weren't...she didn't need that cake.

But the test showed two, bright pink lines, and Whitney braced herself against the counter in the bathroom.

"I'm pregnant."

Pure joy filled her, and she basked in it for a few minutes.

Now she just needed to tell Jeremiah.

She headed over to the bakery to pick up her cake, and the girl working the counter got a strange look on her face when Whitney gave her name. "Sorry it was a little crazy this morning," she said. "I had no idea I could choose coconut lime filling."

The girl flashed a tight smile and went to get her cake. She returned and flipped open the top of the box. "How'd we do?"

Whitney gazed down into the box to find a perfectly

chocolate cake with a smooth, glassy mirror glaze on it. The word *surprise* had been piped on in white frosting, and that was all. No flowers. No balloons. No stars. Just pure class in pure chocolate.

"It's perfect," she said, pulling out her debit card to pay for it. She and Jeremiah still kept separate finances, but she didn't buy her own groceries. She put gas in her car and paid her mortgage to keep the house, though with the new addition to her family, she wasn't sure why she should keep doing that.

She loved Jeremiah Walker. This marriage wasn't fake anymore. She was his real wife, not his bogus bride. She could sell her house.

Determined to talk to him about it that night, after she'd given him the cake and made him guess what the surprise was, she tucked her card away and picked up her cake box.

She'd only taken two steps when someone said, "Whitney?"

She turned toward the oh-so-familiar voice, finding the man she thought she would.

Blake Thurston.

She froze, the cake suddenly heavy in her hands.

He stepped out of line and came toward her, a wide grin on his face. "There you are, baby. I've been back for a couple of days and haven't seen you yet." He took the cake box and set it on a nearby table.

Blake gathered her into his arms, despite Whitney's protests. He never had listened to her, and Whitney's anger started to rise. Everything in her emotions felt a little off, and she knew her increased hormones were to blame.

"I missed you, sweetheart," he said. "I'm going to stay in town this time."

"Right," Whitney said, and before she knew it, Blake leaned down and kissed her.

Whitney struggled, unsure of what to do. He was bigger than her, and she'd never resisted his kiss before.

She pushed against his chest, but nothing happened.

"Hey," a man said, and pure terror moved through Whitney. Her stomach dropped to her toes as Jeremiah pulled Blake away from her. "What are you doing, kissing my wife?" He switched his dark, dangerous, lasered gaze to Whitney. "This is what you're calling an errand?"

"Your wife?"

"Jeremiah."

But he simply glared at her, glanced around the bakery, and spun around. He walked away before Whitney could get her brain to play nice, and the tinkling of bells seemed to scream through the air as he yanked open the door and left the bakery.

Whitney slapped Blake's chest. "You...you...what are you doing? I'm not yours for the taking."

Surprise had etched itself in Blake's eyes. "I didn't know."

"Maybe ask," she said. "Or better yet, just leave town again, Blake. It's what you're good at." She snatched the cake off the table and hurried after her husband, desperate to make him understand.

31

Jeremiah drove away from the bakery, his sweet tooth completely unsatisfied. And to think he'd gone to get some sweets because he knew Whitney would like them. She particularly enjoyed the Rocky Road bars at the bakery on Main Street, but now the thought of them made Jeremiah's stomach turn.

Of course, watching his wife kiss another man had done that. In fact, that had turned his most vital organs inside out, his heart included.

He hoped the twenty-minute drive back to the ranch would allow him to simmer down, but he was angrier by the time he pulled into the garage at the homestead. He slammed the door and took the three steps up to the entrance in a single bound.

Inside the house, he felt caged, and he paced from the mudroom to the living room and back. He took his cowboy hat off and put it back on. Surely Whitney would only be a few minutes behind him, even if he had driven over the speed limit the whole way home.

Her cats snoozed on the couch, and Jeremiah wanted to spray them with water. Instead, he watched them, and when Jones perked up only a half-minute later, he knew Whitney was home.

Sure enough, she walked through the front door a moment later, a cake box in her hand. "Jeremiah," she said, but he stayed in the kitchen.

She came down the hall and found him instantly. It wasn't like he was trying to hide. He pressed his cowboy hat lower, every emotion in the book raging through him.

"That wasn't what you thought it was."

"No?" Jeremiah didn't mean to bark the word. He was just glad Wyatt wasn't home so he and Whitney could have this conversation. "Trust is vital to me," he said. "Absolutely vital." And she knew why. How could she do this to him?

"I was just there getting a cake." She took a few steps and set the cake box on the counter.

"For what?"

"Open it."

Jeremiah made no move to do what she said. "It took you three hours to get a cake?" She still owned her home. She could've met Brock or Brian or Brett—whatever his name was—and been kissing him for hours. She didn't need to do it in public, and something troubled Jeremiah about the kiss in the bakery.

He couldn't put his finger on what, but he knew one thing: his trust in Whitney had just shattered. And it had taken him over four years to learn to trust a woman again.

Jeremiah felt all the carefully glued-together pieces of himself slowly splintering apart. "If I can't trust you, we have nothing."

"You can trust me," she said. "I worked at the store, and I was tired. I ordered this cake, and I couldn't pick it up until one, so I went to my house and took a nap."

Her house. So she had gone there. Jeremiah's mind went through a thousand different scenarios in the blink of an eye, none of them good. All of them ended with him standing by himself while what he wanted drove away from him.

He couldn't believe this. He'd invited this pain into his life when he'd started imagining what it would be like to kiss Whitney's delicious, red lips.

And it had been wonderful. He loved kissing Whitney. He liked holding her hand. He enjoyed sharing his life and his bed with her.

How had everything changed in the blink of an eye?

"I can't constantly be wondering if you're really at work, of if you've snuck off to meet him," Jeremiah said.

"I *didn't* do that," Whitney said, pure desperation in her voice. "You're not even listening to me."

"Nothing to listen to." He felt like he was floating

outside his body, much the same way he had while Laura Ann babbled on and on over the phone as she tried to explain why she hadn't been able to marry him.

Whitney said something, but Jeremiah didn't hear her. His pain spiraled through him, and it wasn't until Whitney stepped right into his personal space and said, "Look at the cake, Jeremiah," that he pulled himself out of his mind.

She opened the lid on the cake box, and he looked down at it dumbly. Nothing made sense, especially not the single word there. "Surprise? What is this? It's not my birthday." They'd celebrated his birthday in New York City. He couldn't think clearly right now. "I have to get back to work."

He left the cake on the counter and Whitney standing next to it. He'd just put his hand on the sliding glass door when she said, "I'm pregnant. Surprise."

He turned back to her, disbelief raging through him. "Is the baby mine?"

Tears filled her eyes and streamed down her face. "*Of course* it is."

"Of course? How would I know that? You were just kissing your old boyfriend, the man you *ghosted* me for earlier this year." He took a couple of steps toward her, anger and hope mingling inside him. It wasn't a pleasant feeling at all. He wanted the baby to be his. He wanted Whitney. But not if she wasn't going to be all his, all the time. Not if he couldn't trust her. "I told you, I'd rather you just told me if you don't want to be with me. So go. Go be with him. He's back in town, and you should see if you can make things work this time."

"Don't do this," she said. "That is not what I want." She shook her head, her dark eyes flashing dangerously now. The freckles he loved so much popped out on her pale skin. "I'm in love with *you*. The baby is yours. Ours."

Jeremiah wanted to believe her, but something inside him wouldn't allow it. "I know I asked you to marry me in an unconventional way. I get that it might not be real to you." It sure was real to him, especially when they made love. "Honestly, I'll be fine. Just be honest with me."

"I *am* being honest with you." Whitney sagged into the counter, as if the conversation was too heavy for her to handle.

"I need to think." Jeremiah turned, opened the door as gently as he could, and stepped outside. He wanted to rip the sliding glass door off its track and hurl it against the wall. He didn't, and he stalked away from the kitchen, from his wife—*from your baby?*—so he could find a place on this ranch where he could make sense of everything he'd seen, heard, and felt.

32

Callie spun honey in the metal container she'd purchased earlier that year, pure happiness flowing through her. Her life this November was drastically different than a year ago, and pure gratitude for all she'd been through, all she'd experienced, and the people in her life filled her from head to toe.

Liam worked in his office that morning, and Callie had put a pork roast in the slow cooker for dinner that night. With Miah married and focused on Whitney, he only cooked on Sundays now.

And oh how Callie still loved going next door and eating with the Walker family. Her family. Her sisters. Everyone, as the family continued to grow and expand.

Callie couldn't help the way her thoughts tumbled down the path toward expanding her own core family. She and Liam had completed their adoption profile a few months ago, but their phone hadn't rung once.

Yet, she told herself. Her relationship with God and her faith had warmed and grown over the past ten months, the same way her family had. And she believed with everything inside her that she would be a mother.

She thought of Evelyn's son's baby pictures among the flowers of Texas, a few carrots, some green beans, and a couple of heads of purple cauliflower. Callie wanted pictures like that of her baby too.

Lake Winters had transformed into Whitney Wilde, and all Callie would have to do was call her new sister-in-law.

The honey finished spinning at the same time her phone rang. She glanced at it, already considering letting the call go to voicemail. But the screen said *Alice*.

She sucked in a breath, every cell in her body trembling instantly. With shaking fingers, she picked up the phone and swiped on the call. "Hello?"

"Callie," the woman said. "Are you sitting down?"

"No," she said, leaning into the counter in the garage where she'd been working. The scent of flowers, wax, and honey filled the air. And her own anticipation.

"Do you want to get Liam? Is he available?"

Callie's heart thumped in an irregular way. She couldn't think. Somehow, her feet moved her away from the honey station in the garage and up the steps to the kitchen. "Let me see." She tapped the speaker button and hurried through the kitchen.

"Liam?" she called toward the front of the house. She wasn't surprised that he didn't answer. He almost always wore headphones while he worked; that way, she didn't distract him during a deadline, and he could listen to the loud music he loved without disturbing her.

The door to his office stood open, and he sat in front of his four screens, working with his headphones on. "He's here. Let me see if I can get him to take his headphones off. I'm so nervous."

"Don't be nervous," Alice said. "This is good news."

Callie nodded, which made no sense. Alice couldn't see her. She tapped Liam on the shoulder, and he jerked toward her. She must've had a crazed expression on her face, because he swiped the headphones from his ears with the words, "What's the matter?"

"It's Alice," Callie whispered. "She wanted us both on the phone."

"Alice?" Liam asked, looking at the phone Callie held in her hand.

"Hello, you two," Alice said cheerily. "Liam, make sure Callie's sitting, okay?"

"Right here, baby," he said, guiding her to his chair. The heat from his body soaked into hers, and he took the phone from her too as her hand continued to shake, and shake, and shake. She was already crying and Alice hadn't even said the real news yet.

"All right," he drawled. "We're ready."

"I'm so pleased to be the one to tell you that your profile has been selected by a birth mother."

Callie buried her face in her hands and sobbed. She was aware of Liam kneeling in front of her, his voice choked as he said, "You're kidding."

"I'm really not, Liam. Not only that, but this particular mother already has a three-year-old in the foster care system, and she'd like to place her with the baby, if at all possible. I told her not everyone is willing to take toddlers, but that I had the perfect couple in mind...then I showed her your profile."

Callie lowered her hands and looked into Liam's eyes. Two kids? At the same time? She barely knew how to hold a baby, and she hadn't known a three-year-old for far too long. Maybe never.

"And I know you said you were open to all kinds of adoptions, and this mother would love to place both kids with you. So." Alice blew out her breath. "I need to know if that's something you can do or not."

Liam opened his mouth, but no sound came out. Callie knew the feeling. She felt like she'd been hit upside the head with a railroad tie, and nothing in her brain seemed to be connected anymore.

"When?" she finally asked.

"The three-year-old can come live with you now," Alice said. "She's been with a foster family for a couple of weeks, and they're not looking to adopt. The birth mother is due in January."

So only one child right now. But *right now*.

Callie started nodding as Liam continued to search her face. He was the one to say, "We'd love both kids," his voice thick and his eyes glassy. He swiped at them as the first tear fell, and Callie loved him with her whole heart and soul in that moment. He'd been her rock this year. Her one comfort among so many changes and adjustments. Besides the Lord, the only constant thing. The one person she could fail over and over with, and he'd still be by her side.

"I knew you would," Alice said with a laugh. "I need you to come into the office and start on the paperwork, just as soon as you're able."

Liam looked at his computer and back to the phone. "Today?"

"Tomorrow morning would work," Alice said. "I want to call the foster family and get Denise from them. I want to be here with you through this, and I have a meeting this afternoon that would prevent me from doing that."

"Tomorrow morning," Callie said. "We'll be there."

"And you can meet the birth mother too," Alice said. "I can set up a lunch if you'd like? She'll be able to say good-bye to Denise, and you two can exchange contact information. Now, the adoption will be open, but how much you interact with her is up to you. Or her. There's no pressure to do anything."

Callie nodded, as they'd been through this before. All she could think was *tomorrow morning. Tomorrow morning.*

Tomorrow morning, she was going to bring home a new daughter.

Denise.

The call finished, and Liam hung up, setting the phone on his desk. Their eyes met, and Callie started crying again. This time, though, it was a soft, low, weep, filled with love and gratitude for yet another change in her life. And to think she'd been so averse to things shifting in her life before.

Liam took her into his arms, and they cried together for a few moments. "I don't even know what a three-year-old needs," he said.

"We'll figure it out," Callie said. "Alice said she'd send a list and come out with us tomorrow afternoon."

"I'll check my email right now." He started clicking, his email opening on one of the screens while Callie watched. The list was there, and it was comprehensive. Everything from clothes to a bed to the girl's favorite foods.

"Do you want to go shopping tonight?" he asked. "This afternoon? I'm maybe three hours from finishing this project."

"Yes," Callie said as the printer whirred. She got up and collected the paper from the printer while Liam sat back in his chair. "I can't believe this."

Someone knocked on the front door, and she spun that way at the same time Miah walked inside. "Liam?" he called. "Oh. Callie."

He did not look good, and Callie glanced at Liam and back to his brother. "What's wrong?"

Liam's chair squeaked as he got up and joined Callie in the doorway to the office. "Whoa. What's going on?"

"I need advice," he said, taking off his cowboy hat and tossing it into the formal living room. He ran his hands through his hair. "I went to town this afternoon and I saw Whitney kissing her old boyfriend."

"No," Callie gasped.

Liam sucked in a breath too, his arm around Callie's waist tightening. "And?"

"And she said it was nothing. He just showed up there. She's not back together with him or anything."

Callie glanced at Liam, who watched his brother carefully. She wanted him to say something, because though she and Miah were friends, it had been a sticking point with Liam in the past.

"Then why are you over here, looking like your whole world ended?"

She swung her gaze back to Miah, who glared. Oh, this was the old Miah. The one who'd shown up at Seven Sons Ranch with a chip on his shoulder and darkness in his heart. Callie mourned for him, because he'd made such good progress, especially the last ten months.

"I'm not," Jeremiah said.

"Okay." Liam stepped away from Callie. "Come with me." He started down the hall that led into the kitchen, and Miah looked at Callie.

"You and Whitney are so good together," she said.

He nodded, pure misery etched in his eyes. "But what if it's not enough?"

"What if *what's* not enough?" Callie asked.

"Being good together. Being in love with her. What if they're not enough?"

Callie didn't know how to answer him, and Liam called to him from the kitchen. Miah tried to put a smile on his face, but it looked all wrong. He walked away from her, and Callie watched him go. She should've told him that love was always enough. That it could grow and expand and heal *any* hurt. She knew, because she'd seen it in her own life. She knew, because she'd experienced it.

And he had too.

"Help him remember that," she whispered, adding more to her prayer that Miah would be able to find the truth, and that it wouldn't break him.

33

Liam took Jeremiah out onto the gazebo in the corner of the yard. "What do you see?"

"Texas," Jeremiah said, his voice full of sarcasm.

He ignored his brother's attitude. Jeremiah was in an immense amount of pain, and he was terrible at hiding it. "Remember when I was upset because I thought you and Callie had more than a friendship going on?"

"Yeah." He sighed as he leaned against the railing and looked out at the horizon.

"What did you tell me?"

"That you should talk to Callie."

"Did you talk to Whitney?"

"I *saw* her kissing that other guy."

"And I saw you hugging my wife. I heard her say she loved you." Liam hated that the memory was still so clear, still so sharp, inside his mind. At the same time, he did not doubt Callie, and a slip of embarrassment moved through him that he ever had.

Jeremiah would feel this way too, once he made up with Whitney and this situation sat in his past.

"But you knew—"

"Did I?" Liam asked.

Jeremiah finally looked at him. "What are you trying to say?"

"I'm saying that I left for a bit to clear my head. To find my own center. To get outside of what I *thought* and remember what I *knew*." Liam didn't know how to tell Jeremiah to do those things. He could stay at the Shining Star tonight, and maybe he'd know for himself in the morning. Or maybe he wouldn't.

"And once I did that, I talked to my wife, and we worked it out. Because, yeah, then I *knew* that she loved me and not you. And I think if you do the same with Whitney, you'll know she loves you and not this other guy."

Jeremiah's jaw worked against itself. "She said she was pregnant."

Joy and surprise, and yes, a little jealousy, moved through Liam. "Jeremiah, that's amazing. Congratulations." He slung his arm around his brother, who turned into him and hugged him.

"I'm a bad man," he whispered. "I may have implied the baby was this other man's."

Horror struck Liam right behind his heart. Still, he

clung to his brother, who likewise wouldn't let go of him. He said nothing, because Jeremiah was already beating himself up for that one.

Jeremiah finally cleared his throat and stepped back. "I need to talk to her."

"Yep."

"I'm sure that baby is mine."

"I'm sure of that too."

Jeremiah looked at him, and Liam watched—literally watched—as light cleared the agony from his face. "I'm going to be a father."

Liam's face split into a smile, his own joy too big to contain. "Me too."

Jeremiah blinked once, then twice. "You too?"

"Our adoption case worker just called, literally a few minutes before you walked in. We're getting a three-year-old and a baby."

Surprise blanketed Jeremiah's face, and he grabbed Liam in another hug. "That's fantastic. Congratulations." He stepped back quickly. "Oh wow. I'm so sorry to interrupt you guys. Have you called Momma?"

"We haven't told anyone yet."

"Let's go then." Jeremiah turned and hurried down the steps of the gazebo.

"Go where?"

"Tell everyone," he said.

Liam chuckled as he followed his brother across the

lawn and back into the house. "What? Should I call a family meeting?"

"Yes," Jeremiah said. "Tonight, at the homestead. Maybe I'll have figured out a way to make up with Whitney by then, and we can share our news too."

Liam thought Jeremiah had more to do than just talk to Whitney, but he didn't say anything. Everyone had their own journey to take when it came to forgiveness and finding peace, and Jeremiah had been on the road for a long time now. He'd figure it out again.

Still, Liam chuckled as he entered the house and said to Callie, "I told him. He thinks we should call a family meeting for tonight."

"Do it," Callie said. "I'll have enough meat for pulled pork sandwiches."

Liam picked up his phone from the counter where he'd left it. "All right. Family meeting tonight," he dictated as he typed. "Shining Star. Pulled pork sandwiches for dinner. Seven?" He looked up.

"Six," Callie said. "No one wants to wait until seven to eat dinner."

"Agreed," Jeremiah said, and Liam put six o'clock in his text and sent it. He looked up and found Jeremiah opening his fridge. So he wasn't going to run right back to Seven Sons and Whitney.

Liam hadn't either, so he couldn't blame him. But he hoped Jeremiah wouldn't let Whitney slip away from him, because they were great together, and Whitney had healed something inside Jeremiah that no one else could.

Texts started coming in from the other brothers. Skyler, of course, couldn't make it, and Wyatt said he'd like a ride. Micah said he'd pick up Wyatt, and Rhett said they'd bring drinks.

Jeremiah didn't answer, but Liam didn't need him to. Tripp didn't either, and his twin was probably working—the way Liam needed to be.

"Okay," he said. "I have to get back to work." He looked back and forth between Jeremiah and Callie. "You two gonna keep each other company?"

"I was spinning honey," Callie said.

"Oh, I'm a pro at that," Jeremiah said, smiling. At least it didn't look like a grimace. "I'll stay and help." They moved toward the garage together, and Liam watched them go. Not an ounce of worry or doubt came upon him, and for that, he was grateful.

"Now help Jeremiah figure out how to trust his wife," Liam prayed as he grabbed a can of cola from the fridge and went down the hall to his office.

34

I vory heard the bell on the front door of the dry cleaner, but she couldn't just jump up and go help whoever had walked in. She leaned over the toilet, pretty sure she was finished. She took another moment, then stood up slowly, her legs shaking slightly. The mirror showed her a red face and messy hair, and she turned the water on cold, stung by it but also needing the shock of it.

She had no doubt in her mind why she'd been sick for the past week.

She was pregnant.

She'd been pregnant before, and it had been exactly like this. Maybe not as violent in how quickly the nausea overcame her. Sometimes, she barely made it to the bathroom. At least she hadn't thrown up in front of a customer yet.

After she'd rinsed her mouth and washed her hands,

she went out to the counter. "Sorry," she said to the woman standing there. "What can I help you with?"

The woman had a ticket for pickup, and Ivory retrieved her dress for her. As she walked out, Ivory reached for her phone. Tripp still brought her lunch every day, and he picked up Ollie from school, and he made sure they had something to eat for dinner. He was a brilliant man, with a kind heart and a good soul, and Ivory loved him with everything inside her.

They'd talked about having more children, and they both wanted them. A feeling like she'd been blessed with an unfathomable gift filled her, and she wanted Tripp to have that same feeling.

When are you coming for lunch? she texted.

Same as always, he sent back. Twelve-thirty, right?

She started tapping out another message, but he was quicker. *Do you need to move it?*

I have a request today, she'd typed. Ivory never made requests. She ate what Tripp brought, and he'd been up and down Main Street, trying every restaurant, deli, mom-and-pop diner, and more. Last week, he'd brought bowls of ramen noodles from a food truck. And they'd been delicious.

She sent the text, a smile forming on her face.

Did you see the text about a family meeting tonight? he sent, clearly not seeing hers. Pulled pork tonight at Liam's.

Ivory hadn't seen it, because she kept the family text string on silent. The Walker brothers and Foster sisters could send a *lot* of texts, and she didn't need her phone chiming every other second while she was at work.

A request?

Tripp had thumbs like lightning, and Ivory leaned against the counter as she thought about what to say.

Yeah, she typed out. *The baby and I feel like a big salad from The Bread Bowl.*

The baby and I. Surely Tripp would see that and know. Ivory thought she was being clever, and she grinned as she sent the text.

Tripp started typing, and in the next moment, her phone rang. Her husband's name sat on the screen, and she swiped open the call, feeling sick to her stomach again.

"No tomatoes on the salad," she said. "They give me heartburn." And she already had enough of that from the morning sickness, thank you very much.

"The baby?" Tripp asked.

Ivory could only giggle, and Tripp said, "Ivory, don't tease me. Are you pregnant?"

"Yes," she said. "I've been sick for over a week. I haven't taken a test, but I just know I am."

He started to laugh, the sound made mostly of air. "I'm coming right now," he said. "I'll get your salad and be there in a minute."

Ivory wiped her tears as she lowered her phone, the call ending. Twenty minutes later, Tripp walked through the door, pure anticipation on his face. He took her into his arms and held her so, so tight.

"I love you," he said.

"I love you, too," Ivory whispered into his neck. "I feel bad I'm going to have to leave Verona's." The dry cleaner, cheesy as it may sound, had been a saving grace for her. She'd worked here for almost eighteen months, and she loved it. She loved Harmon and Verona.

"They'll find someone else," he said. "You've been sick? How come I didn't know?"

"You're at the gym," she said, wiping her eyes and taking her salad out of the bag he'd brought.

"Is it bad?"

"I'm okay," she said. "It usually lasts until about lunch, so I'm glad you brought this early."

"Can we tell everyone at the family meeting tonight?"

"Sure," she said, gazing up at him. He looked like a little boy on Christmas morning, and Ivory sure did love him. "Who called the meeting?"

"Liam."

"He must have news too."

"Who knows?" Tripp asked. "The family meetings can be about anything. I haven't heard how Wyatt's doing in a while. Maybe it'll be more of an intervention-type thing."

"What time?"

"Six."

She nodded, ate another forkful of her salad, and sighed when Tripp sat down beside her.

"I can't believe you're pregnant," he said. "How are we going to tell Oliver?"

"We'll just tell him," Ivory said. "He'll be excited."

"Do you want a boy or a girl?"

"I don't care," Ivory said, glancing at him. "You?"

Tripp just shook his head, a wonderful smile spreading across his face. "Whichever is great with me. I just can't believe it."

Ivory wasn't sure why he was so surprised, but she giggled as she leaned over and touched her lips to his. "Believe it, cowboy. You're going to be a father."

35

Whitney pulled up to her house again, a defeated sigh moving through her body at the sight of the truck there. Brand-new and shiny, the huge blue vehicle set her blood on fire. "Blake," she muttered, her emotions surging. She felt wild, out of control, and angrier than she'd ever been.

She got out of her car and didn't bother to get the small bag she'd packed with a few changes of clothes and some toiletries. She hadn't wanted to leave Seven Sons without talking to Jeremiah, but he'd marched out the back door and disappeared onto the ranch. She had no idea where he was or what he was doing, and he hadn't come back after a couple of hours.

She'd texted him that she was going to spend the night in town, at her house, and she'd love to see him when he was ready. He hadn't answered.

Blake got out of his truck too, and Whitney's fingers clenched into fists. "What are you doing here?" she demanded. "You and I are *not* together. We're *not* going to get back together."

"Hey, wait," he said as if he actually wanted to get back together with her. He held up both hands. "Who was that guy at the bakery?"

"That *man* is my husband," Whitney said. "And you've ruined so many things in my life. I'm not letting you ruin this too." Because Jeremiah was the very best thing that had ever come into Whitney's life. In that moment, she knew she wouldn't stay at her house, waiting for him to come to her. She'd spent so much of her life waiting for a man to come to her. She'd pined for Blake while he was gone. She'd hoped and prayed he'd come back to her when he finally returned to Three Rivers.

"You do not get to kiss me, or touch me, or wait in my driveway like you have a right to be here." She folded her arms. "You should leave. Now."

Blake looked like he had no idea what language she'd spoken. He opened his mouth, but no sound came out. Whitney knew then that he'd played her for years. In the back of his mind, she'd always be there. Steady, stable, stupid Whitney.

Pure humiliation pulled through her. First because she'd given him so much power for so long. And second, because she'd abandoned Jeremiah once for Blake. What a mistake that had been—she would not be repeating it.

"All right," he said. "I'll go." He turned back to his truck and got behind the wheel. Whitney returned to her car too and backed out so he could get to the street. He drove away without looking back, and Whitney knew he had no intention of staying in town, no matter what he said.

Tears came to her eyes, and she didn't even know why. She should be proud of herself for what she'd just done. She'd taken the trash out of her life, leaving space for what —and who—really mattered.

And yet, somehow, it still hurt that he'd just gone. Even though she knew she wasn't important to him. Even though she knew he'd have left in two weeks or two months.

She pulled back into her driveway, but she had no desire to go back into the house where she'd taken a nap that afternoon. She wanted to talk to Jeremiah, and she decided enough time had gone by since texting him to call him.

His line rang and rang, and Whitney's pulse accelerated with every sound. She'd called him dozens of times, expecting to get an angry bark for a response. But he'd always answered, and this silence and way he ignored her sliced through her in a whole new way.

He'd cooked for her once when he was trying to get back together with her. Should she make dinner for him?

She'd thought the cake would help convince him that she hadn't been sneaking around with her ex-boyfriend.

But he'd barely looked at it, and the sneer in his voice had eradicated any hope Whitney had harbored as she'd followed him from the bakery to the homestead on the ranch.

"What do I do?" she asked the empty air around her. She didn't want to talk to Patsy or her mother about this. Dalton had been spending more time after school at Bowman's Breeds, and Whitney didn't want to trouble her teenage nephew with her real-world relationship problems.

The person she trusted most to give her the best advice was the one not talking to her.

Call Callie came to her mind, and Whitney fumbled the phone she flipped it over so fast. Callie Walker was Jeremiah's best friend, and Whitney had her number in her phone.

The line rang once before Callie said, "Heya, Whitney."

"Callie," she said, so relieved the word burst from her mouth. Problem was, she didn't know what else to say. Jeremiah didn't like gossip, and Whitney didn't either. She didn't want to go running to his best friend to see if he'd said anything about her. Not only that, but *she* wanted to be his best friend.

Pushing aside the twinge of jealousy, she asked, "Have you heard from Jeremiah?"

"Yeah, he was here a while ago," Callie said. "He

helped with my beehives for a bit, and then he went back toward Seven Sons."

"Oh."

Whitney had likely left before he'd returned. That, or he'd been hiding out in one of the barns or stables. He liked to take an afternoon nap in the hay loft, and Whitney wondered if she should grab a sandwich from his favorite shop and head back to the ranch. Just because she was pregnant didn't mean she couldn't walk around until she found him.

But maybe he didn't want to be found.

Whitney's heart flopped against her ribs like it was dying, and she couldn't think of anything else to say.

"We're having a family meeting tonight," Callie said. "Did you know about that?"

"No," Whitney said. She loved the Walker family, as well as Callie and her sisters. Moving into the homestead had been easy, natural, for her. She'd experienced several family meetings over the past couple of months, and she always came away with the renewed sense of how much these people loved each other.

They wanted to share their lives with one another. Good things. Hard things. Health concerns. Successes. Failures.

And Whitney wanted that too.

"What time?" she asked, her stomach quaking at the thought of showing up at Jeremiah's family meeting without talking to him first.

"Six," Callie said. "It's here at the Shining Star. I'm making pulled pork."

Whitney didn't want to ask, but she felt like she should. "Am I invited?"

"Of course," Callie said. "You're Jeremiah's wife."

"He's upset with me."

"I could see that," Callie said. "He didn't tell me why. He left with Liam for a bit."

Then Liam knew, and Whitney wasn't sure if she should be humiliated or angry. Or maybe neither. "Will you tell him I'm coming?"

"Oh, I can't do that," Callie said. "You should tell him yourself."

Yeah, Whitney should do a lot of things. Didn't mean she was going to. "Thanks, Callie." The call ended, and Whitney once again looked out her window. She'd left Jones and Jess at the ranch, and the cats were happy there. They roamed the bedrooms upstairs, and they'd even ventured outside, especially to the shed, where they'd found a nice pocket of mice to snack on.

Both cats still curled up on her feet to sleep, and Whitney couldn't stand the thought of being without them for even one night. Without Jeremiah.

Confusion needled her mind, and she ended up laying her seat back and closing her eyes. She couldn't go in the house. She couldn't go back to the ranch. Maybe she'd just stay here for a while.

———

WHITNEY FINALLY DRAGGED herself into her house when the wicked, winter west Texas wind threatened to blow her car over. She didn't have much in the way of groceries, and she ran back outside to go to Wilde & Organic. The store sold meal kits, and she bought one of those, as well as a pound of butter.

With everything else in her pantry, she could make chocolate chip cookies. She planned to eat her lonely dinner for one, make the treats, and head back to Seven Sons and try to catch Jeremiah after his family meeting.

Maybe with chocolate and sugar, she could sweeten him up enough to talk to her.

Six o'clock came and went.

About six-twenty, several texts came in at once, and Whitney's heartbeat pulsed around behind her tongue. Maybe Jeremiah had finally figured out how he felt and what he needed to say.

But none of the texts were from him. One from Evelyn, another from Ivory, and a few from Callie.

You're not feeling well?

Can I bring you dinner?

Miah looks miserable. Have you talked to him?

He says you're sick. Let me bring you the rest of this pulled pork.

Maybe I can bring it by tomorrow. Miah says you work until almost noon?

Whitney pieced together things pretty quickly. Jeremiah had told everyone that she wasn't feeling well, and that was why she wasn't at the family meeting. She frowned at her phone, not quite sure how to answer. No, she wasn't feeling well, though she wasn't plagued with morning sickness. She didn't need dinner. She didn't need pulled pork.

She was sick, but not with anything that an antibiotic or a meal could fix. Her heart hurt, and her stomach clenched, and her hormones seemed way out of control as she started weeping again.

She didn't want to lie, so she flipped her phone over and put her head down as she cried. Only when the timer on the oven went off did she get up to take the cookies out. But she'd lost her drive to finish baking them, to drive the twenty minutes down to the ranch, to face her husband.

36

Jeremiah slept in the homestead alone that night. Well, his two pups had kept him company. Winston and Willow were good friends, and the only time they wanted to be away from him was when they needed to go outside.

Double well, Wyatt and Micah were also at the homestead, and they shared a bedroom down the hall from Jeremiah's and Whitney's. Wyatt hadn't wanted to be alone in case he needed help in the middle of the night, and Micah had been willing to share.

Jeremiah hadn't seen either one of them since the family meeting. Of course, he'd gone straight to his bedroom after returning from dinner at the Shining Star, where Callie and Liam had shared their news about getting two kids by January with everyone. Tripp and

Ivory had shared that she was pregnant. And everyone had wanted to know where Whitney was.

He'd said she was sick. Not feeling well. If she was pregnant, he hadn't lied.

Jeremiah hated the if's in his life. Hated that his wife wasn't with him for dinner and cheerful family announcements. Hated that they hadn't been able to make their own.

He sat in his recliner and read the Bible, trying to focus on the words Paul had sent to the Ephesians. He couldn't. He'd re-read the same passage of scripture over and over, and he finally closed the book and set it on the table next to the chair.

Looking around the room, he was only reminded of how big it was. How big, and now how empty. Whitney had set up her computer and photography needs in the front office, so his desk still sat cleanly, with a lamp on the surface and his puzzle books hidden in the drawers.

His mind raced, though, and he couldn't imagine being able to settle down enough to solve anything.

He'd made a mess of his life, and he couldn't fix that.

"You can," he muttered to himself. "Call your wife." Winston lifted his head and looked at Jeremiah, as if the cowboy had said something of great importance to his dog. Jeremiah reached over and stroked the dog absently, taking comfort from his presence, his pure devotion to Jeremiah, even when he did stupid things like run away and say he needed time to think.

Whitney had texted him and called him, and he'd ignored her. His gut writhed over that, because he knew what it felt like to be on the receiving end of a ghosting, and it was not pleasant. He remembered how uneasy he'd been, how much he'd obsessed over what he'd done wrong, how strong the speculation and self-doubt had been.

At the same time, he couldn't bring himself to talk to her yet.

He picked up his boots and put them in the closet. He showered, though he would again in the morning. He went to bed early, not expecting to be able to fall asleep. But when he did doze off, only to be awakened after full dark had settled over Texas. He slept fitfully all night, seeming to wake up or doze off every few minutes.

By the time he dragged himself out of bed and back into the shower, a sense of exhaustion filled his muscles in a way he'd never experienced before. His ranch ownership meeting was that morning, and he took his time scrambling eggs and frying bacon, making coffee, and serving Micah and Wyatt.

Neither of them asked about Whitney, for which Jeremiah was grateful. Micah worked around the ranch on various projects, but he hadn't done much since moving to Three Rivers from Temple. Well, much more than keeping an eye on Wyatt, driving him to appointments, or keeping him entertained, moving, and medicated.

His brother had been recovering decently well from the back surgery, and now that he was nine weeks into the recovery, he was starting to do more, move better, and return to his normal, confident self.

"I'm goin' to town this morning," he said to them as the three of them finished eating. "Ranch meeting." He stepped over to the back door and let Winston and Willow back inside. The dogs came in, their nails ticking against the wood floor. Jeremiah smiled at them and sat back at the table with his brothers.

"Bring back lunch?" Micah asked, glancing up from underneath his cowboy hat.

Wyatt stood up, only bracing one hand against the table to do so, and picked up Micah's plate and then Jeremiah's.

"Yeah, sure," Jeremiah said, patting Willow's head. "What are you thinking?"

"Soup," Micah said. "There's a cold front blowing in today."

"Feels like soup weather," Jeremiah added, glad he wasn't the only one who could feel a chill in the air. He'd thought maybe his argument with Whitney had just made everything in his life feel colder.

He'd noticed her shampoo and conditioner wasn't in the shower. He'd read her text about where she'd be staying. Perhaps he could just swing by her house that morning....

She'll be at the store, he told himself. And he didn't want to have a conversation with her in public. So he finished his coffee, grabbed his keys, and headed to town.

He was running a bit late, and almost everyone was sitting in the circle when he finally walked in.

"There you are," Bear said. "I was just about to call you."

"Yeah?" Jeremiah had missed meetings before. Not many, but he'd never been called, as if the ownership meetings couldn't happen without him. "Why? What's going on?" He glanced around and saw all the same people. Brit, Squire, Pete, LeRoy, Tammy, Gavin.

Bear handed him an envelope. "Seven Sons was nominated for Ranch of the Year."

Jeremiah's pulse raced as he took the envelope. The official seal of Texas sat in the top, left corner, and a smile started to crawl across his face. "You're kidding."

"Nope." Bear grinned at him and leaned closer. "I think Squire nominated you, so you'll probably win. Three Rivers Ranch has won for the Texas Panhandle region four times in the past twenty years."

"Squire's only been running it for what? Eight years?" Jeremiah asked. He didn't dare take the paper out of the envelope quite yet.

"Seven," Bear said. "And two of those awards have been during that time." Bear turned to the rest of the group. "All right, let's talk surviving the winter." He sighed as he sat down, and the chair groaned. Bear was not a small man. Jeremiah wanted to talk about best winterizing practices for the ranch—particularly for his fields—

but he took another moment to slide the paper out of the envelope.

Sure enough, it was an official announcement from the Texas Ranching Board that Seven Sons Ranch had been nominated for Ranch of the Year for the Panhandle region. Pride filled him, as he'd worked so hard on the ranch these past few years. He'd poured all of his time, energy, and love into the animals, the fences, the land, the crops, the cabins, the buildings, all of it.

His brothers helped too, of course, but everyone knew the ranch was Jeremiah's baby. And if they got Ranch of the Year, everyone would know it was because of him.

He wanted to pull out his phone and call Whitney. Celebrate with her.

Sadness streamed through him, and he shoved the paper back into the envelope before taking his seat next to Gavin. The other man looked at him, but Jeremiah couldn't return the gesture.

Something seethed inside him. Something dark and dangerous and which he'd felt before. He'd worked *so hard* to rid himself of exactly these feelings, as they were debilitating, could overtake his mind in moments, and leave him second-guessing everything and everyone for years. He knew, because he'd felt this unsettled, this dark, this angry after Laura Ann had left him standing at the altar.

He'd brooded as he'd packed and moved from Austin to Three Rivers. He'd poured that negative energy into a relentless drive around the ranch, getting things cleaned up after the tornado, installing better systems, proven protective measures, all of it.

His hard work wasn't for nothing, but Jeremiah liked laying in bed with Whitney a whole lot more than glaring through a ranch ownership meeting. He didn't contribute much to the conversation, and he took the literature Bear had brought with him.

Squire and Pete appeared in front of him, creating a roadblock to the exit, before Jeremiah had even stood up. "What's goin' on with you?" Squire asked.

"Nothing," Jeremiah said.

"Right." Squire looked at Pete. "It sure seems like nothin', don't it, Pete?"

"I'm sure the man's right," Pete said, his voice way too nonchalant. "He comes storming in like a rain-cloud every other week." He cocked his eyebrows and folded his arms. Gavin hadn't moved from the seat next to him, and even Brit was watching the conversation.

The conversation Jeremiah didn't want to have. He simply looked at the other ranch owners—his friends. Sometimes, Jeremiah convinced himself he didn't have anyone but his brothers. But it wasn't true. He had these men and women, too.

"I heard you caused a ruckus in the bakery yesterday," Squire said.

"Where'd you hear that?" Jeremiah asked, his fingers curling into fists. "Because it's not true."

"My momma. Said you and your wife had an argument and you left real fast."

Jeremiah's panic reached epic proportions, and he couldn't contain it.

"Oh, you nailed it," Pete said. He tried to smile at Jeremiah and added, "Tell us about it."

"Whitney was kissing someone else," he blurted out. Everything inside him, around him, under him, was moving at the speed of light. He took a deep, deep breath and things slowed down. "It was her old boyfriend."

"Blake Thurston?" Brit asked.

"Yeah." Jeremiah ducked his head, embarrassment filling him. He didn't want to tell any of the cowboys here why he and Whitney had gotten engaged and then married in the first place. They all had happy marriages, with pretty wives, and thriving families.

Jeremiah didn't care about Ranch of the Year. He wanted Whitney, and he wanted a baby, and he wanted to be the best man he could be for both of them.

"Well, Blake's only been back in town for three days," Brit said.

"How do you know that?" Jeremiah looked up at the other rancher. If that was true, there was no way Whitney had been unfaithful to him to the extent that her baby wasn't also his.

And there was no if about that. Jeremiah knew in his heart that Whitney hadn't cheated on him at all.

"His family lives out on my lane," Brit said. "That boy

is a gypsy at heart. Always drifting from one thing to the next. A couple of days ago, he shows up with this brand-new truck and some story about how he's been working on the premier horse farm in Lexington." Brit shook his head, his expression dark. "I think his daddy has about had it with the boy."

Every eye swung back to Jeremiah. "I get why," he said. "He and Whitney have been off and on for a while. I guess I just thought since we were married...she'd be off him for good."

"I'm sure she is," Squire said. "What did she say?"

"About that," Jeremiah said, misery in his tone.

"Oh, so you just ate some bad sushi for breakfast," Pete said. "I *told* you that was what had happened." He nudged Squire, who chuckled.

"Yeah, all right. Let's go. Kelly wants lunch during an actual lunchtime today."

"Sushi up here?" Gavin asked. "It's so not good."

Everyone burst out laughing, Jeremiah included. Three Rivers had had at least half a dozen sushi restaurants in the few years he'd lived there, and Gavin was right. None of them were ever good, and they all went out of business quickly.

His friends started to disperse, and Jeremiah stood up. He wished he had their confidence, and he wondered if any of them had been standing at the altar when their bride-to-be refused to come out.

Doesn't matter, he told himself. He could—and had—

moved past those feelings of inadequacy, abandonment, and distrust.

At least, he thought he had.

He dialed Doctor Wagstaff's office on his way out to his truck, and said, "Can I get in with him today? It's an emergency."

"He has a twelve-thirty," the receptionist said.

"Great," Jeremiah said. "I'll take it." Wyatt and Micah could order food and go pick it up. Or go next door, where Callie had plenty of pulled pork left over. He texted them quickly, feeling better now that he was doing something about his situation. Sitting and thinking about something never boded well for Jeremiah.

But once he had a plan of action, he could execute it. Up first—talk to his therapist. And then...then he had to talk to Whitney and work things out between them. He loved her. He wanted her. He wouldn't let her go this time, not if there was any chance at all that she wanted and loved him too.

37

Whitney piled all the cookies she'd made onto a paper plate and covered them with a piece of aluminum foil. She'd managed to put the uncooked dough in the refrigerator before stumbling down the hall to her bedroom.

She'd gone to bed far too early and managed to stay in bed until the sun started to brighten the sky. She'd showered and dressed in fresh clothes, and now she stood in the kitchen, wondering if she should toss the cookies in the trashcan on her way to Wilde & Organic or if she should take them with her.

She could put them in the office upstairs and be a hero for her family. Or she should leave them on a high shelf in the back room and take them to Jeremiah when she finished her shift.

It was the second Thursday of the month, which

meant he'd be at his ranch ownership meeting in town today. The IFA stood only three blocks from Wilde & Organic, and Whitney toyed with telling her sister she had to leave a little bit early. Or perhaps she could work much quicker than she normally did and slip away before the meeting ended.

Jeremiah had once waited for her to come out of work, and it had been dark then. She could do the same and park behind him so he couldn't leave without talking to her first.

"It'll be a miracle if he goes to the meeting," she muttered to herself, swiping the plate of cookies into her arms along with her phone and purse. She took everything out to her car and returned to the house for her bag. If she left it here, it would be way too easy for her to come back here after work. Far too simple to stay away from Seven Sons, from Jeremiah.

She packed her pajamas and tucked her hairspray back into the top of her bag. With it on the backseat, she drove the short distance to the store and went in the back door, the same as she did six days a week.

Winter squash went on a main display. Pumpkins. Gourds. Purple potatoes. Broccoli crowns and heads of cauliflower. She broke down boxes and swept up the dirt from the farms around Texas where their produce came from.

The store was ready on time, and Whitney retreated to the back room. She usually marked the charts of what she put out and how many, which produce to reorder and which would probably go on the clearance table. She'd been taking things to Jeremiah for the few months of their marriage, and he could do amazing things with past-their-prime onions, slightly moldy greens, and withered carrots.

It seemed every thought led back to Jeremiah, and Whitney looked at her brother. "I have to be somewhere. I'll come back and mark the produce this afternoon."

Johnny waved, because it wasn't his job to order what the store needed. The back-of-house manager, Tilly, would do that. Johnny worked the farm, and he brought in what they had on the farm, in season, no matter what the other inventory was.

Whitney hurried out to her car, wishing she'd driven away from Seven Sons in her grandfather's truck. It was distinctive, and Jeremiah wouldn't be able to miss it. "He won't miss your sedan either," she told herself, backing up quickly.

She almost gave herself whiplash she put the car into drive so quickly. The IFA seemed impossibly far away, and she had no idea how long Jeremiah's meeting would last. He usually brought lunch back to the homestead afterward, though, and she started praying that whatever they were talking about today would run long.

She pulled into the parking lot, and every vehicle in sight was a truck. She wished she had a cake. She'd even forgotten the cookies she'd made, back on the shelf at Wilde & Organic.

But she wouldn't be going back to get them. Jeremiah's truck sat up ahead, and she pulled right behind the big, black behemoth. He wouldn't even be able to back out now. Her nerves pulled tight, and she squeezed her fingers around the steering wheel.

She should go.

Just go on home. Send her brother for her cats and her computer. Move back into her yellow house, and keep taking her pictures, and somehow figure out how to move on.

You're pregnant, she reminded herself. She could move back into the yellow house, but she wouldn't be able to keep taking her pictures. And she'd never move on if she had to look into a version of Jeremiah's eyes multiple times every day.

So she waited. She wasn't going to give up on Jeremiah. She wasn't going to walk away.

The truck a couple down from where she'd parked backed out, and Whitney watched as the vehicle eased past her, two cowboys insanely curious about staring at her.

Jeremiah would be coming soon. Whitney got out of her car and slicked her palms down the front of her jeans. The sounds of boots against cement met her ears, and she almost bolted. *No*, she told herself. *No, no, no.* She repeated the word in her mind as another cowboy passed her, this one wearing a hat much bigger than any she'd seen on her husband's head.

Another cowboy peeled off the sidewalk, and there stood Jeremiah Walker.

Whitney pulled in a breath at the simple sight of him. The first time she'd laid eyes on him, she'd found him gorgeous and stormy, but full of a spirit she'd wanted to get to know. She could admit that their game of telephone tag had been fun for her, and she'd prayed for a long time that he would come around to her. First, so she could shoot at Seven Sons. And then so they could get to know each other better.

And they had. She knew him so well, she was carrying his child inside her.

"Hey," she said, making her voice as strong as she could. She gestured back toward he car. "I made some cookies, but then I left them at work, and...." Her voice trailed off, because embarrassment squirreled through her.

This wasn't what she'd come here to say.

"Look," she said. "I love you, and I know you love me. We need to talk." She glanced around, but no one seemed to be paying them any attention. "Will you go to lunch with me?"

"No," Jeremiah said, taking a step forward. He glanced to where her car boxed his truck into the parking spot. "But I'll make you lunch out at the homestead." He continued toward her, stopping just out of reach. Whitney could see his anxiety, but he also wore an edge in his eye she'd seen before too.

He did love her. He wanted to be with her. Maybe he

was embarrassed too, and Whitney nodded. "I'll meet you out there." She turned and stepped off the curb, almost going down with the sudden motion. Vertigo hit her, and she flew out her hand to steady herself against his truck.

"Whoa there," Jeremiah said, his strong arm coming around her waist. "Are you okay?"

"I'm just a little...woozy," Whitney said. Her heart raced, and she felt lightheaded. She pulled in breath after breath, but she wasn't getting enough oxygen. She leaned into Jeremiah. "I don't feel right."

"Let's go to the hospital," he said.

Whitney started to protest, but the world continued to spin. She braced herself against him and the truck, feeling very much like she was going to pass out.

"What did you eat this morning?" he asked.

"N-nothing," she said. "Just coffee."

"No wonder," he said. "Whitney, you're pregnant. The caffeine will speed up your heart rate, and you need more calories than normal." He put his other hand on her forearm. "I'm driving your car. Give me the keys."

"You'll never fit in my car," Whitney said, trying once again to breathe in enough oxygen.

"You're right." He looked at her car again. "Get in the truck. Come on. I still need your keys." He helped her around the truck to the passenger side and balanced her as she climbed in. He started it, and took her keys.

With her car moved, he got behind the wheel and

backed out. The hospital was about ten minutes away, and Jeremiah walked her inside slowly. "Feeling better?"

"I need to sit down," she said. Worry gnawed at her. She and Jeremiah had so much to talk about still. She didn't want to be here. She wanted to go back to the ranch and work things out with him, celebrate that their family was going to get bigger, and tell him how much she loved him.

"We need some help," he called instead, and a nurse came forward with a wheelchair. Foolishness moved through Whitney, but she let Jeremiah push her through the doors, where a nurse took her blood pressure.

"This is low," she said. Whitney answered the questions as best as she could while they took her vitals, and they rushed her back to a room, where one nurse put in an IV while another asked her how far along she was.

"Not far," she said. "Maybe a month or two. I just missed my period last week."

Jeremiah stayed at her side, his hand never leaving hers. With the fluids and lying down in bed, Whitney started to feel better quickly. Eventually, all the nurses left the room, pulling the curtain closed and turning out the lights.

"I'm sorry," she said to Jeremiah, who had his head down. He immediately looked up, pure concern in his eyes. It shone like a star in the natural light in the room, and Whitney reached for his face. "I didn't cheat on you. I went to the bakery to get the cake, and Blake was there.

He surprised me, because I didn't even know he was in town. And he kissed me before I'd said three words."

"I know." Jeremiah nodded.

"I took a nap at my house while I waited for the cake," she said. "That was all."

"I know," he repeated. "I'm sorry, Whitney. I shouldn't have walked away from you yesterday, and I did it twice."

Tears filled her eyes. "I'm kind of a wreck right now." Her voice was choked and much too high. "These are happy tears, I swear."

"I love you," he said. "I'm sorry for any pain I've caused."

"I love you too." He hugged her, and the scent of his skin, his aftershave, his shampoo, was so comforting. "What if—what if something's wrong with our baby?" Whitney couldn't fathom the thought of losing something she wanted so much. Something Jeremiah wanted.

"Nothing's wrong," he said. "The doctor will be in soon, and then you'll see."

As if summoned by Jeremiah's words, the curtain snapped open, and someone said, "Knock, knock."

Jeremiah straightened and looked toward the door. A woman entered, a bright smile on her face. "Let's check on your baby, shall we?" She pulled her stethoscope from around her neck and listened to Whitney's heartbeat while Jeremiah looked on nervously.

"Let's do her bp again," she said. "Her heart rate is down from what's on the chart." She smiled at Whitney again. "I'm Doctor Lucas. I'm the OBGYN on call in Emergency. You're about six weeks along?"

"Yes," Whitney said. "Will we...can we hear the heartbeat?"

"It's a little early for that," Doctor Lucas said. "I could do an ultrasound, but I don't think there's anything wrong with your baby." She looked at the nurse. "She's not bleeding?"

"No, ma'am."

"I think you just need to eat," Doctor Lucas said. "And drink a lot more than you ate or drank this morning. You work on your feet?"

"Yes," Whitney said, another dose of foolishness punching her in the back of the throat.

"You need rest, ma'am," the doctor said. "Food, water, prenatal vitamins." She looked at Jeremiah. "You're the husband?"

"Yes, ma'am." He swiped his cowboy hat right off his head, and he looked so darn cute. "I'll take her home and take good care of her."

"I'm sure you will." Doctor Lucas looped her stethoscope around her neck again. "She can go as soon as she feels strong enough."

———

Hours later, Whitney let Jeremiah escort her into the homestead and take her directly to the couch. She'd wanted to leave the hospital an hour before anyone else would let her, Jeremiah included.

Micah and Wyatt fawned over her, bringing her a big glass of water and a bag of pretzels. Jeremiah set to work in the kitchen, making what would be their dinner at this point. Whitney dozed in and out of consciousness, aware of the Walker brothers talking around her. They didn't bother her; if anything, their presence was a comfort to her.

"Whitney, baby," Jeremiah said lovingly, wiping a cool cloth across her forehead. "Wake up, okay?"

She opened her eyes and blinked a couple of times. The homestead was full of people, and she tried to sit up.

"Go slow," Jeremiah said.

"I'm okay," she said even as a sharp pain tore through her forehead. "My head hurts." And her mouth felt like a furry animal had crawled inside and died. "I'm thirsty."

Evelyn appeared with a glass of water, and Rhett had pills in his hand. Jeremiah took them and handed them to Whitney, who swallowed them while everyone watched.

"Family meeting," Jeremiah said. "Whitney's pregnant, and we had a little scare this morning."

Cheers erupted, as did things like, "I told you that was why she wasn't well," and "I knew it. Congratulations, Miah."

"We're going to pray over the food," Jeremiah said loudly. "And then we'll explain everything."

<h1 style="text-align:center">38</h1>

Jeremiah basked in the energy at the homestead. He loved having people over, though he wished he'd thought better of it as Whitney's face didn't get much color into it, even after she'd eaten, had something to drink, and taken some medicine.

He watched her but kept participating in the conversations around him. With so many announcements and meetings lately, he thought maybe they wouldn't have anything to talk about. But the Walkers were all loud, and Callie, Evelyn, Simone, and Ivory had learned how to survive among them.

"And that's it," Jeremiah said. "She's okay. She just needs to rest and make sure she gets enough to eat."

"Good thing she's married to you," Rhett said. "You'd keep us all fed if you could."

Jeremiah chuckled, but he didn't deny it. He did like

taking care of people, because it made him feel useful. Whitney reached over and slipped her hand into Jeremiah's. He smiled softly at her, and Simone said, "We should go."

"Yeah, good idea."

"Okay, time to go."

"Thanks for dinner."

Everyone started standing up and putting their dishes in the sink, throwing napkins in the trash, and giving hugs goodbye. Liam, Callie, and Simone went out the back door, a little girl with them, holding Callie's hand.

Liam whooped and laughed as he scooped Denise into his arms and swung her around to his shoulders. The three-year-old squealed and laughed, and Jeremiah watched Callie gaze up at her new daughter, all smiles and giggles too.

Happiness moved through him, and he whistled for the dogs to come back before he closed the back door behind them. He followed everyone else to the front door, where he hugged Tripp and Rhett, Evelyn and Ivory, and he, Micah, and Wyatt said good-bye to everyone. That door closed too, and a sense of silence descended.

"I'm exhausted," Wyatt said. "Taking Kessler out today was harder than I thought." He limped away from the door, a groan emanating from his throat. Winston went with him, as the dog seemed to want to be around Wyatt when he needed help.

"I'll get him settled," Micah said. "And then I'm going

to go for an evening walk." He wore a mischievous glint in his eye, and Jeremiah knew exactly what it meant. He'd met someone.

"What's her name?" he asked.

"There are three single women out here," Micah said. "You'll have to guess." He grinned as he followed Wyatt, and the two of them disappeared down the hall that led to the bedrooms. He could never go to bed at eight o'clock, as he'd be up by midnight. But he wasn't recovering from major back surgery either.

He returned to the kitchen with Willow, where Whitney still sat the huge dining room table. "Let's get you to bed." He extended his hand toward her, and she smiled those ruby red lips at him, put her hand in his, and stood up.

She stepped gingerly, and Jeremiah moved slowly with her. "Are you okay?"

"I feel about ten years older," she said. "I know I slept, but I'm still tired. I just feel sort of...off."

Jeremiah nodded. "You have to let me know what you need. I'll get it. Do it. Whatever."

"I want to lay in bed and watch something on my tablet," she said. "I need my phone and my appointment book."

He left her in the bedroom to change into her pajamas while he went to get her appointment book from her office. Back in the bedroom, he found her bed, tapping and swiping on her tablet. He handed her the book and leaned over to touch his lips to her forehead.

"We're okay, right, Whitney?"

"Yes." She leaned into his touch. "I'm so glad to be back here. I *hated* sleeping at my house."

"You should probably sell that house."

"Yep," she said with a sigh. "I'll put it on my to-do list." She looked up at him as he stepped back. "Because this isn't fake anymore."

"You know what?" Jeremiah grinned at her. "I'm not sure it ever was, at least for me."

Surprise danced across her face. "Really? You think you would've asked me to marry you only a few weeks after we started seeing each other again?"

He chuckled and took off his cowboy hat, hanging it on the hook on the side of the dresser. "You're right. I probably wouldn't have done that."

"Would you have ever asked someone to marry you for real?"

Jeremiah thought about it for a moment. "I don't know. And it doesn't matter now. You're mine, and I'm yours, and we belong together. We're *good* together."

Whitney received his kiss willingly, and Jeremiah ended up laying down in bed with her, whatever she'd put on her tablet playing while he made love to her, his wife, his best friend, the love of his life.

———

"ONE FOR YOU, WINST," he said to the cattle dog as he hung a stocking with a paw print next to his. The mantel held a variety of stockings, for humans, horses, and now dogs alike. "And Wills, yours is right here." He picked up the shiny teal stocking that looked like it had fish scales on it.

Willow barked at him as if she knew she'd get a rawhide to chew come Christmas morning, and Jeremiah chuckled. He nudged her stocking over a little bit so it was evenly spaced with the others, and stepped back to admire his handiwork.

Everyone would be here in a couple of hours to get the tree set up, as was their custom on the day after Thanksgiving. The past few weeks had been busy, but good. Whitney returned to her normal self—mostly—after a couple of days of rest and a lot of chocolate. She'd rescheduled a couple of shoots to be able to stay in bed, and she'd relied on Jeremiah just the way he'd wanted her to.

He loved her more and more as the days passed, especially when she said, "Oh, look at those cute stockings for the pups." She bent over and scratched both of them. "You guys are so lucky, did you know that? So lucky to have your own stockings."

Jeremiah shook his head at the way she spoke to them like they were humans, but he could admit he loved Winston and Willow with his whole heart.

Whitney's official due date was July twelfth, and they'd talked about not finding out if they were having a boy or a girl until the baby was born. It had been his idea, and Whitney was still on the fence. Jeremiah liked the intrigue of it all, and he didn't see why it mattered if the blankets they had in the nursery were blue, pink, or yellow. The baby wouldn't even know.

The living room held a dozen boxes, most of them open and in some version of being unpacked. But for right now, the mantel was beautiful, and Jeremiah slung his arm around Whitney's waist and held her close. "I love Christmas."

"Me too," she said, leaning into him. "I've been thinking...."

"Uh oh," he said. "Is this thinking like how will we know what clothes to buy? Or thinking like you want to take your next bride out to the far cabin? Or something else?"

"Something else," she said.

Jeremiah shook his head. "Honestly, Whit, I don't know what else I can take. After you lost that kid on the ranch...."

"He wasn't lost," Whitney said. "Winston knew right where he was."

The dog perked up at the sound of his name, cocking his head as if Whitney would give him a command that would end with him earning a chunk of hot dog.

"What have you been thinking about?"

"Just hear me out."

Whenever she started a conversation like that, Jeremiah had to work not to roll his eyes. "I'll listen to the very end," he said.

"I've been thinking that I would like a small, private ceremony where we pledge to each other how we really feel."

"Whit, you know how I really feel."

"I know," she said. "But I want something, I don't know. More official. Our wedding *was* a bit staged, and I hate that's all we got."

"How private is private?"

"Me and you," she said.

Jeremiah didn't see the point. There were plenty of times with just the two of them where he told her and showed her how he really felt about her. "All right," he said, because he didn't have any reason not to. He had plenty of money for cakes and dresses and whatever else she needed to feel like she'd gotten the wedding she wanted.

"And in return, I'll concede about not knowing the gender of our baby."

Jeremiah jerked his attention back to her. "Really?"

She grinned at him, and she was honestly the sexiest, sweetest, most wonderful woman he'd ever known. "Really."

"Deal," he said instantly. "And that wasn't even a hard one."

She laughed as the back door opened and Liam said, "We're here."

Jeremiah turned to welcome his brother and his family to the homestead. They'd all work to decorate the ranch, and while Jeremiah had found it annoying in the past, now he certainly didn't.

"I brought the stuff for the fences," he said. "It's on the front driveway."

"Great," Jeremiah said. "Whitney and I will do that. You and Tripp on the oak tree again?"

"Always," Liam said, crossing through the kitchen and moving toward the front door. "He said he's two minutes out."

"Great." Jeremiah walked around the couches and took Denise from Callie. "Heya, baby."

The little girl smiled at him and reached for his cowboy hat. He chuckled and let her knock it sideways on his head. "Let's go put up some garland, okay?" He reseated his hat as he followed Callie and Liam and Whitney to the front door.

Rhett and Evelyn had arrived, and his brother was hanging a wreath on the front door. "Tree inside?"

"Sure," Jeremiah said. "Everything's out. Recruit Wyatt to help you."

"Help with what?" Wyatt asked, coming up behind Jeremiah.

"The tree inside," Jeremiah said. "Popcorn strands for Oliver and Denise."

"Yeah, I don't think so," Wyatt said, stepping past Jeremiah. He'd turned a corner a couple of weeks ago, and he was so much better now, in a lot of ways. "I'll babysit Conrad." He took the six-month-old from Evelyn, who laughed as she passed him over.

"Deal," she said. "He's teething like mad, so don't blame me if you're covered in slobber in five minutes."

"Let's go get some crackers," Wyatt said, practically cooing at the baby as he went down the hall.

Jeremiah laughed with the others as Rhett and Evelyn went inside. The house started playing holiday music, and Jeremiah had never been happier to have Bluetooth speakers installed on the inside and outside of the homestead.

He and Whitney loaded the boxes Liam had brought over into the back of her grandfather's truck and rumbled down the drive to the fence. Tripp and his family arrived, and Jeremiah waved to him and called, "Liam's waiting for you by the oak tree."

Skyler and Micah had gone to town for pastries, and when they returned, Jeremiah would have them make coffee, sweet tea, and hot chocolate.

A couple of hours later, the homestead was decked out for the holidays, and everyone had gathered inside the homestead for cinnamon rolls and orange scones. Heidi Ackerman made the best spinach quiches in the entire state, and Jeremiah slid a tray of them into the oven to re-warm them.

He loved nothing more than this day-after-Thanksgiving tradition of getting together for a late breakfast, decorating the homestead, and putting on a movie.

"What are we watching today?" Wyatt asked. "Can I pick?"

"No way," Micah said. "You always pick something no one likes."

"Like what?"

"Like that weird documentary about dogs," Rhett said. "Let Callie or Evvy pick."

"I don't want to watch a romantic comedy."

"Evvy likes things that are too sad."

"Let's put on a Christmas movie."

Jeremiah loved listening to all the talk, all the bickering. He lifted his mug of hot chocolate to his mouth and watched as Wyatt continued to plead his case while Micah was not having it.

"They're funny, aren't they?" Whitney asked, joining him.

"Gotta love 'em," Jeremiah said, looking at her. "Should I make popcorn?"

"There's always a case to be made for having popcorn." She grinned at him, and Jeremiah dropped his gaze to those red lips he loved so much.

"I love you," he whispered, dropping his mouth to taste those lips.

Wyatt hadn't spoken to Marcy since the day she'd ran from his hospital room. His body had healed as much as it was probably going to. His back only hurt when he overexerted himself. His heart hurt all the time.

He had no idea how to bridge the gap between them, and he'd resorted to listening to the rumor mill to keep up with the Payne family news. They were a low-drama family, and as far as he could tell, Marcy was still flying planes and her father was still alive.

On Christmas morning, he went with Micah and Skyler, along with Jeremiah and Whitney and Dalton, over to Tripp's estate on the east side of town.

Oliver was really the only niece or nephew old enough to enjoy the magic of Christmas, and he'd agreed to wait for his aunt and uncles to come over before he opened his presents. The scent of maple syrup hung in the air when Wyatt walked in, and he grinned.

"What's for breakfast?" Skyler asked, always the one to bring the spotlight to him. Wyatt had enjoyed plenty of spotlights, seen his name in lights, all of it, and he carried a hat box in his hand.

"Jeremiah!" Oliver yelled, running through the living room. "Wyatt! Skyler! Micah!" One of the best things about Oliver was how happy he was to see everyone. Wyatt grinned at him as Jeremiah scooped the ten-year-old into his arms. Skyler and Micah loved Oliver too, but they didn't seem as interested in children as Jeremiah and Wyatt himself were.

"You didn't open any presents without us, did you?" Jeremiah asked. "Wyatt has the best one right there in his hand."

"Hey," Oliver said. "You got a new hat." He reached up and touched the brim of Jeremiah's hat.

Wyatt waited for his brother to say something. For Oliver to notice all five of the men who'd arrived had new hats, and that they were all identical. No one said anything.

At the back of the house, Tripp flipped French toast while wearing pajamas, and he didn't wear a cowboy hat at all.

"For you," Wyatt said, handing him one of the boxes he carried.

"No way. It's finally here." Tripp took the box and

handed the spatula to Ivory. "How are they?" He looked at Wyatt, and then Jeremiah, and then Micah. "Oh, they're fantastic." He chuckled and opened the box. "I can't believe you have your own line of western wear."

Wyatt couldn't believe it either, and he could only shrug. All the money in the world didn't really matter to him. Neither did the *fantastic* cowboy hats. Heck, he thought he'd trade all of his championship belt buckles if Marcy would go out with him again.

He moved over to the Christmas tree in the living room, which burst with presents. He set the remaining hat box down and turned back to the group. Jeremiah put Oliver down, and the little boy turned toward Wyatt.

He motioned him closer, the little blond boy exactly the kind of child Wyatt imagined Marcy could have.

He was insane for obsessing over her. It had been months since the surgery, and yet her disappearance from his life had left a gash on his heart that refused to heal.

"That one's for you," he said, indicating the box. "I don't think your momma would be too mad if you opened it early."

"Can I?" Oliver asked.

Wyatt nodded, a smile touching his mouth. Oliver lifted the lid on the box and looked inside. Wyatt took the hat out and put it on Oliver's head. "I had Tripp measure your head," he said. "You know, every hat is custom-made." He adjusted it slightly. "How does it feel?"

"Feels great," Oliver said, grinning. He threw his

scrawny arms around Wyatt's neck and hugged him tight. "Thank you, Wyatt."

Wyatt held the boy close, breathing in his innocence. "Yeah," he said, his voice choked. "Merry Christmas, bud."

Oliver ran off to show the custom-made, rodeo champion Wyatt Walker limited edition cowboy hat to his mother, and Wyatt had a moment of looking in from the outside. Everyone stood in the kitchen but him, and he could see everything clearly in that moment.

He wanted what Jeremiah and Tripp had. What Rhett and Liam had found.

And he knew who he wanted it with.

Marcy Payne.

He stood up, his back protesting slightly, and joined the others in the kitchen. Maybe he could call a family meeting and ask for suggestions. He'd talked the most about his situation with Marcy with Jeremiah, and his brother had told him to be patient.

Wyatt felt like he was almost out of patience. Maybe he could just text her. Everyone wanted to be wished Merry Christmas, didn't they?

Before he could talk himself out of it, he brought up her name and texted her quickly. *Merry Christmas.*

Two words. Simple.

"Okay, we're going to eat," Tripp said. "I'm not as fancy as Jeremiah. There's bacon and French toast. After we finish, we'll read the nativity story from the Bible, and then finally, we'll get to open presents."

"Presents!" Oliver yelled over the last couple of words, and Wyatt felt the child-like joy of the holiday.

He wanted the grown-up version too, where he got to spend time with those he loved, and remember the birth of the Savior.

Tripp prayed over their food, and chaos ensued as they all tried to butter and syrup and find a spot at the table. Everyone chatted and laughed, and Wyatt soaked it all in. His phone buzzed in his pocket, and he took it out to check it.

Thanks, Marcy had said. Merry Christmas to you too Wyatt.

His heart turned to pudding, and he gazed at the phone, his mind moving through options at the speed of lightning.

"Something interesting on that thing?"

Wyatt tore his eyes from the phone and looked up at Jeremiah. Instead of speaking, he tilted his phone toward Jeremiah. Surprise filled his eyes as they rounded. "Wow."

"What should I do?"

"Oh, I can't tell you that," Jeremiah said. "I'm terrible at this kind of stuff."

"What kind of stuff?" Whitney leaned closer, and Jeremiah showed her the phone before Wyatt could say or do anything.

"Oh." Whitney looked at Wyatt. "Text her back, that's what you do."

"Yeah?"

"If she didn't want to talk to you, she wouldn't have responded."

"Maybe it's just Christmastime," Wyatt said.

"Maybe she's lonely," Whitney said.

"What do I say?"

Whitney looked at Jeremiah and back to Wyatt. "Invite her to the New Year's Eve parade. We have plenty of room between our two spots."

The New Year's Eve parade. As the idea rolled through Wyatt's mind, it felt more and more right.

"All right," he said, taking his phone back from Whitney. He tapped out a quick message, suddenly unable to make his own decisions. He'd been in such great control in the rodeo. He could tame any bull, ride any horse, rope any calf. He had the titles and the wins and the buckles to prove it.

And yet, Marcy was completely out of his reach.

"This okay?"

Whitney wouldn't look at his phone. "Wyatt," she said with a smile. "You're a champion. Send the text."

"Walkers *are* champions," Jeremiah said with a smile, and he turned back to the conversation with Skyler about something that had happened in Amarillo during Finals Week.

Wyatt read over the text one more time. Would you go to the New Year's Eve light parade with me?

It was simple. Direct. A simple yes or no would suffice.

And if she said no, Wyatt would find a way to move on. He would.

"All right," Tripp said. "Let's open to Luke, chapter two."

Wyatt's phone buzzed, but he couldn't bring himself to look at it. The problem was, he used his phone for the scriptures, and he had to swipe it on and open the app to participate in the part of Christmas he loved best.

Drawing in a deep breath, he did, catching Marcy's text before it disappeared.

Yes.

A smile filled his whole soul, and he felt like punching the air the way he did when he had a good run in the team roping event. Instead, he kept his celebrations to himself and opened the app so he could participate in the story of the Savior's birth with the people he loved.

———

Less than a week later, Wyatt set up two chairs in the plot assigned to Seven Sons Ranch. Whitney's parents always had a spot too, for their store Wilde & Organic, and kids ran around, people went in and out to get food from the table, and the atmosphere was full of light and joy.

Wyatt sat down and tucked his hands in his jacket pockets. He'd been texting with Marcy since Christmas, and she'd said she'd meet him at the parade. Jitters jumped through him while he waited, while more and more people arrived and Marcy wasn't one of them.

He finally stopped looking around for her as the night stole the light from day. The parade would start soon, and Wyatt had the sinking feeling that she wasn't coming at all. His heart beat faster and faster, the way it did every time he got close to getting in the chute with a two-thousand-pound animal. With horns.

And this was just a blonde woman. But she'd roped his heart completely, and Wyatt didn't know how to get loose.

He didn't want to get loose.

"We'll begin in five minutes," a man said over the loudspeaker, and Wyatt bolted to his feet.

"Wyatt," Jeremiah said, but Wyatt just walked away. Left his chairs and walked away. If he hurried, he could get out before the parade began. He did, going over a curb and away from Main Street and all the people.

He knew where Marcy lived. Where her dad lived. And where Payne's Pest-free was. She hadn't texted, and she wouldn't leave town. So she had to be at one of those three places, and Wyatt was going to find her and figure out why she hadn't come.

A pit opened in his stomach as he pulled up to her father's house—the closest spot to the parade route—and didn't see a single light on inside the house. Her car sat in the driveway, and she didn't go to bed by eight p.m.

Fear filled his gut as he got out of his truck and strode toward the front door. "Marcy?" he called. He knocked on the door. Maybe it was a pound. It didn't matter. "Marcy," he said. "It's Wyatt, sweetheart. Open the door, would you?"

She didn't, and Wyatt stalled. He put both hands against the door and held very still. He listened. And something—or someone—told him to go inside. Right now.

He tried the doorknob, and it gave under his touch. He fumbled for a light as an old, stale scent met his nose. He found the switch and flipped it, bathing the room in golden lamplight.

Panic accompanied him as he scanned the room, his eyes landing on Marcy's almost immediately. "Marcy," he said, already moving toward her. She sat on the loveseat, her face tear-streaked and red.

She cried openly as he knelt in front of her. "Baby," he said. "What's wrong?" He took her shoulders into his hands and enveloped her in a tight hug. She gripped him with everything she had and sobbed, and sobbed, and sobbed.

And Wyatt knew then that her father had died.

Sure enough, after a few minutes, she quieted enough for him to turn and look at the other couch, where her father usually lay. He was still there, and he still looked like he was asleep.

"Come on," he said, helping Marcy stand up. "Come sit in my truck. I'll call the paramedics."

His heart wailed, but he knew without a doubt that he was strong enough to carry Marcy through this trial.

After all, he'd just survived a brutal back surgery by himself.

Even as he thought it, he knew that wasn't true. Micah and Jeremiah had helped him immensely these past few months, and he now knew it was his turn to be the support for someone else.

"I miss him already," Marcy said as Wyatt helped her down the front steps.

"I know, sweetheart," he said. "I know."

40

Whitney woke when Jeremiah got out of bed on New Year's Day. He'd always gotten up before her, and he was very good at slipping away like smoke while darkness still filled the world.

What he didn't know was that she'd set her alarm for four-thirty, and it had gone off twenty minutes ago. So she'd dozed, but when Jeremiah got up, Whitney snapped awake too.

"Happy New Year," she said as he pulled on a pair of gym shorts.

"I didn't mean to wake you," he whispered. "Go back to sleep." He pressed a kiss to her forehead. "I'll do my puzzles in the kitchen."

"I have something for you," she said, grabbing onto his hand before he could slip away from her.

"Right now?"

"I said I wanted a ceremony," she said, sitting up and clicking on her lamp. She pulled open the top drawer in her nightstand and removed a black box. "And there's no better way to start the year off right than to remind ourselves of what we want. For us. For this year. For forever."

She opened the box to reveal a silver belt buckle. Jeremiah pulled in a breath, and Whitney looked at him. "I love you, Jeremiah Walker," she said. That was it. She hadn't prepared a fancy speech. He knew how she felt and what she wanted their marriage to be.

"It's beautiful," he said, taking the buckle out and letting the lamplight glint off of it. "I love you, too, Whitney." He touched his lips to hers gently, and Whitney experienced a powerful moment of joy and peace as she kissed her husband.

"I don't have anything for you."

She shook her head and cradled his face in her hands. "It's cute how you think I don't know."

He grinned too and took the belt buckle around to his side of the bed. He opened the bottom drawer in his nightstand and took out a tiny bag. He wouldn't buy her another ring, Whitney knew that. Maybe a bracelet. Maybe her own belt buckle, as Jeremiah had been teaching her the finer points of horseback riding the last few weeks.

He returned to her side of the bed and handed her the bag. "To us," he said.

"For forever," she said, leaning her head against his shoulder. She reached into the bag and took out a small box. It was a ring box, and surprise darted through Whitney.

"It's a mother's ring," he said as she opened the box.

A large green gem sat in the middle with a much smaller ruby on the left side. It looked very Christmasy, and Whitney looked at him with pure love streaming through her.

"The middle gem is peridot," he said. "It's the gemstone for August, which is when we got married."

"It's lovely," she said.

"The ruby is the gemstone for July, when you'll have our first baby," he said. "We can take the ring in when we have more children. Or get a new one."

With shaking fingers, Whitney removed the ring from the box, and Jeremiah slid it on her fingers. "I love it," she whispered.

"I love you," he said. "With my whole heart. And it *is* whole now, because of you." He swept her hair back off her shoulder and kissed her.

And there was nothing bogus about that, or their relationship.

———

Keep reading to find out if another Walker brother can get his happily-ever-after in Three Rivers! Can Wyatt really help Marcy? Or will she be even more unavailable now that her father is gone? Chapter one and two of **WYATT** is next! Keep reading!

Sneak Peek! Wyatt - Chapter One

A groan hissed from Wyatt Walker's mouth as he tried to sit up. He got his legs over the side of the bed and paused, taking a long, deep breath. If he didn't stretch before he stood up, it would be a very bad day.

And today was already a very bad day, so he didn't need his back acting up on him. Because today, he needed to be strong for Marcy, as she was burying her father in just a few hours.

His heart hurt as he stretched his right arm up and over his head, reaching toward the wall until his fingertips pressed against it. Breathing in and out, he held the stretch, finally releasing it. He repeated the motion on the other side, and then twisted side to side as much as he was able.

With the pins in his spine, he didn't have great range

of mobility, but he did what he could. The last surgery was nearly five months old, but he'd endured major back surgery, and that didn't heal overnight, despite his pleas to the Lord.

"Help me today," he prayed as he got to his feet. "Help Marcy be strong." He already knew Marcy Payne was a strong woman. One of the strongest he'd ever met. But he also knew she had a soft side, and she suffered behind a mask of confidence. She'd let that down in front of him several times over the past year, and the memories from last week, when he'd found her sobbing in her father's house after he'd passed away, moved through his mind as he showered.

They'd communicated a little bit since then, but she'd been surrounded by family members, and she'd had a million things to do to prepare for the funeral. Once Martin Payne had been diagnosed with colon cancer, he'd started planning everything. But having the floral arrangements chosen didn't mean they'd be ready without phone calls and follow-up.

Wyatt had stayed away from Marcy's house, her father's place, and the hangar on the west side of town. If Marcy wanted him to come visit, bring food, or anything else, she'd call or text. She always had in the past.

Once out of the shower, he stood in front of the mirror and shaved, keeping the edges of his beard trim and neat. He brushed his teeth and got dressed slowly, making sure all the right pieces were in the exact right place.

Black slacks. White shirt. A burgundy, navy, and white tie knotted precisely at his collar. The navy blue colon cancer pin to show his support. He'd just pulled a pair of black, shiny church shoes from his closet when someone knocked on his bedroom door.

"Yeah, Micah," he said, as he knew his brother's knock by now. Micah had moved to the ranch and Three Rivers just before Wyatt's surgery, and he was Wyatt's best friend.

"Just checking on you," he said, entering the room. "Looks like you're ready."

Micah was too, right down to the red and white paisley tie around his throat too. "I'm ready," Wyatt said, inhaling the scent of coffee and sausage floating down the hall from the kitchen.

"How's the back today?" Micah asked, his keen eyes missing nothing.

So he saw the slight limp in Wyatt's step, though it evened out after only two strides. "Not bad," Wyatt said anyway. "I just want to make it through this day."

"Momma would say you need a hearty breakfast to do that," Jeremiah said, leaning into the doorway. "We've got eggs, sausage, and coffee out here."

"Yep." Wyatt smiled at Jeremiah, who welcomed everyone to the ranch, made them whatever food they wanted, and got them to stay awhile. At least that was how Wyatt had felt when he'd come to Seven Sons last year.

"How are you today?" he asked, following Wyatt

down the hall. Wyatt swallowed a sigh, because he knew his brothers meant well. But there had been a reason he hadn't told them about his injuries for almost eight months. At the same time, he was glad he didn't have to try to hide his bad days anymore.

"I'm okay," he said, turning back once he'd reached the kitchen.

"Really?" Jeremiah asked, moving past him to pick up a plate. "Because it's okay to not be okay."

Wyatt glanced at Whitney, who lay on the couch, her phone up in front of her face. She'd had a scare about three weeks ago with her pregnancy, and Jeremiah didn't let her do more than walk a few steps at a time.

"If you keep badgering me," Wyatt said as he took the plate from Jeremiah. "It'll be a double-funeral we go to in a couple of hours—and not mine." He cocked his eyebrows at his brother, who only laughed at him.

"I hear you," Jeremiah said. "I just want to make sure you're doing all right."

"I am right now," Wyatt said, but he wasn't sure what would happen when he saw Marcy. She had a couple of cousins in town, and Wyatt assumed her brother would come from back east. He couldn't remember where her brother lived, but it was a big city on the Eastern Seaboard, where he worked as a corporate attorney.

The Payne's were a Three Rivers generational family, and Wyatt expected the whole town to be at the funeral.

He wanted to see Marcy today, make sure she knew he was there and available to her.

She knows that, he told himself as he put food on his plate and took it to the kitchen table.

He had the very real feeling he wouldn't be able to spend much time with her today, at least not the way he wanted to.

Tomorrow, everyone else would go back to their regular lives. They'd get up with their own problems and go about their business. Every once in a while, they might think of Martin Payne and the daughter he left behind, but the thoughts would be fleeting and momentary. Nothing would come from them.

Wyatt didn't want Marcy to be alone tomorrow, either, and he already had an alarm set on his phone to call her tomorrow morning to check in.

The back door opened, and Liam, Callie, and their daughter Denise came inside. "See?" Liam said to the three-year-old. "I told you Uncle Jeremiah would have breakfast."

The little girl had tight, dark curls, and they bounced as she ran toward Jeremiah, who scooped her up into his arms. They both laughed, and he asked her what she wanted.

"Toast," she said, and though there was no toast on the counter, Jeremiah set about making her what she wanted.

"Dressed already?" Liam asked, glancing around. "Looks like we're the only ones not ready for the funeral."

"We have time," Callie said. "I just hope Vicki doesn't go into labor today."

Wyatt looked up from his plate, glancing between Liam and Callie. "It's that time already?"

"She's due in four days," Liam said. "So yes, any time now."

"Hopefully not today," Callie said again, and her nerves radiated off of her in every direction.

Wyatt didn't want to sit around the house, and a viewing for Martin had been scheduled for that morning. Though he'd gone last night at the funeral home, he cleaned up his breakfast dishes and said, "I'm headed out."

"Already?" Jeremiah asked, still nursing his coffee while he held Denise on his knee as she ate bits of toast.

"Already." Wyatt took his keys out of the kitchen drawer where he kept his stuff and met Micah's eye. "You want to come with me?"

"Sure thing." Micah downed the last of his coffee while Wyatt ignored the concerned looks on his family's faces. He didn't need their pity. Didn't even want it.

The moment he walked out the front door, the weight of all those eyes lifted from his shoulders, and he felt like he could breathe normally. At least for a minute. Micah joined him on the porch, the front door closing loudly behind them.

The oak tree looked forlorn without all the Christmas decorations it had worn so festively for the past six weeks. Jeremiah loved their Christmas traditions, but he wanted the ranch to "get back to normal" after the holidays too. All of the ranch hands and brothers had worked for the better part of a day to get all the ornaments off the front fence, all the tinsel out of the tree—though the Good Lord had sent plenty of wind last week to help finish that job— and all the decorations snugly in their boxes and in the storage shed out back.

"Where do you want to go?" Micah asked, his keys jangling in his hand as he went down the front steps. He didn't pause and look behind him to see if Wyatt needed help, and he appreciated that. Sometimes the way Rhett or Liam wanted to steady him by holding onto his elbow made him feel infantile. And he didn't need to deal with that on top of everything else.

Wyatt pocketed his own keys and followed Micah to his truck, as it wasn't worth the argument with his youngest brother over who drove. Wyatt would get to go where he wanted no matter whose truck they were in or who sat behind the wheel.

"The bakery," he said, using the runners on the side of the truck to get himself into the vehicle. He sighed as he settled into the seat and pulled his seat belt into place. "And that new hot chocolate shack."

Micah fired up the truck and got the heater blowing, the heated seats warming, and the radio volume adjusted.

"Sorry," he said, grinning. "I like the music loud."

"You always have." Wyatt's head hurt, and he should've taken some painkillers before leaving the house.

He thought about asking Micah to run back inside and grab some, but he didn't. Micah was good at letting Wyatt take care of himself, but if he went back inside, everyone would know why.

"Will you open that glove box and see if I have any pills in there?" Micah nodded toward Wyatt's side of the truck. He turned onto the lane and headed toward the highway. Wyatt did as he asked, thrilled when he found the little bottle of ibuprofen.

"Can I have some too?"

"Of course."

Wyatt shook a few pills into his hand and swallowed them dry. "How many do you want?"

"Three."

Wyatt counted them out and handed them to Micah, who drank from a half-full water bottle to take his pills.

"This is a terrible thing," Micah said.

"It sure is." Wyatt didn't usually mince words, and he wouldn't today either. He let Micah drive him to the bakery, through the lane to get caramel hot chocolate, and to the church where the viewing and funeral would be held.

He didn't see Marcy as he went through the line for the viewing, but he shook her brother's hand and moved into the chapel. They saved seats for everyone in the family, and Wyatt's heart leapt and jumped and rejoiced when the Payne family finally walked in.

Marcy wore a floor-length black dress, enough makeup

to hide the fact that she'd been crying, and a bright white rose on her wrist. She held her head high and her brother's hand, and she didn't even glance at Wyatt as she walked past him.

He wanted to reach for her. He wanted to reach *out* to her. He kept his hands at his sides and sat with everyone else. He wept through the songs, the talks, the advice from Pastor Daniels. He wished he could be the Savior in that moment, and take upon himself all of their sorrows, their grief, their pain.

He watched Marcy more than anyone, and she wiped her eyes several times and bowed her head once. She leaned against her brother, and Wyatt wished it was him. He had so many wishes when it came to Marcy Payne, and hardly any of them had come true.

The funeral ended, and after employing his patience once again, Wyatt left the chapel with his brothers and their wives, their children, and everyone else in Three Rivers.

"Are you going to the cemetery?" Micah asked.

"Yes," Wyatt said, deciding on the spot. He shed his jacket as he left the church, as he ran hot almost all the time, and the sun was out, albeit a weak, early-January light and warmth from above. "I can go alone," he said. "If you want to go back to the ranch with someone."

Liam and Callie were going that way, as were Jeremiah and Whitney, and all their ranch hands. Someone would have a seat if Micah wanted it.

Micah said, "I'll come."

Relief filled Wyatt, as he didn't really want to go alone. He didn't function at his best while alone, but he could do it. He'd usually traveled with other cowboys, a trainer, and his manager while he ran the rodeo circuit, but he sometimes had to go by himself. He could stand near the back of the crowd at a cemetery.

Marcy's brother dedicated the gravesite, and four planes flew over the cemetery. Wyatt looked up at the crop-dusters, a sense of peace filling him. Martin had dedicated his life to flying and dusting the fields, farms, and ranches surrounding Three Rivers, and the fly-by was a nice tribute to him.

He didn't dare talk to Marcy at the cemetery, and he and Micah left as soon as the family started putting their corsages and boutonnieres on the casket. He wept openly on the way back to the truck, his heart so full.

"You okay?" Micah asked as they got in the truck.

"Fine," he said, wiping at his eyes. "Thank you, Micah."

"Of course." They drove back to the ranch in silence, and Wyatt beelined for his bedroom the moment they stepped inside the homestead. He just wanted to be alone.

No, what he really wanted was for Marcy to call him. He knew she was having a late lunch at her house after the ceremony at the cemetery, but he didn't want to go. He didn't want to comfort her in front of everyone. He wasn't even sure she wanted him to comfort her.

Frustration filled him over the situation, and he shed all of his fancy clothes and lay down in bed. Maybe a nap would clear his head. Maybe then he'd know what to do about the beautiful blonde who'd crawled into his heart the moment he'd met her, over a year ago.

Sneak Peek! Wyatt - Chapter Two

Marcy Payne hated the way her vision blurred. She hadn't been able to see properly all day. Her head felt too hot while the rest of her body was definitely too cold. Her skin cracked when she smiled, but she wasn't sure if that was from the excess makeup or the salty tears she'd cried. And cried, and cried.

But she'd made it through the funeral phone calls. Most of the decisions had been made while Daddy was still alive, but there had been a lot of emails, phone calls, and texts that had needed to happen once he'd passed. Flights booked. Dresses bought. Flowers delivered.

She took in the dozen or so vases sitting on her kitchen counter, her eyes moving to the one filled with red, white, and pink roses. That one had come from Wyatt Walker, and she'd cried a quart from the simple sight of her favorite flowers and Wyatt's scrawled, cowboy handwriting on the card.

I'm here if you need me, sugar. Love, Wyatt.

Out of all the cards that had come with the condolences over the past week, Marcy had kept only Wyatt's.

She had not reached out to him. She wasn't sure why she hadn't, only that she had enough balls in the air, and she couldn't stand the idea of him falling to the ground and cracking. She'd broken up with him once before— maybe twice, if her telling him she couldn't have a relationship while she dealt with her father's health counted.

He'd stayed away for a while, eventually coming back every few weeks. And over the summer, their romance had really blossomed.

"That's it," Bryan said, drawing Marcy's attention away from the roses. He closed the front door and looked at Marcy.

She smiled, the gesture wobbling on her face. "Thanks, Bry." Drawing in a deep breath, she surveyed the house. The sink was full of dirty dishes, and the dishwasher was filled with clean ones. She should've served lunch on paper plates, but she hadn't been able to. This was her father, and he deserved more than paper plates for the last meal memorializing him.

"Are you going to take off?" she asked. Daddy's death and funeral had come at a terrible time for him, as he was involved in a huge, important case in Washington D.C.

where he lived and practiced law for one of the biggest firms in the country.

"Unfortunately, I have to," he said, walking toward her. He had the same sandy hair as their father, the same dark green eyes. Marcy had inherited more of their mother's lighter blonde hair, which she enhanced with Golden Sunshine dye every couple of months. She also had blue eyes instead of green, and her father had often said how much he loved seeing her after their mother died, because then he could see a piece of her too.

Her chest constricted, but she held back the sob. She didn't want her brother to go. Then she'd be all alone in Three Rivers. No parents. No siblings.

Your cousins are here, she told herself, and that did bring some consolation.

Bryan wrapped her in a hug, and she clung to him. "I love you, sis," he said. "Please let me know what I can do."

"I will," she said. She'd turned over Daddy's estate to the lawyers, as he had quite a few things to go through. The house. The land. The business. The airplanes. Marcy had known about the estate planning lawyer, and she'd notified Nick Marlow as soon as all the family had been made aware of Daddy's death.

Bryan exhaled, bent to pick up his bag, and went out the front door too. Marcy flinched with the finality of the click and turned to survey her house again. It was a mess, which wasn't that different from when she lived there alone. She could pile up coffee cups and soda cans on an end table until there wasn't a spare inch before she'd finally haul a trash bag into the living room and clean it up.

Her thoughts again turned to Wyatt, who'd come out to the hangar several times to sit with her while she worked. But sitting was hard for him, and he'd gone around picking up trash and discarded mechanic rags, setting the washing machine, and making her heart glad.

She had to go through Daddy's house. Meet with the lawyers. Go visit the cemetery and made sure the headstone she'd ordered was correct. Not only that, but she hadn't been in the air since Daddy had died, and the work at Payne's Pest-free had been piling up. And up, and up.

She had to fly tomorrow, as people were sympathetic for a time. After that, they just wanted what they'd paid for. Marcy wanted to fly anyway, as the only place where she'd ever felt perfectly in place and at peace was in the cockpit of an airplane, soaring over the good state of Texas.

Her black maxi dress floated around her legs and feet as she started cleaning up. Exhaustion pulled through her, but she didn't want to be here alone. She couldn't stand the thought of going down the hall and sleeping in her bedroom alone.

Before Daddy had died, she'd craved being able to come home and go to bed alone. She'd spent the better part of the last year going straight to his house after work and staying with him until he fell asleep. Heck, sometimes she fell asleep at his house too, and she'd spent more than one night on his couch.

Her tears started afresh as she emptied the dishwasher and reloaded it, put a detergent pod in the compartment, and tried to start it. The buttons didn't light up, and she opened the door and slammed it closed again. "Just start," she said, jabbing at the buttons without looking at them. The machine did not start, and her irritation grew. She didn't have time for this. There was laundry to do, and a couple of dogs to feed, and garbage. And, and, and.

Someone knocked on the door, but Marcy didn't want another casserole. Food didn't fix anything. She didn't have room for more flowers. They did nothing to fill the hole that now existed in her soul.

She held very still, hoping whoever had come to the door would assume she was asleep or away, and they would leave.

"Marcy," she heard, and her heartbeat buzzed through her bloodstream. That was Wyatt's voice. "Open the door, sugar. I know you're here."

How could he possibly know? Her car was at her father's house, and she'd been riding with Bryan for the past week.

She took a couple of steps toward the door, and then paused. She didn't want to see Wyatt with streaked makeup on her face. Her house an absolute mess. What a wreck she'd become since her father's death.

He already knows, she told herself as he knocked again. He'd been the one to find her at her father's house, with her deceased dad on the couch. She hadn't been able to do anything after Daddy's last breath, and without Wyatt, she wondered if she'd still be in that living room, crying on the floor.

Marcy walked over to the front door and opened it. Sure enough, tall, dark, beautiful Wyatt Walker stood there. She'd seen him at the funeral, wearing his white shirt and tie, as well as his brand of cowboy hat. His actual brand, as he was one of the most-winning cowboys to ever enter the rodeo circuit, and he had sponsors from here to Calgary, even now that he was retired.

The man was made of gold, from his broad shoulders and hard muscles, to his bank account, to the pure concern in his eyes.

Concern for her.

Marcy wasn't sure what she'd done to attract this man's eye, as he could literally have anyone he wanted.

"Hey," he said, obviously nervous. It was laughable that *she* made *him* anxious when he was the celebrity bull rider, when he was the one with international sponsors, when his face appeared in TV commercials, when he was the one with a western wear clothing line.

She glanced up at his cowboy hat, wishing she hadn't broken up with him before the hats had hit the market. "Hey," she finally managed to say.

"Can I come in?"

"I'm tired, Wyatt." She leaned into the door as if she needed to prove it to him.

"Me too," he said. "Tired of waiting for you to call me." He took a step forward. "Please. Thirty minutes. I had a feeling I should come see you, and I couldn't ignore that."

She was tired of pushing him away, and she didn't want to be alone. Besides, who was she to tell him his prompting to come see her was wrong? So she backed up and let him step past her and into the house.

"Thanks." He paused and surveyed the scene before him, and Marcy wondered what he saw. "How are you holding up?"

Marcy didn't want to answer that question, so she just exhaled and went back into the kitchen. She didn't want to entertain anyone right now. She told herself that Wyatt had come out to the hangar several times and simply stayed with her. They didn't have to talk all the time.

"I miss you," he said next, and Marcy's anger sparked.

She glared at him and snatched up the trash bag. She could put napkins and envelopes and half-eaten sandwiches in a bag while he watched. He made no move to clean up, and Marcy poured her last remaining energy into picking up the house.

She moved a jacket someone had left, and she stubbed her toe against the coffee table. She cried out and more tears—more blasted tears—flowed down her face.

"Marcy," Wyatt said, but she didn't look at him. She finished in the living room and turned to the dining room. He moved out of the way as she started picking up lemonade cans and sweet tea packets from the table.

The trash made a clunking sound as she set it on the ground. She moved into the kitchen and started running the hot water. She could wash the remaining dishes while he watched, though she hadn't planned to do that.

"Marcy," he said again. "Will you just stop for a second?"

"No," she said. "I have to go to work in the morning, and I don't have a maid."

Wyatt probably did, though she knew he lived with his brothers and only had his bedroom to keep clean.

"What do you want me to do?" he asked.

Marcy dropped the silverware she held in her hand, and it made a horrible clanging sound against the plates there. "Why are you here?" She turned toward him, her despair spiraling out of control. She hated this feeling, and she wished he hadn't come. Why couldn't he just leave her alone?

"I want to offer you support," he said. "I know you—"

"Support?" Marcy shook her head, the idea almost laughable. "No, Wyatt, you're not here to support me. You're here for *you*. You're here because you want to ask me to dinner. You want me to be your girlfriend."

He glowered at her and folded his arms. "I do want all of that, but that's not why I'm here."

"Right." She turned back to the sink and plunged her hands into the water. But it was far too hot now that it had been running for a while, and she yelped as she pulled her hands back. Wyatt arrived at her side a moment later, and Marcy couldn't help crying.

"It's okay," he said, handing her a towel. He turned off the water and curled her into his chest. "It's going to be okay."

Marcy opened her mouth to argue, because she could not see how a world without either of her parents in it was ever going to be okay. But all she could do was suck at the air as she started to sob. And sob, and sob.

Wyatt held her close and tight, and she let him, because she needed someone to do it. Bryan had left. Her cousins had families and lives to get back to. The huge turnout from the people living in Three Rivers had comforted her, but they'd all moved on with their regular lives too.

Marcy didn't have a regular life anymore. Not one she recognized, at least.

Wyatt began to hum, and his bass voice soothed her. "Come on, sugar," he said. "It's time for bed."

Marcy wasn't sure how long they'd been standing in her kitchen, the sink full of dirty dishes sitting in hot water, but she knew it wasn't time for bed. But she let Wyatt lead her down the hall to her bedroom. She was aware of him opening a couple of drawers and then handing her a pair of pajamas.

He left the room, and she somehow changed. He knocked before re-entering the room, and he held a glass of water and a couple of pills. "Painkillers," he said.

Marcy didn't want them. "They can't get rid of this pain," she whispered.

"I know, baby. Take them anyway."

She did, and she crawled under the covers. Wyatt laid down with her, a groan pulling through his throat as he did. She curled into his chest and listened to his heart beating. He breathed deeply, and she tried to match her breathing to his.

Finally—*finally*—she drew a breath full of peace and calm, both things she hadn't felt in twelve long months. "Thank you, Wyatt," she murmured just before she fell into unconsciousness.

———

When she woke, she was alone, and panic pulled through her sharply. She sat up with a gasp, searching the darkness for some clue as to where she was.

"It's okay," Wyatt said again, and Marcy looked toward the sound of his voice. He sat in the recliner in her bedroom. "You're safe, Marce."

Marce.

She loved the nickname he used for her, and she sighed as she swung her feet over the side of the bed. "What time is it?"

"Late," he said. "I didn't want to leave you alone."

Reaching over, she fumbled for a moment before snapping on the lamp on her nightstand. Their eyes met, and pure gratitude streamed through Marcy. Everyone else had left her. Wyatt had not.

"Will you be okay now?" he asked. He looked as exhausted as she felt. She wanted him to stay, but she wanted him to get the rest he needed too.

"I'll be okay," she said.

Wyatt got up, pain moving across his face, and stepped over to her. He swept his lips along her hairline and said, "I'll bring breakfast to the hangar in the morning. I won't stay. I know you'll be really busy." With that, he walked out of her bedroom, leaving Marcy to wonder why she'd tried to push him away. Again.

She also needed a plan for tomorrow morning, because she still wasn't sure she was ready for a real relationship with Wyatt Walker. At least not the kind he obviously wanted. She needed to figure out how to live in this new world first. She needed to keep her crop dusters running. She had all the cleaning and estate sorting to do.

She wondered if she actually had room for Wyatt in her life right now, and she certainly didn't think so.

So she'd just tell him tomorrow. With everything else already weighing on her conscious, she couldn't have her poor treatment of a good man adding to it.

———

Read **Wyatt** in paperback today! Get it here by scanning this QR code with the camera on your phone.

Tripp (Book 2): She needs a husband to keep her son. He's wanted to take their relationship to the next level, but she's always pushing him away. Will their trivial tie take them all the way to happily-ever-after?

Liam (Book 3): She's desperate to save her ranch. He wants to help her any way he can. Will their invented I-Do open doors that have previously been closed and lead to a happily-ever-after for both of them?

Jeremiah (Book 4): He wants to prove to his brothers that he's not broken. She just wants him. Will a fake marriage heal him or push her further away?

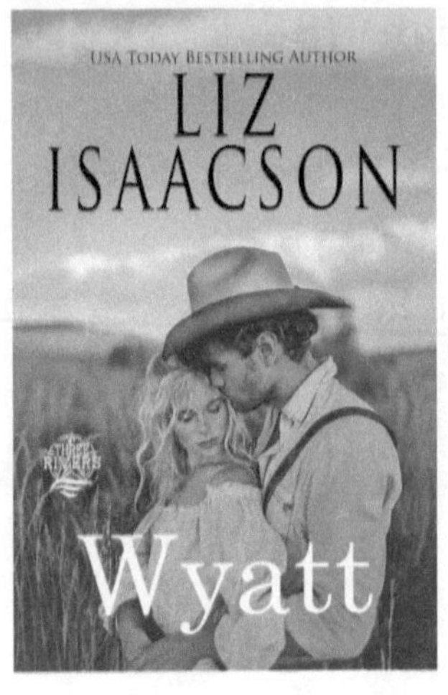

Wyatt (Book 5): To get her inheritance, she needs a husband. He's wanted to fly with her for ages. Can their pretend pledge turn into something real?

Skyler (Book 6): She needs a new last name to stay in school. He's willing to help a fellow student. Can this wanna-be wife show the playboy that some things should be taken seriously?

Micah (Book 7): They were just actors auditioning for a play. The marriage was just for the audition – until a clerical error results in a legal marriage. Can these two ex-lovers negotiate this new ground between them and achieve new roles in each other's lives?

Gideon (Book 8): It's 1971, and Gideon Walker is on the cutting edge of all the technology coming out of Texas. He has big dreams and wants to make something of himself. Then he meets Penny Aarons, and everything changes. He only has eyes for her, but she's got plans and dreams of her own...

Read this origin romance for Momma and Daddy from the Seven Sons series today!

Grape Seed Falls Romance Series

Journey to the beautiful Texas Hill Country for heartwarming, clean cowboy romance with that hint of faith you'll love. This series includes an Army cowboy, a cowboy billionaire, seasoned romance between older characters, Christmas romance, and three brothers looking for a ranch and a the woman of their dreams!

Choosing the Cowboy (Book 1): With financial trouble and personal issues around every corner, can Maggie Duffin and Chase Carver rely on their faith to find their happily-ever-after?

This is an introductory novelette to the Grape Seed Falls Romance series, with full-length books starting with **CRAVING THE COWBOY**.

A spinoff from the #1 bestselling Three Rivers Ranch Romance novels, also by USA Today bestselling author Liz Isaacson.

Three Rivers Ranch Romance Series

Escape to Three Rivers, Texas for small-town charm, sweet and sexy cowboys, and faith and family centered romance. You'll get second chance romance, friends to lovers. older brother's best friend, military romance, secret babies, and more! The Three Rivers cowboys and the women who rope their hearts are waiting for you, so start reading today!

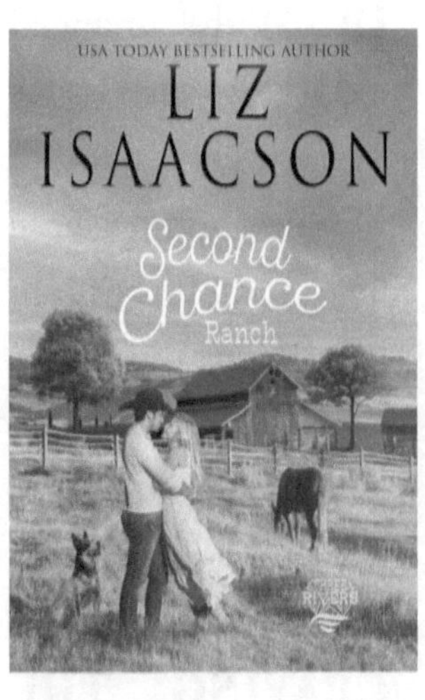

Second Chance Ranch (Book 1): After his deployment, injured and discharged Major Squire Ackerman returns to Three Rivers Ranch, wanting to forgive Kelly for ignoring him a decade ago. He'd like to provide the stable life she needs, but with old wounds opening and a ranch on the brink of financial collapse, it will take patience and faith to make their second chance possible.

Horseshoe Home Ranch Romance Series

Fall for a cowboy today in this inspirational western romance series! Journey to Montana for second chance romance, boss-nanny romance, forbidden romance, and friends-to-lovers romance among an awesome ranch setting in four full-length novels from USA Today bestseller and Top 10 Kindle Unlimited All-Star author Liz Isaacson.

The Redesigned Ranch (Book 1): Jace Lovell only has one thing left after his fiancé abandons him at the altar: his job at Horseshoe Home Ranch. Belle Edmunds is back in Gold Valley and she's desperate to build a portfolio that she can use to start her own firm in Montana. Jace isn't anywhere near forgiving his fiancé, and he's not sure he's ready for a new relationship with someone as fiery and beautiful as Belle. Can she employ her patience while he figures out how to forgive so they can find their own brand of happily-ever-after?

About Liz

Liz Isaacson writes inspirational romance, usually set in Texas, or Wyoming, or anywhere else horses and cowboys exist. She lives in Utah, where she writes full-time, takes her two dogs to the park everyday, and eats a lot of veggies while writing. Find her on her website, along with all of her pen names, at authorelanajohnson.com